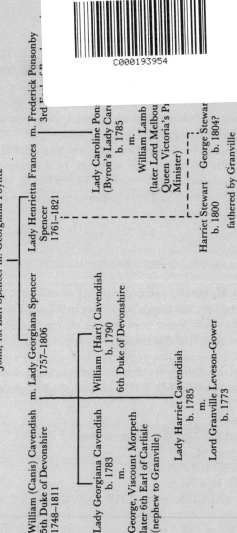

FAMILY TREE

John, 1st Earl Spencer m. Georgiana Poyntz

William (Canis) Cavendish m. Lady Georgiana Spencer   Lady Henrietta Frances m. Frederick Ponsonby
5th Duke of Devonshire   1757–1806   Spencer   3rd Earl of ...
1748–1811   1761–1821

Lady Georgiana Cavendish
b. 1783
m.
George, Viscount Morpeth
later 6th Earl of Carlisle
(nephew to Granville)

William (Hart) Cavendish
b. 1790
6th Duke of Devonshire

Lady Harriet Cavendish
b. 1785
m.
Lord Granville Leveson-Gower
b. 1773

Lady Caroline Ponsonby
(Byron's Lady Caroline)
b. 1785
m.
William Lamb
(later Lord Melbourne
Queen Victoria's Prime
Minister)

Harriet Stewart   George Stewart
b. 1800   b. 1804?

fathered by Granville

Dotted lines indicate illegitimate children

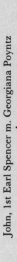

Dear Reader

With AN UNEXPECTED PASSION, Paula Marshall gives us a 'faction'. Written about real people, the story is inevitably different; no exciting moments can be created that didn't really exist. But this glimpse of actuality becomes compelling, and I think you will like Haryo and Granville as much as I do.

We also have Pauline Bentley with SILK AND SWORD, following the fortunes of Eleanor in the chaotic times of 1485 when Richard III lost to Henry VII. An exciting and very different month for you!

The Editor

Paula Marshall, married with three children, has had a varied life. She began her career in a large library and ended it as a senior academic in charge of history in a polytechnic. She has travelled widely, has been a swimming coach, and has appeared on University Challenge and Mastermind. She has always wanted to write, and likes her novels to be full of adventure and humour.

Recent titles by the same author:

AN AMERICAN PRINCESS
WILD JUSTICE
THE FALCON AND THE DOVE

AN UNEXPECTED
PASSION

Paula Marshall

The author would like to thank the staffs of the
Leicestershire County Libraries, Leicester
University Library and Leicester Polytechnic
(now DeMontfort University) for their help in
obtaining books and materials about the
characters and the background of
AN UNEXPECTED PASSION.

*First published in Great Britain 1993
by Mills & Boon Limited*

© Paula Marshall 1993

*Australian copyright 1993
Philippine copyright 1993
This edition 1993*

ISBN 0 263 78055 4

*Masquerade is a trademark published by
Mills & Boon Limited, Eton House,
18–24 Paradise Road, Richmond, Surrey, TW9 1SR.*

*Set in 10 on 11 pt Linotron Baskerville
04-9306-78650*

*Typeset in Great Britain by Centracet, Cambridge
Made and printed in Great Britain*

AUTHOR'S NOTE

THIS book is what is commonly called a 'faction'. That is, the essential parts of the story are true, I have only created scenes and conversations where the facts are missing and the story would not make sense without inventing what was most likely to have happened, based on what we know of Harriet and Granville revealed in the large number of letters they wrote, and from other people's accounts of them.

Both of them entered into marriage with great misgivings — they both said and wrote so. But after their short honeymoon, they were passionately in love with one another, and remained so for the rest of their lives. In an era given to extra-marital affairs, Granville remained entirely faithful to Harriet. The documentary evidence is quite explicit — Granville writes to Lady Bessborough of his love and passion for his '*angel*' Harriet, and for Harriet, Granville first became '*adored Granville*' and then, two years into the marriage, '*adored Granville, who would make a barren desert smile*'. But we have no documents of what happened on the honeymoon to bring about this remarkable change, from doubt, to commitment without reservation. So, given Harriet's virginity, her wit, and the achieved sexual passion of her marriage, plus Granville's known and famous tact, and the body of evidence that he was a remarkably kind and considerate lover to his many mistresses, I invented the wedding night scene.

On one occasion I have departed from fact, by having Harriet renounce her title *before* the wedding — as a Duke's daughter her title would take precedence over

5

her husband's — becoming Lady Granville, not Lady
Harriet. She actually renounced her title in 1815 when
Granville was created Viscount Granville, but I trans-
posed it to demonstrate the extent of Harriet's love for
Granville.

Leveson Gower was, and is, pronounced 'Looson
Gore'. Lord Granville would be known to his intimates
as Granville, or sometimes Granville Leveson — he was
sometimes called that in official correspondence. To all
others he would be Lord Granville, to servants, m'lord.
To call him simply Leveson Gower, if you were not an
intimate, would be insulting.

The surname Cavendish, during the eighteenth and
most of the nineteenth century, was always pronounced
Candish.

Finally, although Lady Elizabeth Foster — 'Lady
Liz' to the younger generation — was known as 'Bess'
to her contemporaries, to avoid confusion with Lady
Bessborough I have made those characters to whom she
is not 'Lady Liz' call her 'Lady Elizabeth' throughout.

CHAPTER ONE

IN A room in a house in a fashionable London street on a sunny morning in May, 1812, a young woman sat at an escritoire, writing. The room was a study, beautifully appointed, everything in it—furniture, break-front bookcases, carpets, curtains, ornaments—in the most perfect taste. Above the hearth hung the portrait of a man by Sir Thomas Lawrence, and the man was as beautiful as the room. 'My masterpiece,' Lawrence had said, when he had finished it.

The young woman was not beautiful, nor even pretty, but she had a strong, humorous face at which most people looked twice. She was dressed with quiet elegance in a sapphire-blue wool morning gown, trimmed with a deep collar of lace, as fine as a cobweb. Her brown hair, a little in defiance of fashion, was dressed high on her head.

She was frowning as she wrote her letter to her brother, who was living deep in the country, for what she had to tell him did not please her.

Two close relatives, who had married in love and hope, were seeing that love, and that hope, disappear; one through wilfulness, the other through what could only be seen as frightful mischance. Both had set out on their married lives with such joy and confidence that the foundering of everything seemed doubly hard. No misgivings had assailed *them*, no gossip had followed *their* progess to the altar. . .and now all lay in ruins, and, whether it was folly or ill-luck, the end for both of them looked like being the same.

The young woman sighed, put down her pen. She

could not help thinking of her own life — and how much that, too, had changed over the past three years. Just over two years ago she had asked herself a question, and had told herself firmly and sensibly that only the passage of time would give her an answer.

Time had passed, and the verdict was in. She rose, walked to the window and looked down at the quiet street where a man was riding up and down, trying out shooting-ponies, and smiled at her thoughts.

She sank into a giant armchair by the hearth and began to muse upon the past, a past which had brought her to this day, and to this room. . .a past which, even now, had the power to hurt her, so unwanted were some of her memories, and yet. . .and yet. . .she must remember it. . .but where to begin. . .there were so many points of entry.

An evening in 1809, late January it must have been, in a crowded drawing-room, a woman coming towards her. . .

'Haryo!' Lady Harriet Cavendish turned her head towards Lady Liz Foster who had just plaintively murmured her name. In the low drawl of the Devonshire House set it had actually come out as 'Hah-yo!' in a breathless bleat, but never mind that, thought Harriet resignedly: the worst thing is having to listen to Liz's maunderings at all. It was easy to blot out the bleat; she had been doing it for years.

'Haryo,' Lady Liz persisted, 'are you listening? Pray pay attention, I beg of you, to what I am about to say.'

'Yes, madam.' Harriet displayed an exemplary and weary forbearance. Despite the helplessness displayed by her pretty, drawling voice, the one gentle hand lightly laid on Harriet's arm, the charming head on one side, patience on a monument vividly portrayed — for all that, when Lady Liz Foster was determined, she stuck to her victim like glue.

'It is not enough, Haryo, my dearest girl, to be yourself as you so often say. You must consider others, who are not as strong-minded as you are, a little. It pains me to say this——' oh, no, it doesn't, thought Harriet grimly; never say that you are not enjoying yourself '—but sticking to your guns as you do, having already refused so many eligible young men of the highest desirability, is no way to ensure your future happiness. Other men will be deterred by such conscious rectitude, such a firm refusal to bend at all towards them. No, do not shake your head at me, dearest girl. I saw your manner to Lord Granville just now. You were almost painfully civil, but painful civility is incivility, as you well know. He was quite put out.'

After this speech, lengthy indeed for Lady Liz, for she was usually given to brief cooings, Harriet looked sardonically over to the other side of the drawing-room at Chiswick House, the Middlesex home of William Cavendish, fifth Duke of Devonshire. She, and his guests, were awaiting the Duke's arrival so that they might go into dinner.

Lord Granville Leveson Gower, having abandoned an abortive conversation with her, was busy charming yet another female who hung on his every word. He did not look in the least put out. Quite the contrary, he seemed, thought Harriet acidly, to be consumed with the most intense self-satisfaction.

'He will think that you are displeased with him again,' finished Lady Liz plaintively.

Harriet's eyebrows rose. 'You do surprise me, madam. I had not thought that Lord Granville could conceive of the notion that he could be other than a source of delighted pleasure to humanity in general, and the fair sex in particular!'

'Now that, Haryo, dear, is exactly what I am complaining of. Such severity in one so young is hardly
pleasing. I put it down to that governess of yours, but
there it is. You are like to gain a reputation as a shrew,
and we all know, dearest Haryo, that you are not *that*.
Think how displeased your dear mama would have been
if she had heard you uttering such sentiments,' and
Lady Liz closed her beautiful eyes in pain, only opening
them to throw agonised glances of reproach in Harriet's
direction.

How dare she speak of Mama to me, fumed Harriet
inwardly, even if she does have a certain amount of
right on her side? Mama would have been pained, I
know, to hear me criticise Lord Granville so severely.
She was always so kind about everyone, and particularly
you, my dear madam, whom she should have turned
out of her home long ago.

But Lady Harriet Cavendish had learned a certain
amount of discretion in a hard school, and if her twenty-
three years had taught her nothing else, they had taught
her to bear the worst pangs of an unhappy existence in
silence — well, relative silence.

So, instead of speaking her mind about Lady Liz *and*
Lord Granville, she said instead, in a freezing voice, 'I
do not particularly wish to please Lord Granville. On
the contrary, I feel it would be salutary for him to learn
that there is at least one woman in the world unwilling
to succumb to his charms. He must content himself with
all the rest.'

'And that kind of speech, my love,' Lady Liz was as
gentle and fluting as ever in the face of Harriet's
intransigence, 'is what I most complain of. And yes, he
is fully aware of your dislike, and no, do not make faces
at me when I speak to you, I know that it grieves him.
He has often assured me that he values your opinion
and your conversation.'

'Oh, madam, I beg leave to doubt that my conduct grieves him, or that a plain Cavendish younger daughter, of little dowry, can be of any consequence to one so armoured in self-love.'

Perforce even Lady Liz, that arch-dissembler and intriguer, a refugee from the pages of *Les Liaisons Dangereuses*, was compelled to retreat a little in the face of such determined opposition, but not before she had fluttered her eyelashes again and sighed at her companion, 'Oh, all my sensibilities tell me that you are mistaken in him,' calling into play, as always, the sensitivity of her nature, so delicate, so fine.

Indeed, as all the world knew, Lady Liz's sensibility was nothing if not notorious. So exquisite was it and so extreme, that when the late lamented Lord Nelson had been killed in the very hour of victory at Trafalgar, her excesses on hearing the sad news were still remembered, nearly four years later.

She had sighed and died for weeks, worn black for months, held a fragile lace handkerchief to those wonderful eyes so often that Harriet was not the only member of society to wonder whether a naval victory won at such a cost was worth it!

And now her target was Harriet herself, and all her many arts were called into action. Graceful, playful taps from her beautiful hands, melting glances from those lovely eyes, sighing, holding of her exquisite head on one side, drawl lengthened even further to convey how much, how very much, she wished not only to be a firm friend of her lover's child, but in the doing to promote her own interests and those of her legitimate and illegitimate children.

For Lady Elizabeth Foster, that enchanting widow, was still inhabiting Devonshire House, Chatsworth, and Chiswick House, or wherever William Cavendish, the fifth Duke of Devonshire, whose mistress she had been for over twenty-five years, happened to be dwelling, three years after the death of her oh, so dear friend the Duchess, his wife, without the presence of the Duchess to give her continued residence there some sort of legitimacy.

Worse, on the beautiful Duchess's sad and untimely death in 1806 she had usurped the place of Harriet herself, for Harriet should have taken over as the hostess of her father the Duke, and as mistress — unless he married again — of all the many and varied establishments which the Duke owned.

Instead of at once leaving the Duke's household, Lady Elizabeth had stayed on, to become his hostess, his wife in everything but name after the Duke had begged her to remain with him — or so she prettily claimed — and leaving Harriet to remain what she had always been: the Duke's least considered, least loved child, the disappointing girl who had been born when he had hoped for a boy. Never mind that the Duchess had later given him his heir, Hart, the Marquis of Hartington; still her presence always reminded him of that sad day when his hoped-for heir had not arrived.

And there was nothing Harriet could say or do about her unhappy situation. Nothing at all, for if her poor mama had been willing to live in a ménage à trois with her husband and her best friend, who had become her husband's mistress, what could she, unconsidered Harriet, do, now that Mama was no longer there to love and protect her?

To leave Devonshire House, to go to live with her Spencer grandparents or with her sister Georgiana, would have been a form of social suicide; worse, would mean admitting defeat at the hands of her father's mistress

But oh, how hard it was to retain one's pride, keep one's integrity intact, behave as though there was nothing untoward about the whole wretched business, especially when it was beginning to look as though Lady Liz's campaign to persuade the Duke to confer respectability on her by marrying her was on the verge of succeeding.

A horrible suspicion of what Lady Liz's praise of Lord Granville really meant struck Harriet. Was it not likely that the reason behind Lady Liz's sudden passionate desire to have Harriet favour him was that by accepting him in marriage she would, of course, be set up in her own establishment, leaving the Duke and Lady Liz free to marry!

Oh, if anything could make Harriet dislike Lord Granville more than she already did it was the thought that they were all, her father's circle, throwing her at him in order to facilitate the final triumph of the Duke's and Lady Liz's immorality; that for her to marry Lord Granville would be the ploy, the master-stroke by which Lady Liz could at last take her mother's place.

And he, was he in the plot? And what was in it for him? Not a vast dowry, that was for sure, although a penniless younger son such as he was badly needed a wife to bring him money.

Harriet suddenly felt nauseated by the whole wretched business, and the nausea showed on her face.

Lady Liz, distracted by the sight, began to flutter; she was good at fluttering, and the fluttering concealed her undoubted cleverness, the brilliant intellect beneath the vague manner.

'Oh, Haryo, dear, pray do not be bilious now. We are about to go into dinner. All I ask of you is that you be civil to everyone, not merely to dear Lord Granville.'

Dear Lord Granville! thought Harriet, a satiric twist to her mouth. Was Lady Liz proposing to add herself to the ever-growing list of his conquests? What a crocodile she was! This last was Hart's favourite description of her; if anything, he liked her even less than Harriet did.

Her father had arrived late as usual to greet his dinner guests — he invariably left doing the pretty, as he termed it, to Liz, as he had left it to Harriet's mama. And, as usual, he smelled powerfully of dog, although everyone pretended not to notice. He offered Liz his arm, ready to lead her into dinner, but she pouted prettily at him, 'Not yet, my dear Canis; Lord and Lady Bessborough have not yet arrived.'

'Damned uncivil of them to be late,' he growled, so that Lady Liz, abandoning her efforts to make Harriet tolerate Lord Granville, began to wail gently about the tardy arrivals.

'So unlike dear Lady Bessborough to be late. She is usually so proper about such matters.'

And what could one say to that? thought Harriet, other than the vastly unsayable, Well, she must be proper about *something*! She was beginning to be a little frightened by her own censoriousness. Perhaps Lady Liz was right, and she was starting to frighten people to the degree that she might shortly be past her last prayers, become an antidote. Oh, not that — the thought of living at Devonshire House forever, an unconsidered spinster, was not to be borne.

Aloud she said, moving away from her tormentor, catching sight of her plain, if not to say dowdy reflection, somewhat distorted in a Venetian glass mirror, the white of her satin dinner dress doing nothing for her complexion, 'Oh, I'm sure that she will be here soon, if only to save Father from a syncope,' for the Duke was beginning to show signs of agitation — and that, if he hears it, thought his daughter, won't make him love me any more.

Alas, moving away from Lady Liz Foster served only to bring her into Lord Granville's orbit. Her arrival in his near vicinity caused him to end his conversation with Frederick Byng, a former suiter of hers, now a friend, long ago nicknamed the Poodle by George Canning because of his beautiful, tight black curls, and turn to her, saying to the Poodle, 'Forgive me, Byng, I most particularly wish to speak to Lady Harriet,' and, 'You appear in spirits this evening, Lady Harriet. Has the war news from Spain been good, or have you had a letter from Lady Morpeth?'

Harriet supposed that anger at Lady Liz's behaviour and her own distaste for him had served to give her a fine flush of colour which might be mistaken for the glow of good health.

Why it was, she did not know, but whenever she was near to Lord Granville the strangest feelings always came over her. So odd and powerful were they, causing her breathing to be affected and her throat to close, and a rapid internal fluttering to begin, that she assumed that it was a strong manifestation of her dislike for him overcoming her.

To keep her self-control in perfect order she said something stultifyingly proper in the order of, 'No, not at all. . .' and what did *that* mean? So that she hastily added, 'I always prefer winter to summer: the cold keeps the intellect on the qui vive; warmth merely serves to stifle it,' a remark which after his usual fashion he gave the gravest and calmest attention and reflection.

His perfect manners added to his cool commnd of himself and his surroundings served only to increase her own feelings of inadequacy *vis-à-vis* both himself and Lady Liz.

Furthermore, she decided, choking back her acute awareness of him, and everything about him, his own appearance this evening was even more outrageously annoying than usual.

He certainly seemed in perfect health and beauty, a

living and breathing Adonis, completely aware, she was
bitterly sure, of all his many charms. His exquisite
profile was turned towards her, his cheeks were glowing
with such absolute health that one might almost have
suspected them rouged, and the long blue eyes for which
he was celebrated were shining at her with what must
surely be spurious admiration.

Spurious because his current target for conquest, the
noted heiress and beauty Miss Susan Beckford, not
being present, he was reduced to practising on poor
Harriet Cavendish, who even managed to look dowdy
in white satin ornamented with seed pearls, a girlish
turn-out which did absolutely nothing for her.

Not only his noble Grecian head but everything else
about him was so totally *à point*, so beautifully presented,
beginning with his chestnut curls, continuing to his
spotless cravat, his black silk tailcoat left carefully,
carelessly unbuttoned to reveal his equally spotless shirt
and his elegant silver and black striped waistcoat, his
black knee breeches, below which his long legs, shapely
in black silk stockings, culminated in the most superb
pair of evening slippers, decorated with silver
rosettes. . . Ugh! His whole disgustingly well-ordered
appearance was such as to make poor Harriet feel even
more plain and dowdy than she already was.

To make matters worse he was so fastidious at all
points that he made every other man in the room,
particularly her father, with dog hairs clinging to him,
look faintly grimy. Oh, he was impossible! No one,
absolutely no one, had the right to look like that. It was
an offence against nature.

Harriet became aware through her distraction that he
was talking to her of her sister, Georgiana, who was
married to his nephew, Lord Morpeth, Lord Carlisle's
son and heir.

'I trust that when you next see Lady Morpeth — for I

hear that she arrives in town any day now — you will convey to her my sincere wishes for her good health. The same, of course, goes for Morpeth, but we do not have much cause to worry over him. He is remarkable for his good health, not his lack of it.'

This was all banal in the extreme, but given with such an air of genial good humour that we might be speaking in epigrams, was Harriet's reaction, accompanied by a strong wish that her aunt, Lady Bessborough, her late mother's sister, would soon arrive to save her from being afflicted by such perfection of appearance, manner and manners.

Surely no one had ever told *him* to watch what he said to others in company? He was talking now of the latest play he had seen at Drury Lane, recommending it to her, some French farce, which yes, she had visited, and said so, adding, 'As in all French farces every room seemed to have at least six doors, through which the characters appeared and disappeared like jack-in-the-boxes. I am persuaded that without doors the French would be unable to write plays at all. Imagine, if they were compelled to keep all their characters on stage throughout the action, they would expire of frustration, or spend their time inspecting the flats for doors which were not there!'

Lord Granville's amusement at this was genuine and unfeigned. 'I am persuaded, Lady Harriet,' he said, 'that you should attempt to write plays yourself. I was inspecting an old book recently — I believe that you share my own bibliomania — which told of a seventeenth-century lady, Aphra Behn by name, who wrote excellent plays. One wonders what they were like.'

'Few doors, one supposes,' offered Harriet gravely, 'unless of course, she *were* French.'

This drew another laugh from him, a perfect laugh, not over-loud, Harriet was fascinated to notice; just enough to convince the hearer of his amusement at what she had said, but not noisy enough to disturb others. Had he been born with such remarkable *savoir-faire*, or was it acquired? If so, could he teach it to her?

The thought amused Harriet, and as he turned to ask her what was giving her such pleasure her aunt arrived, husband and married daughter, Lady Caroline Lamb, in tow. 'So sorry, dear Canis,' to the Duke, 'to be so late, but one of our horses fell, and we are lucky to be here at all. And you do not mind that we have brought dear Caro; she is so low in spirits that I thought seeing you all would quite restore her.'

At the expense of lowering the spirits of all the rest of us, was Harriet's internal comment on this. She was not sure how much she loved either Aunt Bessborough or her cousin, Lady Caroline, known as Caro-William to the family to distinguish her from all the other Caros who frequented both Devonshire and Chiswick House.

Caro had been Harriet's happy playmate when they had both been younger, but growing up had conferred no favours on her; she was flighty and tiresome, and looked like being so tonight, coming over to kiss Lord Granville's cheek whether he wished it or no, forestalling her mother who also came over to bow at Lord Granville and for him to bow back, for all the world as though they were an elderly pair of friends chance met. . .and why did the knowledge of their true relationship give her such a sharp pang?

Harriet turned to Caro, who was a pixie in lemon silk, frail and delicate, her piquant face framed in short curls, alight with malicious mischief, 'And William?' she could not help asking. 'Where is he?' for William Lamb, Caro's husband, was not with the Bessboroughs' party.

'Tiresome,' trilled Caroline. 'He's a naughty boy tonight, gone drinking and gambling—so glad to see you haven't, Lord Granville.'

For once, commented Harriet's internal voice, for
Lord Granville's exploits at play were famous, if not to
say infamous, but he merely shrugged his excellently
tailored shoulders, and whispered indulgently to Caro,
'I do believe that the Duke is waiting for us to order
ourselves so that we may go into dinner. He will
probably wish to find you a partner,' which was a gentle
hint to her not to hold up proceedings, and she skipped
over to do the pretty to the Duke immediately, arriving
before him with her hands held up, almost performing
an entrechat in her apparent delight at seeing him.

And say what you would of the man, granted Harriet
unwillingly, as Frederick Byng took her arm to lead her
into dinner, Granville Leveson Gower always seemed to
have the power to calm poor Caro, to cool down her
inflamed sensibilities without her bridling at him as she
did at everyone else who tried to control her wayward
spirit.

So why was it that he always managed to inflame
Harriet Cavendish? Because she disliked him, she supposed, and later at dinner, with him sitting bodkin
between Lady Caroline and her Aunt Bessborough, she
fell into a musing fit, listening to the Poodle's chatter
with only half an ear.

She began composing a conversation with her sister
Georgiana in her head. 'Would you believe, I had
Doodle opposite to me at dinner *again*; what can they all
be at?' For Doodle was the nickname she had given him
in her correspondence with Georgiana in order to exor-
cise the annoyance he always caused her.

'Doodle', an inconsiderable person, an idiot, and if
the name was unfair, well, so be it, and she said it, she
thought in her head, looking angrily at him as he turned
to speak with Aunt Bessborough, displaying all the
aristocratic langour which was his hallmark.

Only she must have said it aloud, for the Poodle,

turning his head, said, 'Eh, what's that, Haryo?' for he
had known her long enough to use the affectionate pet
name which had been hers since childhood.

She must have been in the doldrums, and no mistake,
Harriet thought later, for she had no more sense, so
cross was she with the man opposite — and herself —
than to say, most impolitely and against all propriety,
'Not Poodle, Freddy, I said Doodle, meaning our inef-
fable friend over there, *il bel uomo*, the beautiful man
himself.'

Something in her tone alerted the Poodle, 'Hey,
steady on, Haryo, my dear. You can't call him that.
Clever man, Granville, damned clever; Pitt's protégé,
you know. Why, George Canning said only last week
that the trouble with Granville is that he's even cleverer
than he thinks he is, which is saying a lot. And if
Canning thinks he's clever. . .! He went to Oxford at
fifteen, which is why he's Canning's friend, ambassador
to Berlin when he was only twenty-five, and to Russia
when he was thirty-one. Can't understand why you
dislike him; your sort of person — loves books, paintings
and witty talk.'

'Oh, dear,' said Harriet on receiving this torrent of
praise from the Poodle of all people. 'Don't you start
trying to pair him off with me. Is all our set in a
conspiracy to make me like Granville Leveson Gower?'

The Poodle laughed at that. It was always a pleasure
to sit by Harriet Cavendish; she might be no beauty,
but her conversation was always witty and to the point.
Funny that she had a blind spot over Granville.

After that Harriet managed to behave herself, even
brought herself to smile back when Lord Granville
offered her his own beautiful smile, which had gained
him the nickname of Beamer from the many ladies who
either adored him from a distance — or no distance at
all!

She really must stop thinking about him, only it was difficult when Lady Liz spent dinner winking and nodding significantly at her, and later, when they had returned to the drawing-room, her aunt brought him over and said in the die-away manner which she sometimes affected, 'You *really* must give Granville a game of chess, Harriet, my dear. He needs one, he says, as a man dying of thirst in the desert needs water, and Caro is no use at such diversions — spillikins is more in her line.'

There was nothing for it. Thus commanded, for Lord Granville always obeyed her aunt, the chess-board was brought out, and they began to play, Lord Granville looking sweetly at her over the men before them, and Harriet trying not to scowl at his attentions.

'Really, Elizabeth,' sighed Aunt Bessborough to Lady Liz, 'I blame that dreadful governess of hers, the Trimmer woman, for making Harriet so. . .strait-laced. I thought that when she left Devonshire House her influence would wane, but she's back again, sent there by Mama, to watch over her, and I know, *sans doute*, that it is she who has inflamed poor Haryo against Granville. Such a pity. Can't you talk to her?'

'Oh, I have, I have,' wailed Lady Liz again; her evening was one long moan, for Canis, the Duke, had left his guests to their own devices, and taken himself off to his dogs, whom he much preferred to men and women. 'But you know how strong-minded she is. However did you get her to play chess with him?'

'Ordered them to,' said Lady Bessborough, grimly for her. 'There are times when I despair of everything, Elizabeth, and tonight has been the very devil. First, Caro and William fell out over nothing at all — you know Caro — and then he flung off drinking with brother George, and I had to drag Caro here, for fear she might go after them, and now she has fallen out with Sir

William Rumbold at dinner over whether Racine is preferable to Molière, of all stupid things, and much he knows about it, and she has disappeared, and I must look for her. . .'

'Oh, poor thing.' Lady Liz's sigh was genuine for once. She knew the troubles which Caro had caused, and would continue to cause, her mother.

She watched Lady Bessborough disappear in a flurry of skirts and thought how badly she was wearing. Like her late beautiful sister she was ageing early, rapidly running to fat, and becoming a grotesque parody of the sylph who had once charmed London society.

And she, Lady Elizabeth Foster, deny it though she might, was also growing old, and if she did not persuade the Duke to marry her soon she would not be able to secure her own future, or that of her children.

If only Harriet would come up to scratch and consent to marry Lord Granville. She was sure that were she to do so the Duke's hesitations over their marriage would end. With Harriet gone there would be nothing to stand in their way. She peered across the room to where Harriet sat opposite Lord Granville. Thank goodness she was not being short with him. Of course, the great advantage of chess was that the opponents need not speak to one another, concentration being all.

Oh, if only life were like that, then she would have no need to plot and plan so busily, trying to persuade others to do what they did not want to do. And Henrietta Bessborough was not returning. What could that poor monkey, Caro Lamb, be doing now?

CHAPTER TWO

HARRIET was quite enjoying herself. Lord Granville was a good player who never offered an opponent any mercy, and, as Lady Liz had thought, the necessity not to chatter had soothed her a little, and taken off the edge of her feelings about him.

Instead, while it was his turn to move she could watch both the chess-board — and him.

Really, she had to admit, all over again, that he was uncommonly good-looking, and at thirty-five he had lost the callowness of youth but had not yet begun to age. She could quite understand why so many women had thrown themselves at him, and why, perhaps, he had chosen to catch so many of them. She tried not to think of the greatest catch he had made, and the effect it had had on her.

'You are not playing your usual cunning game tonight, Lady Harriet,' he drawled. 'Are your thoughts with Lady Morpeth — or with Hart?' For he knew how precious to Harriet were her brother and sister.

'With neither,' returned Harriet, trying to think of something witty to say. After the Poodle's diatribe in his favour she had become uncommonly self-conscious. Was the Poodle right to suggest that she and Lord Granville shared many common interests? She supposed he was. And she couldn't talk about that to him, either, but said instead, 'I feel like the man in the legend who, deciding that three wishes would bring perfection to his life, then discovered that he had frittered away all of them on flim-flam — every time I make a good move, it turns into ashes as you make a better one. And all my wishes are gone, for my invention is as poor tonight as yours is good.'

She was suddenly aware that she was flattering him, and that would never do; for too many people, men and women both, had offered him too much praise for both his intelligence and his looks.

She was rewarded, somewhat unexpectedly, for he raised those remarkable blue eyes from their study of the board and turned their full power on her instead.

'A day I must mark with a stone,' he said slowly, and apparently sincerely, 'for you have chosen to compliment me, Lady Harriet, and that is so rare that if I cannot find a white stone, then I must run up a flag. Which one would you prefer, the Union standard, or the Devonshire arms?'

So, Lady Liz had been telling the truth. He had felt her coolness and disliked it. The question was, did he dislike it out of simple vanity — that anyone should not appreciate him — or was it more particular — that his unhappiness arose from the fact that Harriet Cavendish disliked him?

For if the latter statement were true, then that put a different complexion on things. For it must mean that he wanted Harriet Cavendish to like him because he valued Harriet Cavendish's judgement.

Harriet shied away from this, and said with a light laugh, 'The arms of the Leveson Gowers would be the most appropriate, I think. To fly the Union standard over such an event would be presumptuous, and, as a woman, the Devonshire arms are not for me, as females do not carry standards into battle, so we are left only with your arms — if you feel that the occasion is not too trivial for their use.'

'Not trivial at all,' he said slowly, picking up his queen, and moving it briskly down the board. 'And now

I fear that you are in a difficult position, Lady Harriet. Under heavy attack, with little to defend yourself.'

Their eyes met. Her undistinguished little ones, and his distinguished, large and beautiful ones, and for a moment there was no one in the world but Granville and Harriet — and the board between them.

They were, although neither knew it, nearing a point of *rapprochement*, when what had lain between them of distrust on one side, and disappointment at being unvalued on the other side was about to disappear, but the point was not to be reached that night, for the busy world was claiming them again.

Lady Bessborough, her face grey and drawn, her step hurried, was upon them, etiquette and propriety forgotten, her hand was on Granville's shoulder, her distress so patent that *rapprochement* and chess were alike forgotten.

'Oh, Granville, I need you most desperately. Caro. . .' All her usual charming composure was gone. More, Harriet noticed that Aunt Bessborough was on the verge of tears, nay, hysterics. Behind her, Lady Liz hovered, also in a state of acute distress.

Lord Granville rose. His absolute calm was still in evidence. He took Lady Bessborough's hand, said slowly, 'Now, my dear. Pray tell me what ails you, and what you wish me to do. Slowly, I beg of you.'

The control he had exercised over Caro earlier, he now exercised over her mother. She drew a long sobbing breath, said, 'As usual, G, you are right. Caro has fallen out with Rumbold, announced that she hates all the world, and has locked herself into the little study, saying that she will never come out again. She has begun to throw things about. I fear for her. . .the scandal. . .'

'And you wish me to go there, to talk to her, perhaps to bring her out. Come, my dear. Sit down by Lady Harriet. I will go to see what I may do.'

He turned to Harriet, his manners, she was fascinated
to note, still perfect. 'You will forgive me if I leave you,
Lady Harriet. I am sure that you would wish your
cousin to be calmed.'

'Indeed.' What else could she say? The whole world
knew how unstable Caroline Lamb was, and the distress
she caused to all those who loved her. He walked slowly
away. Even at this juncture he did not hurry himself.
He might have been strolling in the park.

'Come, Aunt,' said Harriet gently. 'Do not distress
yourself, I beg. Caro rarely carries out her threats.'

She thought, like Lady Liz, that Aunt Bessborough
looked old and ill, all her bright beauty vanished, and
when she sagged down by Harriet even the brilliant
social face she had presented to the world for so long
had vanished.

Pity for her aunt, instead of the pained exasperation
she usually felt for her, gripped Harriet.

She took her aunt's hand, said gently, 'Do not distress
yourself over-much, Aunt. I cannot believe that Caro
will do anything really drastic, and Lord Granville is
usually able to calm her.'

Lady Bessborough took a deep choking breath. 'You
are right, my dear. And oh, how I wish that she had
married someone like him. She and William love one
another, I know; but Harriet, there are times when I
wonder whether love is really enough,' and she looked
at her niece, her eyes filled with unshed tears almost as
though she were trying to convey some message which
went too deep for words.

Harriet felt compelled to respond, and worldly though
their surroundings were she also felt the necessity to
respond with, 'Only if the love of God, dear madam,
accompanies our love of man can we ever be truly
happy,' and she felt her aunt shudder a little at her
words, almost as though she sensed them as a reproach,

which they were not meant to be, only, for once, Harriet felt that she had to say what was in her heart.

Then, 'Pray for me, my dear, and Caro, too, for I feel that we may need all the help we can acquire, human as well as divine.'

They were both silent after that, Lady Bessborough occasionally drawing a convulsive breath, and then, when she saw Lord Granville approaching, Caro by his side, and he bending from his great height to speak to her in low tones, she made one last comment, 'Oh, Haryo, there are times when I fear that one day Caro will do something quite unforgivable — and who will save her then?'

'Let tomorrow take care of itself, dear Aunt, since today seems to have solved itself satisfactorily,' replied Harriet briskly, before she rose as Lord Granville and his companion finally reached them.

'I have brought Caro, Lady Harriet,' said Lord Granville in his usual pleasantly languid tones, 'to assist me in what I hope will be your defeat on the chessboard. I know it is unfair for me to bring an auxiliary into action at such a late stage, but Caro needs to relieve her boredom a little, and you, I am sure, will not grudge her a late participation in our game.'

He sat both Caroline and himself down in the most ceremonious fashion, speaking as though he had not recently used all his considerable powers of diplomacy to persuade her cousin to let him into the room where she had locked herself and had begun to throw about sofa cushions, books and ornaments, although none, he had wryly noted, was among the most valuable possession in a room filled with treasures.

He had then calmed her down, talked gently to her, so that her crimson and swollen face had begun to return to normal before he had assisted her back to where her mother and cousin sat. He gave Lady

Bessborough a warning look, Harriet was fascinated to
notice, with a slight movement of his head, so that her
aunt rose, said, rather feverishly, 'Oh, I must speak to
Elizabeth,' and walked away, leaving the three of them
together.

The game proceeded, Lord Granville quietly explaining his moves to Caro, and asking her for advice. But
what, perhaps, was more significant, was that he lengthened the game considerably when Harriet knew perfectly well that he had been on the point of checkmate
when her aunt had come to ask for his help.

Why, he's kind, she thought wonderingly. He's
making the game last so that he can continue to calm
Caroline without creating any undue excitement, and
when, predictably, the game ended in her defeat — long
after it should have done — Harriet replaced her scat-
tered white pieces, and said, 'Thank you, Lord
Granville,' for him to look at her sharply, aware that
she was offering him more than simple thanks for the
game.

'Not at all, Lady Harriet; win or lose, a game of chess
with you is always a pleasure,' and he turned to Caroline
and began conversing with her in a low voice, asking
after her little boy, and generally acting as though
rescuing hysterical women and saving their public face
was an everyday occurrence.

'You will forgive me, Lady Harriet, if I do not offer
you revenge tonight, but I am a little tired. The day has
been a tedious one. I should much prefer it if you were
to play for us, and perhaps Caro could sing. A little
music would soothe all our spirits.'

So it would, thought Harriet, agreeing to his request,
her mind full of her discovery about him — that he was
genuinely moved by a wish to relieve the sufferings of
both her cousin and her aunt, and had done so in the
most unobtrusive manner possible. It was an action

AN UNEXPECTED PASSION   29

quite unlike that of the selfish and self-loving person she
had thought him to be.

Why was she surprised? Was not she, Harriet
Cavendish, inwardly quite unlike the person she showed
to the outside world? Outwardly prickly, with an apparent cold command, she was, in reality, tender and
vulnerable, assuming her public armour to protect
herself from pain. Was it possible that Lord Granville,
that self-assured and confident man, also had depths to
his nature which few were allowed to plumb?

He had come to stand by her, to turn the pages of her
music, and she was suddenly more aware of him than
ever. Something he had put on his hair, or had used to
scent his linen, reached her, a hint of lemon, spiced with
herbs, which pleasantly added to the male aroma which
belonged uniquely to him,

Well, she still could not say that he had reversed her
dislike of him, but at least she had discovered that there
was more to him than she thought. She even managed a
little smile at him when she and Caro had finished, and
he was applauding them, and asking if it would not be
too tiring for them to continue, but he would like to
hear at least one more song from them both.

Looking at Caro, who had by now recovered her
normal colour, and had lost the frenetic energy which
had marked her behaviour ever since she had arrived
with her mother, Harriet could not be other than
grateful to him — an emotion which she had never
thought he could rouse in her!

Later, she sat with Caroline in her bedroom. Caro had
announced that she felt tired and a little soiled, needed
to refresh herself, and Harriet had responded by taking
her to her room, where Caro washed her face, and said
frankly to her, 'I know that I was tiresome earlier, but
oh, Haryo, you do not know how William can sometimes

provoke me. He is occasionally so hard — like his Mama. Now, Lord Granville, he can always make me feel happy.'

'So I saw,' replied Harriet, a little drily.

'What a pity you don't like him these days,' remarked Caro, brushing her silken curls and admiring her piquant face in Harriet's mirror. 'You used to like him a lot — whatever happened to change your mind about him?'

'Oh, I think you are mistaken,' declared Harriet; she really did not wish to discuss Lord Granville with Caro. Caro had absolutely no discretion, and would repeat what you said to her in the most artless fashion, however confidential one's remarks were supposed to be.

'Oh, no, I'm not,' Caro retorted. 'I remember quite well that when we were children — how long ago that seems — we used to quarrel about which one of us he ought to marry, and you seemed very set on him then.'

'I can't say I remember things quite like that.' Harriet felt a little agitated by Caro's reviving these unwanted memories. 'Besides, we were children, and he was so much older than we were. We could have no idea what he was really like.'

'A fine gentleman who is kind to me,' offered Caroline shrewdly. For all her nonsense, Harriet thought, she occasionally showed flashes of good sense and judgement. 'But have it your way, Haryo dear, although I assure you that you are wrong. You were really fixed on him. I wonder what William is doing? Dead drunk with George now, I suppose. Sometimes marriage is nothing but a dead bore!'

These sad words remained with Harriet long after Caro and the others had gone. She could not help remembering the dream of love in which Caro had accepted William Lamb, a little against the wishes of her family perhaps, and the ambiguity which Caro now displayed in her relationship with her young husband.

Harriet liked neither William Lamb nor George, his brother; she thought that they were both unfeeling, coarse creatures, and although William undoubtedly loved his wife, and had been desperate to marry her, now that he had done so he hardly knew how to cope with her changing moods.

Would anybody, even Lord Granville, be able to manage Caro Lamb for very long? She begged leave to doubt it. She could only be happy that Caro had not chosen to wait for Hart, who loved her to distraction, and whose heart she had broken when she'd married.

But was Caro right in saying that she, Harriet, had once admired the man who was now in many ways her *bête noire*?

She sat on her bed in her night-rail, her book, for she always read before she went to sleep, neglected in her hand, trying to remember the early days when she had first met him. Strange that she had erased them from her mind. Perhaps, if she could recover the past, she might discover why he had become so inimical to her; why the sight of him caused her to bridle inwardly, however pleasant he might be to her.

It must have been the spring of 1794, and she not yet nine years old, when he had first called at Devonshire House with commissions and letters from Aunt Bessborough to her mother. . . She closed her eyes, and was back in the past again, a little girl being prepared for the drawing-room by her governess, Selina Trimmer, who was then still a young woman. . .

'Oh, do stand still, Haryo; I shall never finish dressing you. Why cannot you be good, like Georgiana?'

'I wanted to finish my story-book,' little Haryo complained, pulling against Selina's urgent hand. 'I hate dressing up.'

She was always conscious that Selina loved Georgiana
best of all. Georgiana was always so good, while she,
Haryo, even at that early age always spoke her mind,
was not interested in dressing up, preferred lessons to
holidays, and loved Mama, but did not love sitting in
the drawing-room with Mama and Lady Liz, being
quiet and good.

Nevertheless she allowed Selina to tie her blue silk
sash and fasten the strings of the elegant little lace
bonnet Mama liked her to wear. Whatever Selina did to
dress her up she would never look as sweetly pretty as
her cousin Caroline, who was now with her Mama in
Italy, or Caroline St Jules, Aunt Liz's little girl, or
Corise de Grammont, the prettiest of them all.

She was painfully aware that neither Georgiana nor
she were considered to be future beauties as the other
girls in the Devonshire House nurseries were. She had
overheard Mama and Miss Trimmer talking about them
once, and Selina had said, 'Well, the two girls may
never be great beauties, madam, but they both have
something better, Lady Georgiana in particular, and
that is a good heart.'

Well, she, Harriet, would have preferred a pretty face;
who could see, or care for, a good heart? She had felt
quite sore for days after that, particularly because she
could not tell what she should not have heard, for, as
Selina was fond of saying, 'Listeners never hear any
good of themselves.'

'Why are we being dressed so fine today, pray?' asked
Caro St Jules, to be told briskly, 'Your mama is
expecting a visitor with letters from Naples. Your Aunt
Bessborough is sending them by a young gentleman she
met there, and there are other visitors expected, too.'

'Some of Mama's "little men",' said Georgiana
eagerly.

Selina Trimmer, the governess found by the Duchess's

mother, the devout Countess Spencer, was herself the
equally devout daughter of a mother whose pious books
and good works were nationally famous, and she made
a little face.

It was not for her to disapprove openly of the
Duchess's way of life, and the presence of her dubious
friend, Lady Elizabeth Foster, but she could show her
dislike of the Devonshire House set's easy ways after a
more subtle fashion.

By her pursed lips, raised eyebrows and her insistence
on her charges' devotion to *all* the ten commandments,
Bible readings and Sunday observance, she was beginning to influence them more and more, although nearly
nine-year-old Haryo was still unaware of her governess's
intention.

'Perhaps,' was all Selina offered them. 'But whoever
is there, remember to mind your manners. Haryo,' she
said sharply, 'remember that you must not interrupt
your mama or Lady Elizabeth when they are speaking.
Little girls must be seen and not heard!'

'Why?' said Haryo naughtily. 'They do not hesitate
to interrupt me.'

'Do as you would be done by.' Selina, like all govern-
esses and nurses, had a fund of such maxims. 'The Good
Lord says. . .' she began, and Haryo let her attention
wander. The Good Lord was given to saying a lot, and
all of it boring.

Selina gave her a little shake, and said severely, 'I
shall ask the Duchess not to let you attend her in the
drawing-room if you are not prepared to be instructed.
You really must take more note of Lady Georgiana's
behaviour. *She* always knows how to behave with the
utmost propriety.'

'She's older than I am,' said Haryo indisputably.

'Be quiet.' Selina found Haryo's already acute obser-
vation of life more than a little troubling. Whatever

would the child say next? Her preference for Georgiana
and the others arose as much from this as from anything
else. Not that she was unkind, but she left the little girl
in no doubt that she was not so satisfactory a person as
the rest, for all her forwardness in reading, writing and
understanding.

It would be nice, thought Haryo disconsolately, if the
Good Lord had made her more lovable, prettier, and
less spiky — this last was an occasional word used of her
by Selina and the nursery maid who attended them.

So she hung back when Selina led them all downstairs, the other little girls chattering in front of her, and
she found herself wishing that the Good Lord would
smite them all dead, as he occasionally did in the Bible,
but leaving her out of his vengeance so that Mama and
Papa would have only her to love, instead of their
affection for her coming after that given to Georgiana
and her dear little brother Hart. They loved Georgiana
because she was good, Hart because he was the heir,
and then Haryo because, after all, she was their daughter, even if she hadn't been a boy when she was born.

And that was being unfair to Mama, she knew,
because when they did arrive in the drawing-room
Mama pulled Haryo to her and said gently, 'How is my
little girl today?' and kissed her on the cheek, tweaking
her pretty lace cap into a better set before letting her go.

After that they were given wooden puzzles to play
with, cut-outs of the counties of England, which put
together made up the whole country. Haryo would have
preferred a book, but it would not be polite, she knew,
to read in company.

Mama and Lady Liz seemed quite excited by the
coming visitor; they were laughing and talking together.
Mama seemed tired and her eyes were looking inflamed
and sore. By contrast, Lady Liz was prettier than ever,
nearly as pretty as Aunt Bessborough.

Her unpowdered blonde curls were caught up in a blue ribbon, and like Mama she was wearing a pretty cream dress with tiny flowered sprigs on it. Her slippers were of cream kid, with little stars on them.

Perhaps the Good Lord would be kind, and she would turn into Lady Liz or Aunt Bessborough when she grew up. On balance, Aunt Bessborough was probably the loveliest of all, quite Haryo's favourite person.

When all the little girls had been pushed and pulled into position they made a dear little tableau as they played with their puzzles, Selina smiling benevolently over them.

'And yes, *he* comes today,' fluted Lady Liz, making eyes at Mama.

'I hope so, I truly hope so,' answered Mama. 'After all dear Henrietta has written of him, I can't wait to see him. I understand that he has to leave for his duties with the militia at Plymouth, so if he does not come today I do not know when he will come. But he has letters to deliver to us, so I am sanguine.'

Who was the *he* who was causing so much excitement? wondered Haryo; a new 'little man'? And what was amusing them so much, for Lady Liz's tinkle rang out beside Mama's deeper tones, and Lady Liz whispered something which sounded like 'another conquest' just as the butler came in and spoke to Mama and they all laughed again, and Mama ordered, 'Show him in.'

He returned to say, 'Lord Granville Leveson Gower, Your Grace,' and both women put on grave faces — as though ready to receive the Good Lord, thought Haryo, irreverent again — and told the little girls to behave themselves.

And then the *he* they were awaiting walked in, and little Haryo knew at once why they were excited, and no wonder.

For he was like a prince in a fairy-tale, so beautiful

was he in his person and his dress. Yes, it was no
wonder he was expected, and the Good Lord had
certainly chosen to bless *him*. To begin with, he was very
tall, and to the little girl Harriet was then he seemed
even taller than he was.

His chestnut hair was unpowdered and had deep
waves in it, his mouth was soft and tender, and when he
smiled he showed beautiful white teeth. But it was his
eyes which held every woman in the room in thrall, even
the little girls, all staring wide-eyed at him.

They were almond-shaped, long and deeply blue; she
later discovered that he had been nicknamed *occhi azzurri*
in Italy, and without his appearing to mean it — quite
unconscious of the effect he had on all around him — his
looks were, to use a favourite word of Mama's, killing.

Even his clothes were remarkable. Because he was
going on to visit the Prince of Wales he was wearing
white satin court dress, with a fall of fine lace at his
throat, and more lace at his wrists, and his suit was
perfectly cut to show off a fine athletic body, the knee
breeches enhancing the length of his shapely legs.

All the little girls, Haryo included — no, particularly
Haryo — fell in love with him on the spot, especially as
his manners were excellent, too. He spoke in a low
voice, a slight touch of aloof hauteur in his manner,
although the absolute attention he always bestowed on
whomsoever he was speaking with took the edge off an
almost languid pride.

'Your servant, Duchess,' he was saying in a slight
drawl. 'Report had told me of Devonshire House and its
many beauties and for once report does not lie,' and by
his gesture he included the little girls in the offered
compliment.

Even at that early age Haryo saw at once that his
manner to Mama was deferential, but to Lady Liz,
slightly less so, the temperature of his greeting and the

bow over her hand both less than those which he had bestowed on Mama.

'And the children,' he said, at last turning those killing eyes on the little girls, who were accustomed to be ignored by Mama's visitors. 'A bevy of future beauties, I see. One wishes one were a few years younger. I envy their contemporaries.'

Corise de Grammont, a little older than the rest and always almost impudently assured of herself, even at this early age, said, as he bowed gracefully over her hand — he honoured all the little girls in turn, ending with Haryo, 'I shall not complain if you care to wait for me to grow up, dear Lord Granville. I promise to do so quickly.'

Everyone, including the recipient of the compliment, laughed at this, and Haryo wished that she could say something witty too, but if she tried it was sure to come out all wrong, 'That child is almost too sharp for her own good,' being Selina's favourite comment.

Instead she blushed scarlet, and ducked her head awkwardly when the tall boy — for he was little more, despite his cool self-command, being not yet twenty-one, she now realised — bowed over her rather grubby paw. She had been playing with little Hart before Selina had readied her for the visit.

She avoided his eyes, sure that, beside the others, plump and awkward Harriet Cavendish could not interest such a stunner — as Corise called him later.

But his manner to her was as kind and gracious as it was to everyone else, and later the cousins agreed that he was quite the most satisfactory of the 'little men' who surrounded Mama, Lady Liz, and Aunt Bessborough, when she was not holidaying in Italy — where she had apparently met the stunner.

He handed Mama the letters which she had been expecting, and then produced a box of bonbons for the

little girls, 'With your permission, Duchess,' and gave
the exquisitely packed little carton to Selina, whose
expression was not quite so approving of him as that of
everyone else.

Haryo could not keep her eyes off him, and when
Mama said, 'Come here, Haryo, and tell me what
exercises you,' for, unknowingly, her expression was
almost agonised, she blurted out without thinking,

'Oh, Mama, the Good Lord has made him look
exactly like the prince in my book of fairy-tales.'

Her mother said gaily to him, 'There, Lord Granville,
you have already conquered two of the Devonshire
House young ladies, and you have only been here these
ten minutes!'

Harriet, sitting on her bed, nearly fifteen years later,
could not remember what he had said in answer, but
she did remember that, later, when he had gone and
they were back in the nursery, Selina had reprimanded
her sharply for taking the name of the Lord her God in
vain, 'And to praise a peacock like that, too!'

'Oh, but he is so handsome,' Haryo protested,
unaware that society had already christened Lord
Granville Antinous, after the famous statue of the
Emperor Hadrian's favourite, a copy of which stood in
the hall at Roehampton, Aunt Bessborough's home.

'Handsome is as handsome does,' snapped Selina —
another of her favourite sayings — only to have Corise
say curiously,

'Why do you not like him, Miss Trimmer? He has
such splendid manners.'

'It is not for me to like, or to dislike him,' Selina had
said firmly. 'Only time will tell us his true worth.' She
stopped short of informing her charges that the beautiful
boy whom they so admired was most likely the latest
lover of Harriet's aunt Bessborough, and was already
noted as a breaker of female hearts, for all his youth.

AN UNEXPECTED PASSION 39

So Caroline Lamb had been telling the truth. When Harriet had first seen him she had been overcome with admiration — no, you tell the truth, Harriet. Confess, what you felt for the stunner was very like love. True, a little girl's love, no more, but love for all that. And whenever he came, either alone, or with some of his many friends — he was the centre of a little group which included Lords Boringdon, Holland and Morpeth, the Lord Morpeth who later, much later, was to become Georgiana's husband — she always looked out for him.

She thought, now, that the grave little girl she had been, so solemn compared with the rest of the light-hearted children of the Devonshire House nurseries, had amused him.

Aunt Bessborough had returned in the summer, she remembered, and had visited Devonshire House, and she and Mama and Lady Liz had chattered and laughed together, talking half incomprehensibly in front of the little girls. Hart had been there, too, and then a whole group of gentlemen had arrived, so many of the little men, Mama had remarked gaily, that really they should have opened the double doors at the end, and thrown the two rooms into one.

He had brought presents again — a spray of flowers for cousin Caroline Ponsonby, whom he had first met in Naples with her mama, a box of bonbons for the other girls, and then he had handed her a small parcel, smiling at her, saying, 'And something for the little scholar,' and watched her unwrap it.

For some reason any attention he had paid to her then always made the young Haryo breathless and gauche. She had gabbled at him, 'Oh, no, Miss Trimmer always says I am a sad lazy thing.'

The fine eyebrows had arched, and he said with the extreme hauteur he always adopted when slightly offended or annoyed, though why this should annoy him

Haryo could not think, 'Then Miss Trimmer is wrong; the little girl who asked me about the Roman temples and the classical beauties I saw in Italy cannot be a backward or lazy child. I thought of you when I saw the pretty book. Your aunt had told me that you were always reading. I hope you do not possess it already. If you do, then I shall have it exchanged for a new one.'

It was a child's version of the myths of Greece and Rome, done in a question and answer form; she had it still, battered from much reading.

'Do not forget your manners, child.' It was Selina breaking in on her delight as she had inspected the crude engravings; one of Apollo was just like *him*, and so she was about to tell him when Selina had disturbed her thoughts.

Gauche again, she had clutched the book to her bosom, exclaimed fervently, 'Oh, thank you, Lord Granville, thank you,' and then greatly daring, as though she were a romp like Caro Ponsonby or Corise, she had taken his shapely hand and kissed it in gratitude.

It was a gesture so unlike her — she was usually withdrawn and reserved — that Selina had stared at her, and he — what had he done? He had bent and kissed her cheek, patted her undistinguished brown curls, and then strolled off to talk to Aunt Bessborough and Mama leaving her holding his present.

'What did he give you, Haryo?' It was Corise who had watched them from a distance, a little jealous. 'Oh, a *book*! I thought it was something interesting. Only fancy,' she said to Caro St Jules, 'Lord Granville has given Haryo a book,' and they had all laughed as though it were a great joke.

The grown-up Haryo closed the book on her knee. Remembering had taken longer than she had thought it would, and, lost in the past, time had ceased to have meaning.

It was very late. Tomorrow Miss Trimmer would be arriving from Brentford to pay her a short visit. The years had changed their relationship; she had not thought then, when Lord Granville had been a young man and she had been a child, that one day Selina Trimmer would seem a rock, a refuge, and, even though she still preferred Georgiana, the knowledge had ceased to hurt, for second best had its virtues, too.

CHAPTER THREE

HARRIET had not thought to see Lord Granville again immediately after the dinner at Chiswick. Before he left they had talked briefly of Madame de Sévigné's *Lettres*, and he had told her that, in his opinion, those of Madame de Maintenon were also interesting. 'But a cold woman, Lady Harriet; she has not de Sévigné's warmth. Her piety froze her, rather than made her soften towards others — besides —— ' and he hesitated for a moment, then said with a certain gleam in his eye ' — the piety is a little suspect, too, given the lady's career, from marriage to the scurrilous poet Scarron to a so-called morganatic union with Louis XIV. You have not read her, I see by your expression.'

'I have not had that pleasure,' Harriet told him gravely. 'Do you think that Raison Sévère,' which was Miss Trimmer's nickname, given to her by the irreverent Devonshire House children, being loosely translated as Strict Morality, 'would approve of such a doubtful choice?'

'Oh, but whatever she *did*,' replied Lord Granville, 'what she actually *wrote* was as strict as even Raison Sévère could wish.'

'An apt pupil of the late Polonius, then,' said Harriet, who had recently been reading *Hamlet*, and had been amused by Polonius's self-serving morality.

'Indeed,' agreed Lord Granville, picking up her allusion instantly, which was one of the pleasures of talking with him, Harriet thought; no need to explain herself, to see boredom glazing over the eyes of whomsoever she was conversing with. 'George Canning once told me that he thought Shakespeare must have known Elizabeth I's minister, William Cecil, Lord Burghley, Polonius's speech being so similar to those recorded of him.'

'I have often thought,' pursued Harriet, determined to continue conversation with someone who knew exactly what she was talking about, 'that it was no wonder that with such a papa both Laertes and Ophelia went to the bad. No example set, one suspects, nothing but expedience, no good home life in Elsinore and "do as I say, not do as I do", being Papa's motto — and now you will tell me that I ought to set myself up as the new Raison Sévère of Devonshire House!'

She had no idea how charmingly naughty her face had become as she came out with this somewhat provocative speech, transforming it in the process. The witty intelligence which informed her private thoughts was suddenly made plain to the world — and to the man seated opposite to her, for he had proposed another game of chess, which they never got round to playing, he preferring suddenly to draw her out, contrasting her favourably with the volatile cousin whom he had rescued from a false position.

'You would have recommended them Bible readings, I see. Perhaps a course of sermons, a little reading of Paley, whom, by the by, I must confess I have not read myself, and then they might have both been on their feet at the end of the tragedy, instead of underground?'

'More than that,' said Harriet, beginning to enjoy talking nonsense with him. 'There might even have been no *Tragedy of Hamlet* at all! Ophelia could have convinced Hamlet that "vengeance is mine; I will repay, saith the Lord" and then he would have peacefully succeeded his uncle Claudius some years later, and all the characters would have expired full of years and honour in an odour of sanctity.'

'But with the disadvantage,' said Lord Granville

gravely, 'that there would have been no play — and what would Kemble have done then?'

'Oh, indeed,' said Harriet, 'but that need not signify; Shakespeare would have written another, one which we shall never now know, and Kemble would have ranted his way through that, and Lady Liz would have cried her way through ten pocket handkerchiefs, instead of five, when she went to see it, for I am persuaded that it would have been even more moving than *Hamlet* — if you think that possible?'

'You do not like Kemble, I take it?'

'Oh, I do — but "this side idolatry".'

He picked up that illusion, too, proving that his learning was not confined to the classics of university teaching.

'Oh, rare Ben Jonson,' he said, raising an eyebrow. 'Never say that Raison Sévère prevented you from undertaking a catholic course of reading.'

'That evenings in winter are long must be my excuse,' replied Harriet, 'and the libraries at Devonshire House and Chatsworth are large, to say nothing of the instruction I gain from Dr Allen at Holland House. He and I are great friends.'

'Then we have a mutual one,' said Lord Granville, 'for Dr Allen is a bibliomaniac, like myself, and you seem set on the same course.'

'Yes,' said Harriet rapidly, 'I am determined to be one of those old ladies, wearing black, carrying a great bag of books, and, to make myself thoroughly incomprehensible, I am thinking of learning Greek, or Hebrew, and writing a book so dull that no one will want to read it, but everyone will say, "Oh, what a brain was there — and we never knew!"'

And I never knew, either, thought Lord Granville, what Lady Harriet Cavendish is really like, and presumably, for some reason at which I cannot guess, she has chosen to show me a little of her true self tonight, a self which she had never shown me, or others, before. Such witty playfulness — there is a flavour of her Aunt Bessborough there, but more serious, I think. The influence of Raison Sévère, one supposes.

But he said nothing aloud, and they both threw ideas about, half seriously, speaking together of Boswell's *Life of Johnson* which Harriet had recently read, and whose high opinion of it she found Lord Granville shared, although he was more tolerant of Boswell as a person than Harriet had been.

And after all, one must not forget what a worldly man Lord Granville is, she thought, but he won her over by remarking carelessly, 'Seeing that you spoke of learning Greek, dear Lady Harriet, you may perhaps remember that Johnson said of Greek that it is like lace: every man gets as much of it as he can.'

'But he said nothing of women and Greek,' said Harriet mischievously, 'and I do not think he had much reverence for the intelligence of my sex.'

'Ah, but he had not the advantage of knowing you,' was his rapid response to that.

The *occhi azzurri* were hard on her as he spoke, and for the first time she gained the impression that he wished, not so much to please her in an idle way, but to be approved of. An idea which shocked her a little, because the approval he appeared to seek was not that of himself as *le beau* Granville, the beautiful conqueror of so many lovely women, her aunt's long-time lover, but as someone with whom she might wish to converse, to share ideas with — as she knew he shared them with her aunt, but no other woman.

How dangerous he was! He seemed determined to overcome what he knew, quite plainly, was her dislike for him. Another aspect of his vanity perhaps, and why should she succumb to it?

As an Indian brave collected scalps to show how courageous he was, to demonstrate what the Romans called *virtus*, was he metaphorically collecting her scalp? To walk away with that charming smile on his face, having overcome yet another woman, this time out of bed, but overcome, all the same.

Her face changed, the lovely spontaneity disappeared from it, she became cold Harriet Cavendish again, and Granville wondered what he had said or done to provoke such an alteration, not knowing that merely for him to exist, to be his usual self, was enough to provoke Harriet Cavendish to unreasoning anger.

All her old suspicions of him, and his motives, had returned, and being a man who understood other men and women — perhaps too well — he knew that it was time for him to go. He rose, bowed, and said, 'You will forgive me if I take my leave. I have had too many late nights recently, and I should like to continue our conversation again — at an earlier hour, perhaps?'

She had let him go, only to retreat upstairs to try to remember what she had originally felt about him, leaving to another time an attempt to discover when her unreasoning admiration for him had turned to an equally unreasoning dislike.

She was standing in the drawing-room the next day, awaiting Selina's arrival from Brentford, the Devonshire coach having been sent for her, a compliment she — and her neighbours — would appreciate, when the butler came in and announced that Lord Granville Leveson Gower had called, and was asking to see her; was she at home to him?

A little agitated, Harriet replied, 'Indeed, you may admit him,' and, even more agitated, rushed to the mirror to check her appearance. It was, as she knew, perfectly proper if a little dull; she hardly looked a

Duke's daughter in a virginal grey wool dress, with a Quaker-like linen collar, a dress as sensible as she was, while he, she assumed, would be as perfectly turned out as ever.

He was. Quite perfect, and one of the reasons for which she disliked him was because his perfection reproached her. He was wearing a black tail-coat, a rather splendid waistcoat embroidered with irises, and charcoal-grey pantaloons disappearing into perfect boots.

His bow was exactly the right depth — oh, why did he not do *something* ungraceful or gauche? It would certainly restore her own confidence. He said, 'How good of you to see me, Lady Harriet. I shall not detain you long. I am on the way to see George Canning — matters political are at a kind of crossroads, he says, a story I must confess I have heard before — but I wished to see you most particularly.'

Harriet saw for the first time that he was carrying a small parcel, which reminded her of her last night's memories, and the little book he had given her not long after he had first met her. Was this another book? It appeared it was.

'I spoke to you of Madame de Maintenon's *Letters*,' he continued, 'and I thought that you might be interested to read them at your leisure. I recently acquired a rather charming edition, in the original French, which I know you can read, and it would give me great pleasure to lend it to you. I hope you will accept this offer in the spirit in which it is meant — that of one book-mad person to another.'

Why, he was almost pleading with her, thought Harriet astonished.

'Of course,' she said. 'I am honoured that you will entrust a treasure to me. True bibliomaniacs do not care to lend their books to anyone, I know, but I shall guard it like a dragon guarding its gold.'

He laughed a little at that, handed the book over, and she opened the parcel to discover a small quarto, bound in green leather, beautifully decorated in gold leaf, with his arms on the front, and when she opened it she found his signature, boldly written beneath a bookplate, the Leveson Gower arms again, opposite to the title page.

'It is not the first book you have handed to me,' she said on impulse, wondering if he would know to what she referred.

'True,' he said, 'I thought that you might have forgotten. I gave you a child's book of Greek and Roman myths when you were a little girl, I believe.'

'*You* had not forgotten, then,' said Harriet, a little surprised.

'I never forget the presents I give to friends,' he replied swiftly, 'and when you have read the *Letters* I shall expect you to speak to me of them, as you did of the myths.'

Harriet had forgotten that; memory was selective, she knew. She wondered what else he had remembered of those distant days which she had not.

'You have not time to take tea,' she offered.

'Alas, no,' he said. 'I should like to stay, but I visited you on impulse.'

On impulse, thought Harriet, greatly surprised. All the way from Stanhope Street to Chiswick in Middlesex on impulse. She wondered what strange impulse that was, but she accompanied him to the door, and promised that she would discuss Maintenon with him when they next met.

He left her feeling a little astonished. She could not flatter herself that he was courting her—she knew that it was common gossip that he had renewed his interest in Miss Susan Beckford—so why this sudden interest in Lady Harriet Cavendish?

Allied to Lady Liz's hints and flutterings, it was all

rather disturbing. He had singled her out last night, and she knew that gossip would enlarge on *that*, which did not please her.

Perhaps she was refining too much on what was, after all, a piece of courtesy — from one book-mad person to another, as he had said.

She was still troubled about his sudden interest in her when Selina Trimmer arrived, and after suitable greetings, and tea being brought in, Selina asked, her voice quite neutral, 'Was that Lord Granville leaving just as I arrived.'

Harriet felt strangely defensive, which was ridiculous; after all, she was a grown woman now, not a nursling in the Devonshire House nurseries.

'Yes,' she said. 'He came to leave a book for me. He thought that I might be interested in reading it.'

'A book?' said Selina, a little astonished. 'What kind of a book?'

'Madame de Maintenon's *Letters*.' Harriet's tone was defensive, despite herself.

'Madame de Maintenon?' Disapproval rode on Selina's face.

'He says they are most extremely moral — even if the lady herself wasn't,' was her somewhat feeble reply.

'Hmmph!' was all Selina had to say to that. 'But you are old enough to choose your own reading, I suppose.' This came out after a fashion which presupposed that Harriet wasn't.

'I hope so.' Harriet most fervently wished Lord Granville and Selina had not overlapped. Selina had always disliked him. Perhaps it was Selina who had changed her mind about him? She really must organise her memories to find out when and why her opinion of him had changed. She must not blame poor Selina on no evidence at all!

CHAPTER FOUR

GRANVILLE GEORGE LEVESON GOWER, the youngest child of the late Marquis of Stafford and his third wife, Susanna Stewart, daughter of the Earl of Galloway, was preparing himself for the day with the help of his faithful man, Frederick Saxe.

After a cold bath he had been carefully shaved, and then Saxe had rubbed his hair with a new preparation which contained oil of lemon, the scent of which Harriet Cavendish had detected on him that evening at Chiswick House.

And after that he had been carefully eased into his clothes, all of them new and clean each day, and in perfect order, no button loose, no seam undone. Oh, my lord was a real credit to him, thought Saxe gratefully; the whole world knew what an excellent valet he had, that he should always be so completely *à point* in every way. Why, even when they went on their diplomatic missions, sailing, or driving into danger, as he did at the battle of Austerlitz, my lord was always more fearful of being caught with dirty linen than being shot at by the enemy!

'Never give anyone an advantage, Saxe,' he had once said. 'The art of diplomacy is to be ahead of your man, without appearing to try,' and, goodness knew, no man could criticise him for that; my lord always looked as though anything energetic was beyond him, even though he kept himself in trim, not at Jackson's gymnasium as many did, but on the tennis court.

Only Saxe knew, now that my lord's mother was dead, that behind my lord's mask of smiling confidence dwelt another man altogether, a man who was genuinely unsure of his powers, a man who only surfaced publicly when he was compelled to speak in the House of Commons. In private, in the office, the drawing-room, and yes, the bed, my lord was supreme, but when called on to speak in public he suffered the agonies of the damned.

His friend Mr Canning knew, and pelted my lord with good advice, which, Saxe privately thought, made my lord's diffidence even worse. Saxe had advised my lord, once, that he get drunk before he spoke, only for my lord to give a wild crack of laughter, quite unlike himself. 'Oh, damn that, Saxe, I shall make a big enough cake of myself sober, but drunk...why, they might as well cart me off to Bedlam after.'

Not that he had ever broken down, and no less a man than Mr Pitt, the Prime Minister himself, had commended my lord on his performances; but there was no saving him; the blue devils flew away with him every time he was called on to rise to his feet and and publicly address those fellows of his who, in private, could not hold a candle to him for wit and self-command.

But he was not going to the Commons today, even though he was to see Mr Canning in the morning, to discuss the political situation, with the country going to the dogs as usual. And at two, he was off to see 'that old woman', as Saxe always thought of her, who had got her hooks into my lord when he was a boy, and had never let go, preventing him from making a good marriage and settling down — that would have solved his House of Commons megrims, for sure.

Lord Granville, his stock finally settled to his satisfaction — it fell white and snowy, a perfect butterfly, 'A cabbage white, presumably,' he had once observed to George Brummell, who had complimented him on it — caught something of Saxe's mood. They had been

together since Granville was a boy, and now my lord
raised an eyebrow at him, and said, 'All to your
satisfaction, my good sir?' as though he, Saxe were the
master, and my lord the man. He was a good fellow, my
lord, and would have been a better one if he had never
met that woman.

Something with which George Canning would have
agreed. That masterly politician, leader of a fragmented
opposition, had known Lord Granville since he had
arrived at Christchurch, Oxford, a precocious fifteen-
year-old, to become the best friend of the eighteen-year-
old Canning. That friendship had been sealed for life
when Granville had invited him to his parent's home at
Trentham, where he had been royally entertained.
Nothing was too good for the young man who so plainly
showed his admiration for the much loved child of the
Marquis of Stafford's old age, the darling of his mother
and older sisters, all of them immensely proud of
Granville's looks, charm and intelligence — he did everything so easily that he had to be pushed to do anything
at all, as Canning already knew.

'Tell me, Granville,' he said later that morning, 'why
do I trouble with you? Here you are, still unmarried,
still keeping up your acquaintanceship with. . .that
woman — even though I gather the liaison is long over.
Make your friends happy, get yourself a wife, settle
down, and when I become Prime Minister you may
have what office you want.'

His tone was not angry, but one of friendly remon-
strance, even when he added, 'You need someone to
steady you, to go home to at night, have your slippers
by the fire. . .' He burst out laughing at his own folly
when he had said this, choking over his friend's
expression. 'No, no,' he finally achieved through his
mirth, 'never slippers by the fire, not you, no, never
that. But you know what I mean; find some useful girl

to feed you gruel when you're sick, breed you a couple of fine children, and I dare swear the world will never know you!'

He looked at his friend with affection, 'I do believe, my dear Granville, that for all your skimble-skamble you were formed to be a family man. I have never forgotten that what first drew me to you at Oxford was the great affection with which you spoke of your father and mother.

'And that is enough of that. Tell me what you think I ought to do about the Chancellorship of the Exchequer. If we do achieve office, I am torn between the claims of Tierney and Huskisson. Huskisson is my man, but I have to offer the others something since a coalition is the only way we shall ever gain power — and if we do get there, I promise you, you will be my Secretary for War. I am sure of that, if nothing else; all your Continental experience fits you for it. Oh, I shall make you work, never fear. I know you, Granville, details bore you, but in the understanding of the overall situation, and its infinite possibilities, and how to deal with them, there is no one to touch you. I have known that since we were boys together.'

Granville knew that this was no old friend's mere flattery. He and Canning had gone beyond that. Besides, all his loyalties were given to the man before him, had been pledged long ago when the older man had befriended the younger boy, and would, he was sure, last a lifetime.

'And you are to say nothing of this to anyone,' went on Canning, energetically, 'particularly to that woman——'

'I thought that you liked Lady Bessborough,' drawled Granville mildly.

'Oh, I do, I do,' said Canning, picking up a map and staring at it, 'but not when she holds you in her toils.

Free yourself of her, and I shall be her friend for life, as well as yours. The War Office is only a promise, remember, I've taken no blood oath on it, and you know politics, but if I can manage it we shall wage war together. After all, how many of my friends were present at Austerlitz?'

'A spectator merely.' Granville was a little dismissive.

'Did you drive away from the battle — or towards it?' Canning was also dismissive — of false modesty. 'You forget, I have heard Saxe on the subject. "I told my lord we were getting too near to the gunfire, and his answer to that was 'Good, let us push on faster, then. My only regret is that Harrowby is not here with us'," and then Saxe always says mournfully, "And it was my only regret, too. Lord Harrowby has more common sense where battles are concerned than my lord".'

'There are times when I wish I had defied my father, and gone into the army, instead of into diplomacy,' said Granville, frowning a little.

'And a fine old waste that would have been,' said Canning cheerfully. 'Plenty of younger sons have made good soldiers, but good diplomats are harder to come by, particularly ones who look so charmingly innocent as you do.'

Granville took the thought with him to Roehampton. The night before, a letter from Lady Bessborough had been delivered to his home in Stanhope Street, asking him to call on her at two this afternoon.

After all these years she had only to express a wish for him to carry it out. The expedition was not convenient, but, driving there in his curricle behind the matched whites which had excited the admiration of more than one connoisseur in horseflesh, he could not help asking himself why she was so urgent. They were to meet at Chiswick again in two days' time, and whatever it was could surely have waited until then.

Nothing of this showed. He carried his perfect manners in with him, to the room where she awaited him, before a roaring fire; the early February day was cold. She was as carefully dressed as she had always been, but the changes in her, which had begun shortly before he left as ambassador to Russia for the second time in early 1807, were more marked than ever.

He had left behind a woman who, if ageing, was still slim and lovely, her airy playfulness still intact, masking the ravages of the years. He had returned in early 1808 to find that the siren who had been his mistress had turned into his mother. She had grown immensely fat and was dreadfully and consciously aware of it.

Passion between them had died, leaving behind friendship—which had always been there, even in the days when merely to see her had been enough to excite him. The habit of loving confidence, of dependence, still remained.

And she, how did she feel about their changed circumstance? he thought, as he bowed over her beautiful hand, which seemed to have escaped the general ruin which had enveloped her. Oh, he loved her still, would always love her, but the love had changed, as the years had taken their toll, the toll of which she had spoken so long ago when she had finally consented to be his mistress.

Lady Bessborough could hardly have felt worse. Allied to the consequences of her sudden and rapid ageing was her consciousness that her liaison with Granville had prevented him from making the marriage which he should have made long ago. If he had been selfish in his passion for her, she had been selfish, too, as George Canning had half hinted to her more than once.

But in the end, what she saw in her mirror—and hated—exercised her the most. That fat old woman she saw there seemed to have little to do with herself. Inside she felt the same as ever, the beautiful Henrietta Frances Spencer, later Lady Duncannon, later still Lady Bessborough, who only had to enter a room for heads to turn.

But, if they did so now, it was not because of her graceful beauty, it was her lack of it.

And he—unknowingly she echoed her niece Harriet—with his cool perfection of dress, his damnable sureness, for which she had once loved him, was now a reproach to what she had become. How could he know of the passions which tore at her? Was he enduring the torments of the damned, as she was? She had lost him from her bed; was she to lose him from her life?

'My very dear,' he said, bending over her hand as though nothing had changed between them. 'You honour me with your invitation,' and he spoke with no intent to deceive, for he could see her suffering, marked plain upon her face.

She turned away from him; she could not bear to look at him, to see the difference between them so starkly expressed, and said, 'You know why I have sent for you, I am sure.'

'No,' he answered her, bowing his head. 'No, my love. I only know that you wish to see me privately, and so I came. Your wishes have been my command these past fifteen years.'

'Not quite fifteen years yet,' said this other Harriet in his life, although why he should remember Harriet Cavendish as he spoke with her aunt was a small mystery, perhaps best not investigated. 'And the time of which I spoke to you when we first met has at last arrived. My dearest G, we can no longer pretend that what we once felt still exists. The dream is over, for you as well as for me. The years between us have at last taken their toll. I must let you go, for, even if we are no longer lovers, you are still tied to me by iron bonds — and they must be broken. It is time for us to part, and you must marry.'

'No,' he said, moving swiftly, taking her hands in his; more, he dropped her hands, and held her, held her lax body, so unlike the supple one of her youth. 'I must not desert you. We may, we must continue as we were. . .'

Henrietta Bessborough pulled away from him, placed her palm over his mouth, and stared into his eyes, in which, as she later wrote, 'I have looked my life away.' She said, 'We can never again be as we were, Granville. You know that as well as I do. The years between us are the wrong way round, and are too long for us to reconcile ourselves to them.

'Look, look in the mirror,' and she swung him, unresisting, towards it. 'Look at you, and look at me. You are almost the age I was when I first met you — and you, you were a boy then, and now you are a man in his prime, and I am an old and fat woman. I can no longer give you a child, and, like the others I have given you, if I could, it would have no real name, no existence. And I cannot go on depriving you of what, in the end, all men need and, despite your protests to the contrary, what I know you want. A settled home, a wife and children you can acknowledge, not the children of the mist, Granville, such as our two are.'

He would have liked to shout, No, you are wrong, but she was only too dreadfully right. He hated what the mirror showed him: that she was a bloated caricature of the sylph-like creature who had enchanted him for so long, and that even if he insisted, said he wished to continue as they were, she was so old and tired that their liaison had come to seem a burden to her.

He still loved her dearly — but differently. . .they were like an old married couple, an ageing husband and wife, comfortable with one another, reduced to sharing only confidences, not the passion once so fiercely felt.

They could no longer pretend. Truth stared them in the face. From the beginning their love had been a doomed one. They were separated, not only by her husband and her beloved children, by the codes and conventions of their world, but also by the relentless years between them, which were now demanding their cruel payment.

What had his loving, but stern mother once said to him?

'Payment is always demanded of us, Leveson; never forget that. God may forgive us our sins, but he does not fail to exact from us the punishment which those sins entail.'

Punishment was upon them. For, in his heart of hearts, he knew that Henrietta was right. He did want his freedom. He wanted a settled home, a family, a wife, who, even if he could not give her the love which he had given his mistress, would be his to care for, and who would care for him. Above all, he wanted children.

He turned away from her, put his hands over his face in a gesture of despair quite unlike his usually urbane, almost impassive manner. The man of iron self-control for once showing weakness. He felt that his youth was leaving him, that the cruel years were claiming him, as well as his mistress — as they were.

'I would have married you, had you been free, but I could not ruin you by asking you to leave him — and he did not deserve that either.' He meant the husband they had both deceived.

'I could never have left him, you know that, G.'

The pet name she had always used for him; it further undermined him, 'And you wish me to marry.'

'Yes, a marriage of convenience — love would be too much to ask. I wish it, because you wish it.'

'You know that I have tried for many years, my dearest, to do exactly that.' He had dropped his hands, stared at her with a ravaged face. 'But I have never been successful. It was not for the want of trying.'

'No,' she said sadly. 'You have never really tried, Granville. It has always been a game with you. You were never serious. . .then.'

'Never serious? But what of Sarah Fane, the Barbarian. . .?'

'You always found some means,' she said, and again, 'to make sure that you were not successful. Now, you must be successful. For my sake, as well as your own.'

'You know that I have been courting Susan Beckford,' he said. 'To little avail.'

'Ah, yes, the Sapphire,' she answered him lightly, alluding to the pet name by which they had spoken of her in their letters. 'Not remarkaby pretty, but rich. They will not let her marry you, Granville. They want an heir to a grand title for their money, not a younger son, however handsome and gifted. And have you any feeling for her at all? No, I think not. Why not try for a Pearl?'

'A Pearl?' he echoed, intrigued despite himself.

'Yes, a Pearl, whose relatives would be happy to see you marry her, a Pearl who would. . .keep us still in touch, if only at a distance, who would look after. . . them, perhaps, later on, when she has given you legitimate heirs.'

He was still bemused. 'I cannot think of whom you speak?'

Weary amusement rode on her face. 'Not, indeed, not? You surprise me. I mean my niece, Harriet Cavendish.'

And now she had surprised *him*. Emotion spent, he had become cool, distant almost, she thought, as though he were negotiating with her over some treaty, each concession argued for and hardly won. From being warm, moved, he was suddenly as cold as ice. She hardly knew him.

'Ah, now you do astonish me, madam. The very last name I might have thought you would put forward. She does not even like me; she has made that plain enough, many times.'

'You seemed to be enjoying your conversation with her the other night at Chiswick. A good basis for marriage, one might think, better than dangling after a pretty face, or some chit's money-bags.'

'Do I hear you aright, madam? You are proposing that I marry Lady Harriet for her *conversation?*'

'There *are* worse reasons for marrying, G. And you haven't seemed really enthusiastic about marrying for money, or looks. And reflect, all your many mistresses have been required to be witty and amusing as well as beautiful — will you have many mistresses if I encourage you to marry Harriet, I wonder? Am I doing her a favour? Although I think that she would be very good for you, and, I am sure, marriage to you would benefit her.' Her face twisted a little, with grief, regret, or even possible jealousy. 'Harriet. . .she has only to be known to be loved.'

Granville was suddenly not sure how serious his mistress was, until he saw and heard the pain beneath the light utterances.

'I own,' he said slowly, to please her as much as anything, 'that she struck me very differently the other evening, was not like my previous impressions of her at all. I found myself thinking of her, visited her yesterday to lend her a book, we were. . .cheerful together. But marriage. . . I had not thought of that.' He looked up, said firmly, 'No, it will not do. She might have been briefly pleasant, but I fear she detests me——'

'Oh, no,' said Lady Bessborough, emotion making speech difficult. 'I think not. I don't think she detests you, Granville, no, not at all,' and seeing his disbelief, said softly, 'Take another woman's word for it, I beg of you. I know she adored you as a little girl — and then something went wrong. . .'

Oh, Henrietta Bessborough knew quite well what had gone wrong, that for some reason adoration had turned to jealous hate when Harriet grew up enough to understand what handsome young men like Granville Leveson Gower got up to, and with whom. She knew the secrets of the human heart, and had read Harriet's body language correctly. '*Odi et amo*', the Roman poet Catullus had said, 'I hate and I love', and Harriet Cavendish's feelings for Lord Granville were, her aunt thought, equivocal, to say the least.

'But, if you do decide to court her, Granville, be sure of one thing: Canis will not give her a good dowry. They have been at outs too much. Harriet is good — and honest — and her father resents the clear eye she turns on him. Will you give her occasion to turn that clear eye on you? Will you be faithful to her? You were never faithful to me.'

For once he coloured, looked at a loss, said, 'You were never my wife, which, as you know, was my greatest grief. Had you been so, I would never have looked at another woman. I will be faithful to my wife, I hope, though God knows I have broken enough such vows to you, about love and other matters.

'And this is what Lady Liz and you have been plotting,' he added suddenly. 'Oh, women should be diplomats — devious deception comes to you all so easily.'

'And you have never deceived anyone?' Lady Bessborough was satiric. 'The Barbarian, for example.'

She meant Princess Galitzin, whom he had met in

Russia, whom he had thought of marrying after she had
divorced her husband, but she had never understood
that in England a divorced woman could not be
received. Even though he had been prepared, like Lord
Holland with Elizabeth Webster, to live with that, she
had not. Besides, she had deceived him with other men,
he had found, while protesting purity.

'I never lied to the Barbarian,' he said stiffly, 'and
she was never my mistress.'

'But not for the want of trying.'

'Oh, you wrong me,' he said. 'Besides,' and this was
unlucky, 'she was clever, I enjoyed her conversation. . .'
He suddenly realised what he had said.

'So is Haryo clever, and you enjoy her conversation —
but I forgot, the Barbarian was beautiful. . .'

He was stung, thought of Harriet's eager amused face
as she had spoken to him. 'Beauty is not everything.
There are better things than beauty in a woman.'

'A good heart,' his mistress agreed, and added with a
pang, 'Harriet has that, too. And she would be faithful,
and not because she is not a beauty, but because she
would wish to be.'

A marriage of convenience, to his former mistress's
niece! Cold-blooded was hardly the word for such a
scheme. He thought of the two women hatching it. Was
that why Lady Liz had been fluting and fluttering at
Harriet? Why Lady Bessborough had persuaded him to
play chess with her, thrown them together?

And yet. . .and yet. . .did the idea attract? He had
gone to see her, drawn by her wit, before this monstrous
proposition had been put to him — but he still felt like a
character in a bad French novel, something hidden
among the sofa cushions, gloated over in secret.

But what he would achieve by this convenient marriage would be a middle-class domesticity, a faithful
little wife, even though he did not love her, children,

Canning's 'slippers by the fire'. He thought with a pang of what he had, what he had lost. . .and because after all he had no knowledge of what he *might* gain, being a man who always contemplated branching possibilities, remaining aware that such speculation was simply that — that no speculation, however clever, however informed, could determine the future — so he knew that any such gain might not be a simple equivalent of what he had given up for it.

The face he turned on Lady Bessborough was the mask with which he stared down the world. She saw it with profound regret. Only in the depths of passion, when quite alone with him, had she ever felt that she knew the true man who was Granville Leveson Gower, stripped of the armour he assumed to guard himself from failure and the world's despite.

'No,' she said violently, 'do not look at me like that, Granville, not like that. For all that we have meant to one another, do not let me become one of the. . .others, those whom you hold at a distance. . .'

He had to control himself, she must understand that, but he must offer her something, here at the world's end.

'Oh, my dear, my very dear, for you are still that, I do not wish to end completely everything that we have been to one another. You will still let me write to you, will you not? And you will write to me — there would be no treachery to a wife in that, for what I wish to continue is the meeting of our minds, which was always as important as the meeting of our bodies, and which has survived that. You will allow this, I know you will.'

The pleasure she took in retaining this last tie was a mixed one. For, if what he said was true, how was it possible that he could withhold that same mind from the woman he married? And more, did not this explain his half-hearted pursuit of marriage to women with

whom he instinctively felt he would never be able to
forge such a bond — so that when he did marry, inevitably he would choose someone with whom he would
share that which so far, for all his *affaires*, he had only
shared with her?

Oh, it was heaven, it was hell, that the one woman he
might find with whom he could enjoy such a bond was
her niece! Heaven because if he married Harriet she
would not lose his company, would constantly see and
speak to him; but hell because if he married Harriet she
would lose him in the deepest sense, because he would
offer Harriet what he had so far only offered her —
himself!

Something of all this showed on her anguished face,
for he took her in his arms again — for the last time,
groaned a voice sounding deep within her — and said,
'That we always knew that it would one day come to
this is no consolation when it happens. Grant me what
I wish.'

'Yes,' she said. 'Yes, with one proviso; if such an act
distresses the wife I know you will now take, then it
must end. You must grant me that.'

'Willingly,' he said, his eyes closed, his lips against
her hair, memory fuelling desire a little, but the little
that it did underlining the end they had come to.
'Willingly.'

'And now you must go,' and she detached herself
from him. 'If the end crowns the work, Granville, then
let us be a little proud, for we have ended in amity,
without reproach, what could only have begun in
reproach, our condition being what it was, and is.'

'Like the old Romans,' he said softly, 'falling on our
swords to kill, not ourselves, but our passion; but, unlike
them, rising to live again — a different life.'

And later, driving towards Stanhope Street, the reins
in his hand dictating his journey, so often had he made

it that he knew every stone, every landmark on the way, the sense of an ending so strong in him that he felt old, older than his years, unknowingly like Harriet he took himself into the lost past. The past where only a beginning existed, and a boy could convince himself that an ending would never come.

CHAPTER FIVE

LORD GRANVILLE would never forget those magical months he had spent in Italy in early 1794, never. They would be with him until he died, and only when he at last faced death would he know how true that feeling had been — joined with another which at the time of his liaison with Henrietta he did not know he would possess.

Oh, he had already, despite his youth — he was not yet twenty-one — visited Paris, *Ville de Lumière*, City of Light, and loved that, another love which he would retain to life's end, and then Potsdam, whose stiff Prussian classicism was not to his taste, and St Petersburg, where the barbaric splendours he encountered fascinated him, as well as the ageing Empress, who had admired the handsome boy he had been, barely eighteen then. But Italy — Italy was quite another thing.

Ironically, he had not wanted to visit Italy, had been ordered there against his wishes on a further extension of the young aristocrat's Grand Tour. His father had written to him sending him instructions to leave Plymouth, where he was stationed with the militia, and where a military life had begun to attract him.

'No,' his father had said. 'You are to be a diplomat, not a soldier. You must know languages, and the countries with whom you will be dealing,' and he had been given leave to join the Royal Navy ship *Dido* that was leaving for the Mediterranean, and, after changing ships and an exciting voyage, he had at last arrived in the golden land with which he had fallen into a deep and abiding love once he had set foot there.

The blue skies, the scenery, the remnants of both the

classical past and the glorious Renaissance of which he had so often read enchanted him.

He had not been alone. His friends from his schooldays, Borino, Lord Boringdon, and Henry, Lord Holland had accompanied him on his journey south, and, although they did not share his enthusiasm completely, they, too, were half in love with the romantic land through which they travelled.

Early on they met Elizabeth, Lady Webster, the great heiress, already bored with her bucolic husband Sir Godfrey, and looking for adventure. She had made a dead set at him, but he was fastidious, found her coarse and loud, had no desire to make such a woman his mistress. She would bully him, as she bullied everyone, and already he was becoming discriminating in his conquests.

So she turned to Lord Holland, and bullied him, first into an *affaire*, and then, when Sir Godfrey divorced her, into marriage, being a little spiteful about Lord Granville Leveson Gower, who had rejected her, ever afterwards.

But all that was to come. In the here and now he admired statuary, paintings, frescos, ruined temples and villas, haunted bookshops to find interesting texts and prints, the love of beautiful objects already strong in him. The others laughed at him a little, but kindly. Everyone loved Granville Leveson Gower. He was a beautiful object, too, with charming manners, and already possessed the gift of making people think that he cared for and was interested in them for all his haughty pride of manner.

And then they reached Naples.

He knew that there was an English colony there, many of them fellow aristocrats. Some he already knew, and some he did not. His poor mother, when told where he was bound, had sent him a long and agitated letter

warning him against the female sirens there, and one in
particular whom she did not mention by name, nor did
she need to.

Granville, thirty-five years old, now a man of the
utmost and cultured sophistication, could look back and
appreciate his mother's alarm for her beautiful son who
needed to use all his energy and talents to make his way
in the cruel world, in which a younger son was required
to create his own destiny, and not be side-tracked by
chasing women, least of all experienced beauties such as
the one he had been about to meet, whom he could
never marry, when what he needed most was a rich and
single heiress.

For Henrietta Ponsonby, Lady Bessborough, in her
mid-thirties, was one of the most famous belles of her
day. She had been born a Spencer, one of the legendary
Spencer beauties produced in every generation. She was
even more lovely, some said, than her more renowned
sister, Georgiana, Duchess of Devonshire, 'the face
without a frown'.

More than that, she was witty and intellectual, celebrated for her sparkling conversation, just the kind of
person, thought his mother, writing feverishly back in
England, who was most likely to attract a young man,
clever himself, who loved cleverness in others and
particularly, most remarkably in his generation, in
women.

He did not call on her immediately. Tired after the
journey, he and his companions waited until the following day to visit her in the villa which she had rented for
herself and her children.

Naples was all and more than he had expected: the
bay, broad and beautiful beneath the endless blue sky,
the pines and cypresses all about it, the beautiful
classical villa where on arrival he was told that milady

was in her garden with the children and was expecting them for they had sent a messenger before them.

He walked through the scents of the spring flowers, along a winding path, past statues of the gods, and stone cherubs playing among the grass, fountains spouting through the mouths of bronze dolphins and tritons, down a small avenue of cypresses to a shaded lawn — to see her.

Granville, remembering, knew now that she was at the very crown, the zenith of her beauty, before it began slowly to fade. Rumour, for once, had not lied, he had never seen anything quite so lovely. She made Elizabeth Webster seem even coarser than she was. She was unfair to all women, for they paled before her.

She was wearing a gown of the lightest blue, with a white sash, belted high around her waist, and her little feet were clad in white kid slippers. On her floating blonde curls she wore a cream straw hat, with a huge brim, and a pale blue ribbon around the crown.

But it was the lovely face which all this perfection framed which was the magnet which drew his eyes, banished all other considerations from his mind but that this beauty should be his.

The perfect oval of her face, the deep blue eyes, the high-arched nose, the adorable kissable mouth, and the humour which informed everything she said and did, and which was present even when she rose from her seat on an elaborate iron bench to greet them, captured him immediately.

'Lord Holland, Lord Boringdon and Lord Granville Leveson Gower, I am happy to welcome you here. You have come to relieve my boredom a little,' and, seeing the surprised look on Granville's face, added, with a deepening of her slight smile, 'Oh, even living in paradise becomes boring after a time, Lord Granville. Perfection palls in the end.'

He was bending over her hand as she spoke, and he said, like the conceited puppy he must have been, 'Oh, if I have to ruin perfection to please you, madam, then consider it done!' And his eyes gave off the message which he wished them to, and, seeing them for the first time, Henrietta, Lady Bessborough, nearly thirteen years older than the boy before her, knew that she would need all her self-control to keep him at arm's length — even if she wanted to.

The others were equally enchanted by her, and by her little girl, Caroline, a fairy of a child, like something in a Renaissance painting, so fine and delicate was she, but Lord Holland was already captivated by the dominant woman who had made him her target, and Lord Boringdon, taking one look at the expression on the faces of his friend Granville and Lady B. when they first spoke to one another, knew that any hopes he might have had of impressing the lady were doomed to failure. Lord Granville had done it again!

Only, Granville thought wryly, where, before he had met her, the pursuit and capture of the desirable fair one had been all that had mattered to him, with Lady Bessborough his feelings were quite different. Oh, yes, he wanted to conquer her, make her his mistress, but he also wanted her love — and, perhaps more importantly, her friendship.

His poor mother, he thought, all these years later, had had the right of it. The lady had not even needed to sing her siren's song, and she had netted him!

Oh, yes, he would always remember those few weeks they spent together, laughing, talking, riding and walking in the beautiful countryside, sharing their joint delight in the treasures all about them. Her husband, Lord Bessborough, made nothing of their friendship — he was used to his Harriet being admired, loved her, and stayed in the background; drawing and sketching were his passions, not his wife.

Her mother, Lady Spencer, smiled on the handsome boy, too young, she wrongly thought, to be interested in her beautiful daughter, merely a nice safe companion for her—which he was. . .then.

Once, they all jaunted out together, a fine family party, even seven-year-old Willy, who had taken Granville in affection—everyone loved him then, he remembered wryly—to see Vesuvius in eruption. They did not progress far up the mountain; Lady Bessborough was too fearful for them all, 'You included,' she said, laughing up at him, maddening him by her nearness— which was yet so far.

'Oh, yes, G,' she said to him one afternoon, as they walked on the beach, the children running about them, Lord Holland and Lady Webster talking earnestly where they sat on the sand, her husband drawing, as usual, Willy tagging along behind him, like a faithful dog, 'you have ruined perfection for me, to create—dare I say it?—a new kind of perfection.'

He was already growing a little bold, held her with his amazing eyes, said, again like the puppy he was, 'Oh, you can confer a perfection on me that no one else could touch, any time you care to, Lady Bessborough. You have only to say the word, and I will be your willing slave forever.'

'Ever and always?' she queried him. 'What nonsense, G. You are young enough to be my son.'

'Ever and always,' he replied, taking her little hand and kissing it. 'And you must have been most amazingly precocious in the nursery, madam, if you are to propose yourself as my mama.'

'No more precocious than you, sir. Your reputation runs before you, for all your lack of years.'

'Dust and ashes,' he said. 'Mere fall-out from

Vesuvius, dead lava, all its glow gone, if I may not be allowed to worship at your shrine, and offer you a lustration. They say the gods still live in these parts, but it is a goddess I would wish to worship,' and again he looked at her, and again she hardened her heart.

Oh, she had told him years later, she was as dazzled as he, but she was wilful, wanted to have the handsome boy at her heels, worshipping her, but she would give him nothing. He must learn that not every woman was willing to worship at *his* shrine. He needed to be taught a lesson, and who better than Henrietta Bessborough to teach him one?

Had they become lovers then and there, as he so passionately wished, it might have finished then and there, the long liaison never growing between them. But no, she held him off, tantalised him, reminded him of her husband, her children, her reputation, and the net grew tighter and tighter about the poor fish, who, for the first time, was denied what he had come to see as his rightful prize. When they parted—for he was recalled to England and the militia, the war having grown more urgent—she wrote to him constantly, long amusing letters; a modern Madame de Sévigné, he called her once.

He laughed at himself at last. Dismounting from his curricle, calling for his boy to take the horses in, for he had driven alone to Roehampton, it was as though, now all was over, he could judge himself a lot—and his lost mistress a little.

Rejecting him for so long, she had bound him to her the more securely. Every woman he took as his mistress after she had refused him, and before she finally became his, reminded him of the one woman he might not have. What had begun in Naples in spring and sun was not to end until this day of winter and cold.

And now he was to start another life, a new incarnation, as though he were widowed, he thought, and thought again of the niece she had recommended to him, who had looked at him with such a grave face, until something she had said had informed her whole face and, yes, her body, with such delighted wit, wit of a totally different order from that of her aunt's, as salt was different from sugar — and yet both were related.

Attic salt — a delicate wit, he told himself, and. . . I could do it, make it mine. Time and chance must have their way with me, for planning will not answer. I have woven my deceits for too many women, but for this one I shall forget them. Let Henrietta and Lady Liz plan; I shall not. I shall go to her innocent in that sense, if none other.

'Georgiana,' said Harriet Cavendish, to her sister Lady Morpeth — she was visiting Park Street where the Morpeth tribe, Georgiana, her husband and their six children had arrived from Castle Howard, the noble family home in Yorkshire. 'Georgiana, have I told you how strangely Lord Granville has been behaving to me? Morpeth said that he is coming to supper tonight, and I thought I ought to warn you of his changed manner. I hardly know what to make of it.'

Georgiana looked affectionately at her sister. She was cocooned in a large armchair, suffering from she knew not what — Georgiana's hypochondria was famous, and no wonder, Harriet always thought, with so many children born so rapidly, one after another. If she, Harriet, married, would she have a child a year? She sincerely hoped not.

'Yes,' Georgiana said patiently. 'It is the third time you have mentioned his name, although you have not told me before that he has altered his manner to you. Have *you*, perhaps, altered your manner to *him*?'

Harriet coloured, tossed her head a little defensively.

'No, indeed no, not at all. I have remained politely cool
to him, as I always am.'

'Poor Doodle,' said her sister irreverently. 'I know
your polite coolness. It would freeze the Sahara. It
certainly froze both Duncannon and Althorp.'

Harriet coloured again. 'I think we ought to stop
calling him Doodle,' she said. 'It's not really appropriate. After all, he cannot be one, if he was Mr Pitt's
protégé and Lord Malmesbury's favourite diplomat, as
well as being at such ins with George Canning.'

'Oh, we are singing a different song, are we?' commented her sister shrewdly. 'What has brought this fit
on?'

'Nothing, something,' said Harriet restlessly. 'He
showed me a different man at Chiswick the other
week—we had some sensible conversation. I thought
that he had changed a little.'

'Still very taken with Aunt Bessborough, then?'
Georgiana's question might seem irrelevant, but was
most decidedly not.

'Yes and no, to that as well,' was all Harriet could
find to say. 'The temperature there seems to have
dropped since he came back from Russia.'

'Not surprising,' yawned Georgiana. 'They are both
growing old.'

'Oh, I wouldn't exactly call Lord Granville *old*,' was
Harriet's answer to that, so sharply that her sister stared
at her, and diplomatically changed the subject. Evi-
dently any comment at all about Lord Granville might
be the wrong one.

Georgiana was thinking of this conversation with her
sister when she changed the table seating at supper,
putting Harriet bodkin between Sir William Rumbold
and Granville. Before it, she would have kept Harriet
away from *il bel uomo*, but she was suddenly curious to
see them together.

After all, Morpeth liked Granville, thought him a good fellow beneath all the diplomatic lacquer which years of negotiation, both at home and abroad, had given him. Pitt, and later Canning and the leaders of his party, often used Granville's powers of persuasion, behind the scenes, to reconcile foes and keep friends happy.

Harriet had taken more care with her toilette than she usually did. She thought ruefully that there was not much she could do with her little eyes, or her overlarge arms, but at least she could wear something more attractive than usual, and she dressed herself in a new bluey green silk, with a gauze overdress, and wore the little pearl necklace dear Mama had given her, and the ring and bracelet which went with it.

She also brushed her undistinguished hair hard, and persuaded Walker to make it look a little less severe, so that when Lord Granville took her in she was feeling more pride in her appearance than usual.

Before that he had come straight to her after bowing coolly to Sir William Rumbold, in a way she had come to recognise as his own. He was perfectly polite to a man for whom he did not care, but without any hint of the rapport which he usually appeared to offer to his hearers — even to herself, when she had to admit that she was often provoking him by her own cool manner.

Freezing the Sahara, indeed! Did Georgiana really mean that? It was a little dismaying to learn that she was quite so forbidding. She supposed that it arose from her determination not to share in the charming falsity of the manners of both Lady Liz and Aunt Bessborough — who had sent word that she and Caroline would not be here this evening, for poor Caro was unwell again.

She would edit her tone a little — try it out on Lord Granville, emulate his, perhaps. And the only result of making *that* resolution was that when he arrived before her she was conscious of her mouth twitching at the very idea that spiky Harriet Cavendish could ever be as coolly charming as he was, so that, having bowed over her hand, he said, 'You appear at evens with the world this evening, Lady Harriet. You have enjoyed your happy day at Park Street?'

Goodness, he must be a mind-reader as well, to pick up her amusement so quickly. She was unaware that her eyes and her body were giving off their own message—which was one Granville had trained himself to pick up long ago, one of the essential qualities of a good diplomat being the ability to detect what the other fellow might be thinking, rather than what he was saying.

'Oh, indeed. I am always at ease with Lady Morpeth. On paper, or when we are together, our minds meet, and that is a great consideration for friendship—for sisters are not always friends, you know.'

'True, Lady Harriet, and we are both fortunate, are we not? My own sisters not only love one another very much, but are happy to share a little of that love with me.'

Well, that was something he did not need to tell her! The whole world knew that the Leveson Gower children had spoiled their baby brother from the moment he had been born to the very day that he stood before her saying this.

What was it like to be loved and spoiled? Would she ever know? She was painfully aware that no one in the whole wide world ever put Harriet Cavendish first—not even Georgiana.

Disgusting self-pity, Haryo, her grandmother Spencer would have said to this. Count your blessings, child, for few in this world have so many: health, wealth, position—do you want happiness as well?

And all the time that these wild and subversive

thoughts were running through her head Harriet continued her conversation with him, wondering if his thoughts were running at cross purposes to what he was saying, as hers were.

'And Madame de Maintenon? How do you find the lady? I must insist on a proper report as to your opinion of her, and her letters, you being such an excellent letter writer yourself, Morpeth tells me.'

'Oh,' said Harriet, eyes shining again, 'what a fraud she is. Only the exquisite nature of the book in which her pious hypocrisies are printed enabled me to continue reading her at all! The excellence of the binding, like silk to one's fingers, the beauty of the type, and the width of the rivers of space which run on each side of her. . .*litany* of self-deception quite make up for the nature of what I am having to read. Not that I reproach you for lending her to me, you understand. Oh, no, you have furthered my education, and that must be a consolation to you for my lack of enthusiasm for what has done so. I am sorry if my feelings about the lady offend you after you have been kind enough to trust me with your treasure.'

She had rarely spoken so frankly or at such length to him, or to any other man for that matter, revealing so much of the true Harriet Cavendish, the mordantly witty woman who dwelt beneath the plain and serious aspect she showed to the world.

But it was apparent that he was enjoying what she said, and when she had finished, looking up at his own more than six feet of height from her five feet six — which was pleasant in itself, for her height usually made her self-conscious with many men, who were little taller, if as tall as she was — he said approvingly, 'No, Lady Harriet, far from offending me, I am wondering what else from my library to give you to read that I might enjoy such trenchant and informed comment. Have you read Machiavelli? There is a fine gentleman for you to report to me on!

'I have half a mind to treat you as I might one of my acolytes, and ask you to write out, in a fair hand, and in detail, all headings neatly underlined, your judgement upon *The Prince*. Only do not let Raison Sévère know that you are doing so. Were she to read it she would expire at the end of the very first chapter from mortification at the mere notion that such a corrupt fellow could exist at all,' and he looked across to where Selina Trimmer was sitting, occasionally casting disapproving looks at them both.

'Oh, I think the fact that he was an Italian, not an honest John Bull of an Englishman, would comfort her — after all, it is only what one would expect from foreigners, is it not?'

His perfect laughter was provoked again. 'And have you heard the old sixteenth-century saying, Lady Harriet — "An Englishman Italianate is the devil incarnate"?'

'No, but I have now. And do you believe that, Lord Granville?' And, greatly daring, aware that suddenly she was flirting with him — flirting? With Lord *Granville*? — she added, 'After all, are not you a little Italianate yourself?'

'You flatter me,' he riposted softly. 'I had hardly dared to think anyone had noticed. Not that I am not at heart a true John Bull, but one refined a little, I hope, by acquaintance with those who are his cousins.'

'I am perfectly well aware of your John Bullishness, Lord Granville. I shall never forget your distaste for Georgiana and Lord Morpeth when you thought at the time of the short peace they were growing over-fond of the French. Your strictures on their conduct ring in my ears still.'

Harriet did not know that she had given herself away

a little, by showing him how much she remembered of their past conversations. It was nearly eight years since he had said that to her, and the man opposite, thinking of what Lady Bessborough had said of her — that she did not truly dislike him — thought that love and hate were different sides of the same coin, and that he would like to turn the coin over, to see the other side, so that the face she showed him would be a different one.

'I am happy to hear that my opinions are so well worth remembering — particularly as upon that occasion the French so obligingly proved me correct in my judgement of them. One's excesses are not usually so rapidly rewarded.'

It was Harriet's turn to laugh, and to reward him for a little self-criticism. 'Your judgement, I believe, is usually good, even if you do belong to the wrong party.' For the Devonshires were prominent members of the great Whig oligarchy which had ruled England since William of Orange came over in 1688, while Granville was a member of the opposition to them, not so far to the right as his friend Canning, being more a middle-of-the-road man, hence his value to both parties, although it was also known that Canning considered him his principal adviser.

'Wrong party?' he drawled, raising his beautiful eyebrows. 'Now, Lady Harriet, there is a conundrum for you. Who is to say which is right, and which wrong? Upon what authority do you make such a statement? Come, inform me quickly, a verbal answer only. I do not demand a manuscript with neat ruled headings, merely the exercise of your sound common sense.'

Oh, he was singling her out, no doubt about it, and, if she felt a little easier with him on the surface, beneath it her mind was a-buzz. And what's his little game, eh? She asked herself in an inward imitation of eighteen-year-old Hart, talking of one of his school fellows and doubting his motives, as she was beginning to doubt Granville's.

She had a great mind to tell him that it was his cousin, Susan Beckford, on whom his interest was supposed to be fixed, but she had told herself before he had arrived that she would mend her manners to him, but. . .but. . .

As she had surmised at Chiswick a couple of weeks ago, was it possible that there was a conspiracy to foist him on her, led by Lady Liz—and if so, why?

She could not believe that she genuinely attracted him. His taste in women was so different from herself. She thought of the procession of beauties—apart from her aunt—who had fallen to him. She remembered an evening when several of them had had nothing better to do than sit there pulling faces all night, watching him in adoration, united in one thing only: their mutual admiration of the man who had been their lover. No wonder he though all women were in love with him!

And not one of them could be called plain, or inexperienced, and she was both.

Meantime she must answer him; he was looking expectantly at her, waiting for her to spark at him, no doubt, so she duly obliged by looking slightly arch, and simpering at him, 'Oh, dear Lord Granville, pray do not expect me to answer a question so *difficile*. It quite moithers my poor brain. I am sure you know much more about such things than I do. It is surely for you to instruct me?'

This rather cruel imitation of someone who was a cross between Corise de Grammont and Caro St Jules at their silliest when speaking to young men almost deceived him, until a slow smile crossed his face when he grasped what she was doing.

'Oh, no, my dear girl,' he said softly. 'You are not getting away with that piece of charming impudence.

You may flim-flam others, but I have spent a good deal of my life seeing through flim-flam. You forget, I now know perfectly well what a good mind is hidden behind your innocent exterior.'

'Check,' she said. 'I see I must interpose a piece, or mate will shortly follow. Suppose I answer that to the mind of God, as Bishop Berkeley or Dr Johnson might say, all political parties are at one in being insignificant—would that restore my position on the board? Or do you have some other cunning move to offer, such as that the Pope has issued an encyclical to demonstrate quite otherwise?'

Now this was truly witty, for she knew that Granville and Lady Bessborough had nicknamed his friend Canning the Pope, and the allusion would not escape him.

Nor did it. His smile, from being his courtly diplomatic one, grew into something much more human; she dared swear she might call it a grin.

'Oh, stalemate, Lady Harriet, stalemate. I see I must take care when we converse. For you have offered me three proofs of your quality. An understanding of Berkeley's philosophy—we must discuss his concept of the mind of God as an explanation of human understanding one day soon—the knowledge that Dr Johnson half approved of Berkeley, and the cunning to play on my good friend's nickname. You will allow me to pass the witticism on; it is the kind of thing he most appreciates, and will give him a different understanding of the Devonshire House ladies.'

'Of whom he does not completely approve,' said Harriet shrewdly. 'He thinks we lead you astray, and have done since you first came a-calling. And now I must share in the blame, you think?'

'Oh, he would approve of you,' was his answer to that. 'For you are Raison Sévère's prize pupil, and as such the Pope, being infallible, will hold you in esteem. He will think that *your* friendship can do me nothing but good.'

He thought of Canning's 'slippers by the fire' as he spoke, and knew immediately that what his friend had said was true. Harriet Cavendish, despite her name and family, was the kind of person of whom Canning was thinking when he spoke of the necessity for him to make a stable marriage with a good woman who would care for him.

Were all events conspiring to make him think of a marriage with his former mistress's niece? How would she view such an offer? He was well aware that beneath her playfulness and her acerbic wit lay a stern rectitude — although it was also plain that she judged herself more harshly than she had done others.

And in her beleagured situation, the false position which her father's retention of his mistress had placed her, she had so far not put a foot wrong, behaving perfectly without antagonising the artful woman who was busy carving herself and her family a future, and yet not compromising her integrity.

For the first time he truly felt for her, and when they were, immediately after this, called to supper, he put out an arm for her, and the expression on his face, although he was not aware of it — although Georgiana Morpeth was, and raised inward eyebrows — was a tender one.

And also, for the first time, Harriet felt for him more than the plain dislike which she had told herself was the staple of her attitude to him. There was more to him than she'd thought, and she again asked herself why the simple worship she had once felt for him had changed to the hard antagonism of recent years. She must examine herself and her conscience, as Grandmama Spencer was fond of saying, for the fault might lie in her, not in him.

CHAPTER SIX

'I DON'T like walking in the grounds since that nasty deer tried to gore me,' confided Walker, Harriet's personal maid, to Sam, Harriet's footman, as they walked behind her in the grounds of Chiswick House. She was carrying an extra cloak for her, and Sam held a large green umbrella.

'That's why I'm here, ain't it?' was Sam's somewhat grunted reply to that. They neither of them shared Harriet's passion for walking, particularly on a raw late February day. Behind them lay the fireside, comfort, tea and Cook's scones.

Harriet, ahead of them, was walking as if her life depended on it — and thinking as she walked. She had seen Granville twice more at Park Street for a few brief moments. Georgiana had fallen ill, and she had nursed her.

He had been all gentle and friendly solicitude, saying, 'You look a little weary, Lady Harriet. You must not let your concern and care for your sister damage your own health,' and his eyes had shown that what he was saying was more than simple politeness.

What could it mean? She shied away from the obvious explanation for it seemed so improbable. If only she could talk to someone, but when she wrote her letters to dear Hart she could not bring herself to say anything, to ask his advice. Lord Granville, whom she was suddenly aware had figured so largely in them, had disappeared.

Unconsciously she quickened her pace, Walker and Sam groaning and muttering behind her, unseeing of the wintry beauties of the landscape — Chiswick's glories usually delighted her, and the animals which lived in the park, many of them acquired because of Hart's strange passion for the exotic. They might frighten her a little, but they also intrigued her.

She had reached a stretch of water on which Muscovy ducks paddled, and stopped for a moment, sinking on to a bench, Walker and Sam on another, although neither wished to linger in the cold of the grey day.

And while they sat there, a man came towards them, walking briskly, covering the ground with long strides. As he drew near she saw that it was Lord Granville, for once almost hurrying — most unlike him!

He smiled slightly on seeing her, and she rose to greet him, her surprise showing.

And, as she turned towards him, the park before her, the winter all about her, and he, standing there, a hedge behind him, the sun trying to struggle through low cloud, she had the oddest sense of *déjà vu*, something like a migraine, for the world swirled about her, and then steadied again.

'A good day to you, Lady Harriet,' he was saying. 'They told me that I would find you here, and needing the exercise — I have spent the day in the office — I thought that I would join you. Chiswick's grounds are not so large, but you kept up a fair pace.'

'I was thinking,' said Harriet faintly. The sight of him lately was beginning to do strange things to her. Her breath shortened and strange quiverings began inside her. He had always had a strong effect on her, usually lost in anger — but this was ridiculous, she must be getting some unusual kind of megrims.

'Walking is useful for that,' he agreed, 'and if one's thoughts are strong, then one's pace quickens, I find. The mind and body sometimes work strangely together. But I did not come to talk natural philosophy with you.

I came to bring the Machiavelli I promised you. I have left it with the librarian for you to claim when you return. You will allow me to escort you back to the house?'

'Willingly,' said Harriet, wondering again at him. 'And I will return Maintenon, or you will think I belong to the race of book thieves, forever damned to the lowest hell in Dante's *Inferno*. I must admit that I was sorely tempted to hold on to it, with cries of, "Oh, dear, Lord Granville, I have quite forgot to return it. Tomorrow, perhaps", and then, when tomorrow comes, "Oh, but I have mislaid it quite. Never mind, another day", and so on, *ad infinitum*.'

She was talking so foolishly and so rapidly to dispel the almost distress which his presence was beginning to cause, unaware again that what she was saying pleased him, her conversation being so wittily unlike that to which young girls usually treated him.

He began to talk of Paris, of Paris as it must have been at the time of the Sun King, Louis XIV, whom Madame de Maintenon had married secretly in his old age, and she listened with interest, saying, 'I have never been to Paris, but I should like to. This wretched and everlasting war makes it difficult for us to achieve all our wishes. Will it ever end?'

'Only when Bonaparte is defeated,' he replied, refusing to call him the Emperor, as he always did. To Granville Leveson Gower Napoleon would always remain an upstart who had seized his titles by force, and by force must be compelled to relinquish them.

'We shall be singing *Rule, Britannia* together at this rate,' said Harriet, forgetting her reaction to him, and incapable of resisting a joke, when one presented itself so easily.

'Oh, I refuse to stand to attention too long in this keen air,' he said laughing. 'I am happy to have found a fellow patriot. Too many Englishmen admire Boney because he is successful, and because anything foreign is to be admired for its own sake.'

'A strange sentiment for one who possesses and loves so many things one might term foreign,' said Harriet, compelled to quiz him a little, to provoke him perhaps, into losing a little of his unbroken calm.

'Oh, no,' was his answer to that. 'One accepts the best and most beautiful of what one finds, both at home and abroad, but we must never forget what we most truly are—and defend it to the utmost.'

What was it about him? The charm he displayed so effortlessly, the charm which almost frightened her with its power, so that—and here was a discovery—she armoured herself in anger against him.

She remembered something Lord Morpeth had said, one evening at super to Poodle Byng, when the Poodle had been talking about why one liked or disliked people—that there were some people whom everyone liked and some whom no one did.

'Difficult to find someone everyone likes,' Lady Greville had remarked, only to have Morpeth look up from his plate and say in his common-sense way,

'I can think of one quite easily. Lord Granville, now, he has a genius for friendship, and yet he remains very much his own man, which is perhaps a little explanation of his power.'

Harriet had longed to say, You are wrong there, for *I* do not like him, but truth, as well as propriety, kept her silent, as silent as she was now, for he had begun to talk about the war in an interestingly informed way—not patronising her as a woman, she suddenly understood, but explaining a little when he spoke of those things of which women, even the cleverest of them, were not informed, such as battle order, and the nature of strategy, which he told her, in answer to an interested question from her, was not at all the same as tactics.

'Tactics on the battlefield only,' he said, 'but strategy, now *that* is the overall conduct of a war, you understand,' and when she questioned him a little further, again enlightened her in his cool way, so that she said to herself, Now, I know why people like him; it is because he subtly tailors his speech with them so that one gains the notion of two minds in rapport—a delightful sensation. Why have I never noticed that before?

She was thinking of this later, when he had gone, taking his beautiful copy of Maintenon away with his beautiful self—for she could no longer deny, or laugh at his attraction.

It is urgent that I understand my long-held dislike for him, a dislike which I fear is still there, hiding under my new-found pleasure in his company. She thought of the strange moment of *déjà vu* which had overcome her, when they had turned back to the house, the feeling that if she pursued the origin of this almost occult sensation she would understand something of herself and her heart.

And then, as she settled herself in bed, the wintry landscape of Chiswick suddenly rose before her, like a transformation scene at Drury Lane, and it was not Chiswick she saw, but beloved Chatsworth, on a day even more wintry—and she knew when her blind adoration of him had turned to something resembling hate—and why. . .

It was the winter of 1801, she was a gawky sixteen-year-old, a backward child, she knew now, in one thing only. The knowledge and delight of there being two sexes had not really touched her. She had laughed at the two Carolines and Corise huddled together in corners, whispering and giggling and talking of their beaux, Morpeth, Duncannon, Althorp and the other heirs to

great names, who clustered about them, and who were
beginning to take an interest in the flock of pretty girls
at Devonshire House.

Only I was not a pretty girl and in my superior way I
thought them silly. I did not want to know about the
forbidden thing, of *that*, and in a way I might have had
the right of it, except that I was as stupidly fixed in my
determined ignorance as they were in their eternal
obsession with the opposite sex.

It was a cold day, she remembered, snow still lying in
small heaps, and most of the great party assembled,
spread about Chatsworth's noble rooms, were enjoying
themselves indoors, the house full of conversation.

The girls were chattering about one of society's sexual
scandals, she could not remember which one, now, and
she looked up from her book to say wearily, 'Have you
nothing else to giggle about? Not all men and women
are so concerned with love and intrigue as you seem to
think.'

'Much you know about it,' retorted Caro Ponsonby,
once Harriet's favourite playmate, but who had changed
so much during adolescence that she and Harriet were
now almost strangers to one another. 'They are all the
same. One must expect one's husband to behave like it.
They are not at all like the heroes and heroines of the
books you read, by no means.'

'Oh, I cannot believe that,' she replied, and then,
unwisely, 'Lord Granville, now——'

She got no further; all the girls screeched together,
and began to laugh.

'Oh, come, Haryo, dear,' said Corise, when she had
got her breath back. 'You surely cannot mean that?
Particularly Lord Granville, why everyone knows of his
affairs with nearly every beauty in society, he's the
worst — or the best — of them all. . .'

'No,' she had said wildly, 'I do not believe you, he's

not, I know he's not. . .' Oh, he could not be, her beautiful prince. Perhaps at the back of her mind there was some silly belief that one day he might come for her, older, and still spotless, untouched — an innocent girl's dream.

Their laughter grew cruel, Caro St Jules saying, a little maliciously for her, 'Silly Haryo, is he still your fairy prince? He's everyone's fairy prince!'

She knew that they were speaking the truth, even knew, at the back of her mind, that she, too, had known, but had not wanted to know, that the beautiful man who had been so kind to plain Haryo would, of course, have his pick of lovely women — and would enjoy them.

It was too much. She rose, scarlet in the face — she had a horrid habit of blushing in the most coarse way — and saying, 'I am stifled, I need air,' she had almost fled the room, she so desperately wanted to be away from them all, nearly knocking over Selina Trimmer, who had just come in, in her haste to get away.

She had not even summoned Walker, or Sam, she had fetched a greatcoat, and pulled on some stout shoes, and alone, as she had always been forbidden to be, she had opened the door to the outside world and begun to walk through the beautiful gardens, their beauty a strange frozen one, winter having its delights as well as spring and summer.

She had not been truly happy for nearly a year; growing up had been a penance for her, since she was coming to understand that she would never be a beauty like the other girls, and that hurt, how it hurt. She was so conscious of her lack of looks, and, although no one was unkind, she knew that she was forever doomed to be plain Harriet Cavendish, was she not?

Their mocking laughter rang in her ears still, and the knowledge that her idol was flawed, was no better than

the rest, and that she could not come to terms with her
own growing sexuality, was like a weight to be carried.

She knew now that she was a late developer, but she
did not know that then. The other girls were pretty,
rounded things, already exuding sexual desirability,
while she, she felt a gawk, and gauche with it. They
giggled, simpered, looked through their fingers at men,
endlessly they whispered their secrets to one another,
Harriet left out. On and on, they never stopped, speaking so boringly of this and that, boys, men, marriages,
affaires, until she wanted to scream.

No, they must be wrong about him, they must be, she
did not want to believe them, or even her own treacherous heart.

Feverishly she galloped down the avenue of box
hedges, past the stone nymphs and satyrs, touched with
hoar frost, as though the whole world had become a
black and white engraving, and she alone, forever alone,
in it.

And then, she saw them.

They must have thought they were safe, they two,
quite alone. They must have slipped out together,
because they could not bear to be apart, Lord Granville
and her beautiful Aunt Bessborough. They were standing together, face to face, only just touching. Her aunt's
hands were by her side, and he, and he, was holding
them with both his hands, looking down at her, as she
looked up at him.

The young Harriet knew nothing of passionate love,
the demands it made on the body, and yes, on the mind,
too. Her love for Granville had been hero-worship only,
a child's love for someone who had been kind to her,
but the expression on their faces needed no explanation,
no, none at all. What they felt for each other was written
there plain for all to see.

No, no explanation was needed; everything about

them told its own story, and for Harriet the little world of her imagination, the world where Aunt Bessborough and he were separate, both beings whom she adored — she had always wanted to be like her aunt — was shattered. And the idolatry she had felt for him dropped dead on the spot.

They did not speak, and they could not see her, and how long they stood there, motionless, she never knew. A minute — or was it minutes? — the lovers quite unaware of the child, for she was still a child, who watched them, with grief and anger, and yes, jealousy, all intermingled.

Then he bent his head, lifted up his left hand to cup her aunt's graceful head with it, his intent to kiss her unmistakable, and perhaps, she thought now, she had already known what lay between them, but had refused to recognise it, to shatter her dream of him, and her.

She could not, must not, watch them further. She broke and ran, the tears silently sliding down her face. Oh, he not only loved every lovely woman, but he adored her Aunt Bessborough, the woman's heart which suddenly occupied the child's body informed her of that. The passion he and her aunt felt for one another was a replica of all the grand passions of which she had read in her books — and she hated them both for it.

And the hate was stronger and more bitter for all the love she had previously felt for them both before.

Somehow she reached her room without anyone seeing her. She could not have spoken to them — her throat had closed, and he whole body felt numb. Why did she feel so shocked? She knew as well as anyone else that the married women in their world had *affaires*, once they had given their husbands legitimate male heirs, and that their husbands looked for consolation outside the home.

Not that kind Uncle Bessborough did, and the

thought that they were deceiving him as well as herself added to her shock. She was not to know that Uncle Bessborough did not mind—or was used to his wife's life, was only too happy that she had taken for a lover someone as discreet and careful as Granville always was, so that no open scandal ever ensued.

He was even happy to give, later on when they left Chatsworth, his wife's young lover a lift back to town. Like everyone else, he valued Granville Leveson, as he called him, as a good companion.

But the young Harriet, the true pupil of Selina Trimmer and of her sternly devout grandmama Spencer, could not tolerate such goings-on. They seemed shameful, and she sat in her bedroom alone, not crying—she had gone beyond tears—facing at last the true nature of the society to which she belonged.

It was not, it could not be right, to behave so. And when she finally dressed herself to go downstairs, she looked so careless in her person, and so ill in the face, that Mama said to her, 'Haryo, my darling, are you unwell? Should you be going in to dinner? Would not you prefer a tray in your room?'

'No,' she said, 'no. I walked too far in the cold this afternoon, I am tired merely.'

But she could not eat her dinner, was conscious of the other girls' covert amusement, for they had some notion of what disturbed her, although they knew nothing of what she had seen.

She could not help it: she was surly with Aunt Bessborough, who also commented that she did not look well, and later, when Lord Granville came up to ask her to play chess with him, she did not possess sufficient self-control not to be rude to him. The fact that he was so kind to her, was quite the most splendid person in the room, looking more handsome than ever, made matters worse, not better.

Before the afternoon's revelation she had meant to ask him, the next time that she played chess with him, to speak to her only in French while he did so. Lord Morpeth, who sat in a corner with her sister Georgiana, whom he was shortly to marry, had told her of the perfection of Granville's French, and she wished to improve her own, but when he spoke to her, her throat closed again, and she said, stiffly, 'Thank you, no. I prefer to read tonight, Lord Granville,'

Her manner to him was so strange and stiff, so unlike her usual eager friendliness, that her Mama noticed it and frowned. Haryo was sure that she was thinking, yet again, how very prickly she was, compared with the two Caros and Corise, who were almost unnaturally sophisticated for their years.

As always, his manners were perfect. 'Another night, perhaps, when you are feeling more in the mood for mimic warfare — and I, of all people, know how potent the lure of a good book is.'

And other lures, beside that, thought Haryo nastily. Looking at him, at the perfect face, and the splendidly athletic body made her feel worse than ever since for the first time the eyes she cast on him were not innocent. She knew that he was no Prince Charming in a fairy-tale, but a man, and a desirable one, who had pleasured many women, and her head buzzed and rang with the knowledge.

'Perhaps,' she said, giving him her shoulder, being so short with him, that her Mama, hearing her, sighed again, and called her over.

'My dear,' she said, 'Lord Granville intends only a kindness to you when he asks you to play. There are many in this room who would account it a favour for him to give them a game.'

'Well, I don't,' she had said, almost rudely, so that Selina Trimmer, overhearing her, spoke sharply to her

before she went up to bed. Selina did not like Lord
Granville, 'Such a bad example to us all,' but that was
no reason for a sixteen-year-old girl to be impudent to
him, and to her mama over him.

'Really, my dear Harriet,' she had said, 'you must
learn a little polish. You are growing too old to behave
as wilfully as a child would. Whatever you think of
people—and I am far from an admirer of Lord
Granville, as you well know—the civilities must be
preserved.'

'Must they?' she had said. 'Why, pray? Is hypocrisy
to be admired, then? I thought not, from all you have
said to me, over and over, down the years,' earning
herself yet another stiff reprimand.

'You really do chop logic all the time, which is not
admired in a man, still less in a woman,' Selina said.

She was rude to Aunt Bessborough, too, and ever
after found that she felt for her aunt the strangest mixed
emotions which she could hardly control.

Harriet was not old enough then to know how much
sexual jealousy informed her feelings towards them.
Indeed, she made her new dislike for both of them so
plain that Lord Granville knew that he had lost the little
worshipper at his shrine, and Aunt Bessborough became
aware that Harriet, who had always behaved so lovingly
to her before, was now quite rough in her manner, to
the degree that she became defensive towards her niece.

Niether of them, or indeed anyone else in their world,
knew what had brought about her change of heart.
'Poor Haryo is always so spiky,' said Corise in her pretty
broken English, 'and the older she gets, the spikier she
grows.'

Lately, the spikiness seemed to be disappearing a
little, the grown-up Harriet, lying in her bed at
Chiswick, thought. Age must be smoothing me down,
and she felt herself beginning to giggle. I am even

becoming a little frivolous. I must not take myself *too* seriously, especialy now that I have chosen to remember why I changed towards him so dramatically.

And it is also quite plain, to me, and probably to all the world, that whatever existed between him and my aunt in the way of a passionate affair is quite over — and if that is so, and he seriously wishes to marry, and not pretend to chase heiresses, can it be possible that he and the rest of them are thinking of a marriage of convenience between the pair of us?

For Harriet knew, and the thought was painful, that after the years of coolness between them any marriage with him would perforce be one of convenience. After which, no doubt, he would feel free to continue his career among the pretty married women of their circle.

She shivered, staring into the darkness. Be honest, dearest Haryo, she thought mockingly, for without self-knowledge there is nothing — tell the truth, that your childish love for him has never died, merely hibernated, and if you have ever truly desired any man that man is Granville Leveson Gower, and his existence, and his alone, has killed off every attempt at marriage which Mama, Grandmama Spencer and Aunt Bessborough have made for you.

And now you might be able to have him.

Harriet sat up, eyes wide in the dark. 'Not on those terms. No, never. If I marry, it will be in honour, if not in love, and my husband must be mine. I do not wish to share him with others. And if that dooms me to be a spinster — so be it!'

CHAPTER SEVEN

'HARYO, dear. . .' said Georgiana Morpeth to her sister, as they sat in Park Street, for Harriet was paying her a visit from Chiswick, and had informed her that as the months were wearing on they were probably returning to Devonshire House, as more convenient to see their friends; town was filling up a little, early in the year as it was. 'Haryo, dear, you were quite right. Lord Granville has become most particular in his attentions to you. It is beginning to occasion comment. Has he given you any hint as to why this should be so? Everyone had assumed that he was making a leg at Susan Beckford, but he quite neglects her these days.'

'I think,' said Harriet carefully — for some reason she did not want to discuss Lord Granville with Georgiana any more than she cared to do so with Hart, and this was strange, for she usually confided in them both, 'I think that he merely likes talking to me, and playing chess.

'He said the other night that he found my conversation refreshing. A lukewarm tribute to someone you are making a leg at, I think — and what a stupid phrase that is. Why not say courting, and have done with it?'

'Morpeth seems to think that Lady Liz would be happy to have you accept him, if only to get you out of Devonshire House, so that she might then marry Father.'

'Well, she certainly spends all her time cooing about him and his excellences to me,' conceded Harriet, 'that is, when she is not spending it admiring with equal enthusiasm Papa's new litter of greyhound puppies. I hardly know which particular delightful spectacle she is asking me to praise the most, the length of the dogs' legs, or Lord Granville's resemblance to Antinous or Apollo, or whatever god in the Pantheon is exercising her at the time. I am reduced to sighing, "Oh, yes, Lady Liz, quite so, Lady Liz", or, "Indeed, quite superb, I agree"—comments which serve equally well both for him and the dogs.'

'One thing is certain,' answered Georgiana when she had finished laughing at this, 'you are droller than ever these days. Morpeth was saying the other evening that you are better than a Drury Lane farce——'

'Which is hardly difficult,' interjected Harriet.

'—and Granville was agreeing with him. He said that a really witty woman is a pearl beyond price, because it is a quality so unexpected that to secure it must be a trophy for the most demanding man.'

'Did he, indeed?' said Harriet, opening her eyes wide. 'I suppose that is making a leg by proxy, since the recipient of the compliment was absent.'

Georgiana laughed again. She thought that since Lord Granville had suddenly begun his attentions to her Harriet had blossomed. She was more careful with her toilette—she looked quite striking today in a plum velvet, trimmed with silver braid—and her wit was less sharp, more urbane.

'I wonder what Aunt Bessborough thinks of all this,' she pursued, watching Harriet's face carefully.

'Very little, I believe,' answered Harriet. 'You know we had the whole Bessborough tribe yesterday, including Duncannon and his wife, and her manner to me was as half and half as usual. Apologising to me for living one moment, half reproving me for not being sufficiently polished the next. Sometimes I think she is putting Lord Granville up to this, and sometimes I think that she is discouraging him, and I don't know which supposition I like the least.'

'And do you never regret refusing Duncannon?'

'I never refused him,' said Harriet quickly.

'Discouraging him, then.'

'No,' said Harriet slowly. 'He is a good fellow, but not my good fellow, and I am still not sure how much she wanted me to accept him, and I know that she did not want me to accept Althorp when Grandmama and all the Spencers were wild for me to have him.'

'And you are not sorry that you stood him off?'

'Not at all. Oh, Georgiana,' she said, rising, and going to the window. 'There are times when I do not feel formed for marriage at all. Such a bore, constantly having to please a man, "dwindling into a wife" as that old play which I should not have read — Selina would have died if she had known I had — said so cleverly.'

'Selina Trimmer,' said Georgiana reflectively. 'I am not sure that she has been a good influence on you. Oh, I do not mean in terms of virtue, but that she has given you the notion of making impossible demands of the world and of men. There is no perfection to be found in it, Haryo, either human or divine. I am happily married, I know, and I love my children, but to breed at the rate which I do. . . I would not have chosen that beforehand, even if I do love my little ones to distraction now that I have them.'

'Lord Granville does not approve of Miss Trimmer, either.'

'So one would expect.' Georgiana's face was suddenly full of the kind of wicked amusement more usually found on her sister's. 'Can you imagine what such a worldly creature makes of such a charmingly naïve one? They are chalk and cheese.'

'And I am like Selina, you think?'

'Not at all, but she has. . .inoculated you. . .'

And at this critical point in the conversation Lord Granville was announced.

He had come, he said, as much to see Morpeth as anything else, something which Georgiana begged leave to doubt, for Morpeth was usually absent of an afternoon, but he was delighted to see the pair of them together, consented to sit with them, and his manner to them was as coolly charming as it always was.

He made no distinction between the sisters, paying them an equal respect, laughed at Harriet's mild jokes, asked after Georgiana's children, refused tea, said that he must be off, duty called, by which he meant the House of Commons, they supposed, which he confirmed by saying that he was needed to vote there—he had been an MP from the early age of twenty-one.

After he had gone, Harriet fell silent, and did not speak until Georgiana rang for the tea board—and muffins. 'I feel like a muffin,' she announced, and they came, oozing butter, disgracefully difficult to eat, but delicious for all that.

'I shall grow fat,' Georgiana announced, mouth full. 'What are you thinking, Haryo? So unlike you to be silent for so long.'

Harriet stared at her untouched muffin, said, almost painfully, 'I was thinking that men have a life of which we know nothing. To us, Lord Granville is a charming man in the drawing-room, the dining-room, and the ballroom—or in Hyde Park. But, and this is important, he has a whole life of which we really know nothing. A life of great affairs, of politics, of diplomacy, life which hardly touches us, and which we cannot share, not even the cleverest of us.'

She paused, and said, 'It is a shocking thing to say, but we women live on the periphery of men's lives, Georgiana, for beside all that there are their little dinners, their clubs, the gaming houses, and as you know, worse than that. . .of which we may not speak. How little they have to do with us, after all.

'And that is why they hardly understand *us*, our letter writing, our enthusiams for discussing the affairs of the heart — while they discuss affairs of state — so that what we do and say seems unimportant.'

She fell silent, picked up her muffin, while Georgiana looked at her compassionately. 'You are so clever, Haryo,' she finally said. 'It makes you unhappy, doesn't it? Could you do what men do, do you think?' She genuinely seemed to want to know.

'I don't know. Perhaps, if we were properly educated, instead of trying to educate ourselves, as I do. I love Hart, but there he is, fooling about at university, wasting his time, while I. . . I know that I would have loved to go, and would really have worked there.

'Oh, I am being stupid — I suppose most men are right when they think of us as fools. They certainly treat us as such. Even Althorp, perpetually fixed on hunting, considers himself superior to the best of us, and I sometimes think that Lady Liz might have been less of an ass if she had been properly trained to do something, instead of having to spend all her life pleasing men, so that she might not starve.'

She finally bit into her muffin. 'Do you think Granville wanted to meet Morpeth so that they might go gambling together?'

So that is what has brought this on, thought Georgiana shrewdly, but she answered calmly, 'Morpeth gambles, I know, they all do, but not like Granville when he has the fit on him. Morpeth says that when he is out of it he always vows he will never game again, and then. . .when it returns, he cannot resist it.'

'Like an illness,' was all Harriet had to say to that.

'Indeed. Morpeth says it is most strange, for Granville is otherwise so careful, so prudent and cautious, weighing up risks, so calculating, whether he is being the politcian or the diplomat, but on the gaming tables, no such thing — he is a wild plunger, all caution gone, no notion of prudence.'

'Perhaps,' said Harriet slowly, 'it is a relief for him, not to be the man he usually is.' She saw by his sister's face that she was being too deep for her, and decided to talk trivia, forgetting Granville and politics and what women might or might not be able to do, chatting instead about little George, a delightful child, who loved Aunt Haryo dearly, and all the petty domesticities and gossip which made up even a great lady's life.

They talked easily of Caroline St Jules, and her determination to marry George Lamb, William Lamb's brother. 'I own I do not like the Lambs,' said Harriet, 'which is uncharitable of me, I know. Selina thinks that I ought to like everyone, and then judge them, regretfully but firmly. I tend to begin with the judgement — and omit the liking.'

'She is set on marriage, then,' sighed Georgiana. She was never as stern about people as her sister, being gentle in all her ways, earning Selina Trimmer's approval so easily because she need make no effort, Harriet supposed. 'I am not fond of him, or the rest of the Lamb tribe, either, and that includes Emily. I can just about endure William, but George. . .' and she shuddered delicately.

Both sisters contemplated large, loud, red-faced, red-haired George Lamb, the son of Lady Melbourne, but not of his putative father, her husband. The whole world knew that the Prince of Wales had fathered him, as Lord Egremont had fathered his elder brother, William. 'He is exactly the opposite of anyone whom I would have thought Caro would have preferred,' said Harriet. 'The attraction of opposites, one supposes, she being so

fine and delicate and good-natured.' George was not
famous for his good nature, both sisters knew.

'She must truly love him,' continued Harriet. 'As you
and Morpeth used to do, they sit in corners, lost in one
another's company, "the world forgetting, by the world
forgot", an example to everyone as a pair of turtle
doves.'

Inwardly she laughed. Could one conceivably imagine herself and Lord Granville ever doing any such
thing? Well, she might, but Lord Granville? No, no, sit
in corners, lost to the world, forgetting one's party
manners, never, never; one could never imagine him
showing emotion in pubic.

'So, they will marry, you think?' queried Georgiana.

'Why not? Given her circumstances, she cannot hope
for the best, so the fact that she is settling for very much
not the best is fortunate, which is unkind, I know, but
that is the way of the world.'

Both sisters had long ago became aware that Caroline
St Jules was their illegitimate half-sister, the unacknow-
ledged daughter of their father and Lady Liz. It made
no difference to their affection for her, but they were
keenly aware that, that being so, she could not hope to
make a grand marriage. They resigned her, regretfully,
to George Lamb, with the hope that there were depths
to George they had not plumbed — Georgiana's wish.
Harriet was not so sanguine.

They passed on to consider other fascinating gossip.
Like all their world, she and Georgiana were intrigued
by the Paget scandal, unable to understand how Lord
Paget could desert his wife and large family to run away
with Lady Charlotte Wellesley, who had deserted her
own husband and four little children. Would there be a
duel? Would there be a series of divorces? Who would
marry whom? Naughty to dwell on such a thing, but
delightful, too. 'Selina would say that no good can come

of it,' remarked Harriet, 'and one wonders — if the first partner did not answer, will the second?'

'So bad for the children,' sighed gentle Georgiana, to whom a stable family life seemed the be-all and end-all of everything, with which her sister wholeheartedly agreed. One more reason, perhaps, for not marrying Lord Granville — should he ask her, of course.

Harriet was developing an empathy where Lord Granville was concerned, for he *had* been looking for Morpeth, not only to go to the House, but later to accompany him to Watier's. He never knew when the gambling fit would strike him. There were times when he could play whist for small stakes and be happy, and then, without anything to warn him, small stakes and whist seemed foolish, and he would begin to plunge in earnest, which was foolish for a younger son with little cash and only a modest estate.

He remembered what his mother had said to him once, when he had been a boy — and even more foolish than he was now, he supposed. 'Oh, Granville Leveson, the trouble with you is that you are a younger son who was born with the tastes, ambitions and manners of the heir.'

It was a just criticism then, he thought, and there were times when, for all the love he had been given, he had resented his position. But, thanks to that same mother, he had early been made to understand that he must make his own way in the world, create his own fortune — and so far, life had been kind to him. The one thing which he had subconsciously balked at was marrying for money.

He wondered — if he could win a really great fortune at the tables, would the desire to gamble disappear, or did it go deeper than that? He thought that it might, but was not sure. That night the cards ran well for him, but on quitting the game he overheard something which annoyed him, and he showed the man who was speaking the imperious face which Lady Bessborough told him that he always assumed when he was deeply annoyed — which was not often, for he had trained himself never to show his feelings publicly, and rarely dropped his charmingly impassive mask.

He was standing at the sideboard, pouring himself a glass of wine — he had already plunged to some effect, was six hundred pounds to the good, and thought that he would go home — when a man he had never seen before, some country squire doubtless, up in town to enjoy himself, said loudly to a friend, as though he knew Granville, 'I hear that Leveson Gower is after the Cavendish gel, and that they are taking bets on the marriage.'

Being called Leveson Gower by an oaf he did not know was bad enough, but to hear Harriet's name coupled with his own after such a fashion, enraged him.

He put down his glass, turned a freezing countenance on the fool beside him, and said, 'I wonder who gave you leave to bandy my name about so freely? And for your further information, anyone who chooses to bet on my marriage, and name a lady into the bargain, shall be no friend of mine in future. By what means did *you* find your way into the company of your betters?' And he turned his shoulder on the man, who stared drunkenly at him, saying, 'And who's he, to speak to me so?' to be dragged away by embarrassed friends, who had recognised Granville, and did not wish to offend him, he being one of the men of power in their small world, someone whom it did not pay to annoy.

As usual, going home, he regretted having lost his calm temper, but he knew that were he able to go back to relive the incident he would do the same again. He had been annoyed for Harriet, as much as for himself, and this brought him back to the enigma of his feelings for her. He was trying to go slowly, not commit himself, while he explored himself and her, his native prudence strong within him.

Confess it, Granville Leveson, he thought, using his mother's name for him, you were annoyed as much because such betting might tend to force your hand as for any slight on your — and Harriet's — honour. Even at this late hour, when marriage, a settled home and children have become a necessity, you still hesitate.

But *festina lente* — 'make haste slowly' — had always been his motto, in private life, as in diplomacy — gambling always excepted. Now, he thought, if I could be as reckless in life as I am on the tables when the fit takes me, it is I who might be Prime Minister one day, and then he laughed again self-mockingly. If I could bring myself to speak in public with equanimity, that is!

CHAPTER EIGHT

ONLY the months changed—everything else remained the same. Lady Liz fluttered and twittered, the Duke grunted to himself and played with his greyhounds and their puppies—never was a man more accurately nick-named Canis, or 'dog'—Georgiana's pregnancy increased, Lady Bessborough was as two-faced as ever, Caro Lamb even madder, alternately screaming at and fondling her husband in public, Caro St Jules and George Lamb became even more determined to marry, and Lord Granville grew ever more polite and friendly to Lady Harriet Cavendish, but whatever was between them did not progress an inch.

Oh, he sought her out, talked to her, manifestly enjoyed her conversation, was thrust on her by Lady Liz—and the whole world knew what game *she* was playing.

But what game was Lady Bessborough playing? And her erstwhile lover—was he still in her toils? Was he still jumping through every flaming hoop she set up before him, like a dog at Astley's Amphitheatre, thought Harriet inelegantly, willing to offer himself to Harriet Cavendish, but fearful of her aunt's reaction, like a demented parody of the man in the poem—'Willing to wound, and yet afraid to strike'.

The worst of it all was that a woman could do nothing; the initiative always lay with the man. How pleasant it would be to beard him, to say, What exactly are you at, Lord Granville, pray tell?

And yet, was she being fair to him? For although the whole world gossiped about them, his interest was still little different from what it had always been, the charming, slightly impersonal older man, being pleasant to the younger woman. Taken at face value he had said and done nothing which could lead her to believe that he had any deeper interest in her.

So, why the bets — she knew there were bets — the curious glances when she went out in public, the sense of everyone waiting with bated breath, to see whether or not he would throw his handkerchief in her direction? Where did the talk come from? She only wished she knew.

She feared that she might dislike him again, but ever since she had revived those long-hidden memories she knew that she never could. She could never be indifferent again.

And then, in early May, the first ice broke. George Lamb and Caroline St Jules gained the approval of the Duke and Lady Liz for their marriage. They need no longer hide in corners, looking sad but determined. They had gained their hearts' desire, and, even if Harriet was a little surprised that uncouth George was Caro's heart's desire, she could not grudge her half-sister her happiness.

Lady Liz was ecstatic. She seemed to have reached some pinnacle, some mountain-top where she could look back over the distance she had come from the dark days when she had been a poor Irish gentleman's neglected wife. Her two legitimate and her two illegitimate children — for Caro St Jules had a brother, also fathered by the Duke, known as Augustus Clifford — looked like being settled for life so far as marriage was concerned, and if she could now persuade the Duke to marry her she could set them up financially as well.

But in the meantime it was all little shrieks and taps, and delicate lace handkerchiefs pressed to eyes still beautiful, if growing old.

'Say you are happy for me, Haryo,' whispered Caroline, that day at Devonshire House, when her father's approval had been granted, and she was in a delirium of happiness at the prospect of marrying loud, red-headed George at last, 'and perhaps it will be you next. Who knows?' Happy herself, she wanted everyone to be happy.

'Oh, come,' said Harriet, lips a little numb, all the world marrying except herself—had she been wrong to discourage so many, after all? 'I am resigned to being an old maid, one who will visit you to look after your babies, as I look after George and the others for Georgiana.'

Caro threw her arms about her half-sister. 'Oh, you are so good, Haryo, you shame us all. I wish you your heart's desire, as I have gained mine, and I cannot say fairer than that!'

My heart's desire, thought Haryo, and what is that, I should like to know? And for a moment, she thought the unthinkable—Granville's arms around her, loving her, and only her. She thrust the impossible dream away, said aloud, 'Oh, my dear, give me but a touch of that, only a touch, and I shall be satisfied. Now, go and make the others happy at your news.'

She watched Caro run off, her own heart full of she knew not what—no, not jealousy, but heartsickness, not made any better when her cousin, silly young William Ponsonby, came up and tried to persuade her, in his puppyish fashion, that there might be a future for the pair of them, an idea which filled her with an almost sick amusement. Nice boy that he was, she had no desire to marry him, and the servants had already had one go at persuading themselves that she and William might be a thing.

But what in the end threw everyone into a real flutter, causing such a tohu bohu as never was, was the Duke's decision over Caroline's dowry. Almost as though he were determined to demonstrate that his illegitimate children meant as much as, if not more to him than his legitimate get, he settled on Caroline exactly the same amount of money as he had given Georgiana at her marriage to Morpeth, no less than thirty thousand pounds.

When the news of this emerged, after the marriage settlement was signed and the lawyers had gone home, the uproar could have been heard as far as Chatsworth itself, as Harriet said with some amusement to a shocked Selina Trimmer. Never had sin been so rewarded, Selina was heard to declare indignantly.

Ironically and astoundingly, and much to Harriet's further amusement, the person who made the most noise, and displayed the most annoyance and indignation, was Caroline's mother! Lady Liz excelled herself, the crocodile thrashing about and bellowing, if Lady Liz's plaintive cries could be called bellows, and if crocodiles bellowed. Harriet reminded herself to ask Hart about that — he seemed to know everything about strange animals!

Later reflection caused Harriet to believe that Lady Liz had immediately seen an opportunity to blackmail the Duke into marriage.

'Oh, my dear,' she wailed, shedding genuine tears on Lady Bessborough's shoulder — the pair of them were unlikely bosom bows these days, thought Harriet, her amusement growing with every twist in this unlikely tale. 'He might as well have shouted to the world that I am his whore and had done with it. What will everyone think?'

The truth, madam, the truth, was Harriet's mordant and inward comment. After all, the world already knew exactly how matters went at Devonshire House, and the parentage of Caroline St Jules was no secret, however much Lady Liz twisted and turned.

The handkerchief came into play again. 'He is being so unfair. I ask myself, dear Lady B., who else would have sacrificed their life to him, and to dear Duchess Georgiana? And now — to insult me so!' and the sobbings redoubled.

Surely the first time a noble gift of thirty thousand pounds was so designated, thought Harriet, who was more disturbed than ever by her own internal censoriousness. She had promised Grandmama Spencer that she would not say aloud the highly critical witticisms which the self-serving conduct of others inspired in her, but she could not prevent herself from thinking them.

Later that evening, the Duke called her into his smelly study, his greyhound bitch and her fast-growing puppies disposed before him on the expensive Bokhara carpet, and doing it no service by their behaviour. 'And you, Lady Harriet, when can we expect you to be announcing your marriage?' and he looked dourly at her in her plain gown of prune-coloured velvet, which hardly gave her that highly desirable air to be associated with young women much sought after in the marriage mart.

'When someone finally offers for me, you shall be the first to know, I promise you.'

She could not prevent herself; the sentence came out in the satiric fashion which she fell into every time she spoke to her unsatisfactory father. She so desperately wished to love him, and it was so patent, looking at him — more interested in fondling Lille and her puppies, as dishevelled and poorly dressed as one of his stable boys — that he felt far more for Augustus Clifford and Caro St Jules, than he ever had for Georgiana and herself.

He knew, of course he knew, how much she resented Lady Liz, but he must also know that, advised by her

Grandmama Spencer, her behaviour had been impeccable — and that did her no service; he simply resented her the more. He had always disliked his late wife's mother. She had the most judgemental eyes of anyone he knew.

'Elizabeth still got the megrims?' was all he could offer her, and what could she say to that? The only truthful answer would be, Yes, she has, and surely that is the most preposterous thing of all, to be annoyed that you have blessed your child so royally, when in the normal course of things you would have given her nothing at all.

It was not that she wanted to hurt Caro, or deprive her of her prize, but she could not help thinking of her poor dead mama, since everyone else seemed to have forgotten her, and the insult — if there were one — was to her, the legitimate wife, posthumously demeaned by his mistress and her supplanter, still being a resident of Devonshire House, now supplanting her daughter, and *still* complaining, forsooth.

She held her tongue, said meekly, 'She does not seem very happy. As Hart would say, she has been ringing a peal over Aunt Bessborough.'

He threw titbits at the puppies, and they fought for them noisily.

'You should have married Duncannon — or Althorp. Foolish to let them fall to others.'

'Yes, Father. But I did not greatly care for either of them. Althorp seems totally fixed on hunting. I think that he probably goes to bed in his jockey cap and red coat.'

She could not prevent herself; the last few words had flown out, and she could tell that they had displeased him, for he simply grunted 'Humph,' and then, 'You may leave me, Lady Harriet. I hope you do not reject the next man who offers for you — should any do so.'

Before she was out of the room he had forgotten her, dismissed her as though she were nothing to him, which she was. Always, to him, she would remain the unsatisfactory girl baby, who should have been a boy, who would have saved him from having to take his beautiful Duchess to bed again.

Lady Liz's ploy failed, predictably. The Duke refused to be netted, however much his mistress wailed at him. It was, as Harriet confided to Georgiana, too ridiculous to call such a splendid present an insult.

Lord Granville called at Devonshire House on the next day, to bring Harriet yet another book. 'He is running a positive subscription library,' giggled Caro St Jules to Harriet, after he had gone.

'With the advantage that I do not have to pay a subscription,' replied Harriet, determined to raise no stupid hopes of another marriage in Caro's, or anyone else's mind.

They had talked together so amicably that one might have thought them an elderly husband and wife prosing together, Harriet sighed to herself later.

He made no comment on the great news, except to say that he was a little surprised at Caro's accepting George Lamb.

'She loves him, you see,' Harriet felt bound to explain.

'And that is a good basis for a marriage, you think?' His tone was quite impersonal; they might have been discussing the weather, or some abstruse point in philosophy, not something which occupied the minds — and bodies — of men and women every day.

'It is usually considered so,' was all she could find to say. He looked particularly splendid, she thought feverishly, and how dared he raise such a subject with her, when he must know of all the gossip — but he seemed genuinely interested in her reply.

'Few societies consider love as a reason for marriage,' he replied to that. 'They are arranged for family or dynastic reasons, or to secure the retention and transfer of land and estates, or for convenience.'

Harriet thought of the lawyers who gathered every time one of her family or friends married, and wondered, with an inward chill, what he was trying to tell her — if he was trying to tell her anything. Was he hinting that, if they married, it would be for convenience?

She decided to take his words at face value, said coolly, 'Only the poor can afford to marry for love, you are saying?'

He laughed; he had spoken to test her in some way, he knew, and that was unfair — but oh, she had passed the test supremely well. She had neither simpered nor blushed, but instead had calmly considered the proposition he was offering her as a man might have done. Not only her mind was good, her control, her temper was admirable, which surprised him, for in the past she had often sparked angrily, without thinking, at those she considered fools.

Granville always remembered what his mother had written of the young George Canning: that it was unwise of him to let others know that he considered them fools. Better to suffer them gladly, she had advised. Fools they might be, but they could have their revenge on those who slighted them as well as, if not better than, clever men, and a politician must temper his language — for he might have to depend on fools.

The prudent man he was, who lived behind his romantic façade, had told himself that given his station and situation as a politician, a diplomat, who might again serve his country abroad as an envoy, or an ambassador, he would need for a wife a person who would be both discreet and tactful, who would ensure that never, by word or deed, would she cause unnecessary offence by careless or reckless speech. He needed a person who would be a gracious hostess, who would support him, not subtly undermine him, as many wives did.

Would Harriet Cavendish be that person? Could she temper that sharp tongue, that impatience with fools, which he shared with her, but which with age he had learned to subdue? For when his mother had written of Canning he knew that she had also been warning him. He was beginning to think that she might. After all, she was the descendant of Dukes, a grandee herself, despite her lack of a consequential manner. He admired her for that, too. He thought that, once married, she would assume the consequentiality necessary for the wife of the husband she would take.

'You offer me a paradox, Lady Harriet,' he replied, 'for the poor can afford nothing, and have no choices. Only wealth affords one choices, as I suppose you know.'

'Men have choices, being rich,' was her riposte to that. 'Women being poor, however rich their family, have none.'

'Not so,' he returned swiftly, 'for did you not refuse both Duncannon and Althorp? So you had choices, after all.' His manner was so composed, the blue eyes on her so steady, that his words were robbed of any offence they might have held.

'Limited choices, then,' and her face was alight with amusement and the joy of playing with words and ideas.

'But still choices, and men's choices are limited, too, but after a different fashion.'

'Of which, being a woman, I know little. My choices are limited to the excitements and adventures proper to being a woman. For after the wedding, we have the excitement of the christening of Corise's baby, and what we shall choose to wear for that will occupy us all for days.'

Corise de Grammont had left Devonshire House to marry her chosen love, Lord Ossulston, Lord Tankerville's heir, always known as Little O, because of his small size, and she was on her high ropes at having produced her first child.

To Harriet, Georgiana's pregnancy, Caro's coming marriage and Corise's new baby all seemed to emphasise her growing spinsterhood. Would she ever share in such maternal and marital delights? She was beginning to doubt it. Her father's statement on the previous evening rang in her head like a passing bell. . . 'I hope you do not reject the next man who offers for you' — and then the cold qualification offered with it — 'should any do so'. . .

Lord Granville was still talking pleasantly about the current state of the political situation; it appeared that his friend Canning thought that it was very likely that if the present Government was reshuffled, by virtue of the coalition of parties disagreeing, there was a fair chance that some of his cohorts, among whom Lord Granville was prominent, might at last join him in office.

Harriet knew George Canning quite well. While not entirely approving of Devonshire House and its effects on Granville, he also found its habitués, Lady Bessborough included, pleasant and agreeable company. Harriet was not sure that she quite cared for Mr Canning; his cleverness was so obvious that it sometimes jarred — something which no one could say of Lord Granville's.

She did not know that, speaking to Granville at dinner on the previous evening, Canning had said approvingly with reference to the growing gossip about him and Harriet, 'I hope there is some truth in what I hear about you and the little Cavendish. You will be marrying a

woman of great sense, wit and virtue, if not in the first
stare for beauty. But what of that? Beauty passes, as
you of all people should know,' which was a broad hint
about what had happened to Lady Bessborough's fabled
looks.

And then he had added, 'You will never want for
conversation, which should please you. Think of the
long winter nights of old age. The fire of wit will warm
when the flame of passionate love has long expired.'

'If it was ever lit,' he had retorted. The constant
pressure and hints that he ought to leap on 'the little
Cavendish' — and what a misnomer that was, in view of
her height — were calculated to dampen, not to inflame
him. He hated to feel under pressure, would make up
his own mind, not have it made up for him.

After that they had talked politics and then become
pleasantly fuddled, not so much that they lost control,
but enough to feel happy, as Canning said, 'And damn
gout in our old age, eh?' a saying Granville was to
remember wryly in later years.

'And will you like office?' she asked him, a little shyly,
odd to think that Granville was one of England's more
revered senators, a privy councillor, and an ex-ambassador; he would always be to her the handsome boy she
had first met so long ago.

'Oh, I shall not mind office. It is, after all, what all
politicians strive for, the laurel wreath, the crown of all
our efforts; but having to speak in Parliament, that will
not be so pleasant.'

This surprised her a little. He was always in such
command of himself that she had assumed, if she had
assumed at all, that he would be as easy on his feet in
the House as he was in the drawing room, and the state
rooms of embassies and palaces where, she had been
told, his performances were superb, bringing off *coups*
beyond the abilities of other men.

Her face must have revealed this, for he laughed, and said, showing her a little, just a little, of the man behind the mask, 'Public speaking is, of all things, the one I most abhor. When I rise, everything flies out of my head on seeing all those faces turned towards me. My sufferings on the night before I made my maiden speech were indescribable. There, I have disillusioned you, I know, but now you know the worst of me, when I had hoped always to show you only the best.'

He surprised himself a little, saying this to her. His reward was her immediate sympathy, for Harriet exclaimed impulsively, putting out a hand, and then withdrawing it, 'Oh, I know how you feel, a little, if only a little. Whenever I go into a ballroom, or a place where there are many people, I quite want to die. I feel suffocated.'

'Exactly. Well, they say confession is good for the soul. Do you think we shall both rest easier tonight after such noble frankness?'

What a pleasure he was to talk to, never condescending to her, and what a pleasure it would be to talk to him for life! Her throat almost closed. Dear God, say that he was not toying with her, that this interest had some point to it, beyond the entertainment of the moment. Every time she met him, her longing for him grew. It was as though, having lost her hate, she had fallen into something uncommonly like worship — which was more uncomfortable than hate, because it meant that she wished to be with the loved object as much as possible.

With an, 'Excuse me, Lady Harriet,' he was pulling out his watch. 'My pleasure in talking to you has been such that I have quite forgot the time. I have an appointment at the Foreign Office. They wish to speak to me of Russia, and the agreement I concluded there. I have no wish to offend by being late. We will speak again soon, I hope.'

'Of course, Lord Granville,' she said, and then deliberately, 'You are always welcome here, or at Chiswick House, or Park Street, you know that.'

She had left out Roehampton where her aunt lived, but her aunt had had him for fifteen years; it was time to let him go.

He bowed his pleasure over her hand, and left her. To feel as she always did these days after his departure — as though the sun had gone in, and she was left alone in a cold, grey world.

CHAPTER NINE

LADY BESSBOROUGH was nearly as exercised as her niece about Granville and his intentions — but for quite different reasons. One half of her wanted Granville to settle down, marry and have the family life which — as she unknowingly agreed with George Canning — he needed and deserved. The other part still did not want to lose him — and particularly to Harriet — yet Harriet was manifestly the person he ought to marry, the person who was most likely to make him happy, even if he never shared with her the love he had shared with his mistress of nearly fifteen years.

Every day, when she entered the vestibule at Manresa House, Roehampton, she was reminded of him. For there, among the great pots of flowering plants, stood the plaster statue of Antinous, the cold image of the warm, livng man in every respect, as she knew from the long nights of loving him.

She thought that she had been foolish to discourage him from marrying before. She should have let him marry some shallow fool like Sarah Fane, now the gossiping, vacuous Lady Jersey, and then she would at least have remained his Egeria, his adviser, the empty beauties having nothing to offer in that line. Increasingly, as he had had more to do with Harriet, she was coming to realise that if he did marry her he would have no need of an Egeria — Harriet would fulfil that function for him.

Lady Bessborough knew this because when he spoke to her of Harriet and their conversations she could plainly see that her niece was giving him something

119

which even she could not — intercourse with a mind as sharp as his own in intellectual terms. Oh, she knew that she was intelligent, wise; but that crystal clarity, that pointed brilliance which her niece possessed had not been hers. More, Harriet had an integrity of mind and spirit which was rare indeed.

If he did marry Harriet, then, she would lose him. Duty and selfishness struggled inside her breast, made her feel older than ever.

She must stand back, not intervene, still be the wise counsellor if he asked for advice, and her heart told her that, whatever else, she must not betray him, nor Harriet.

'You speak much to her,' she said, later that afternoon, when Granville looked in, to talk to her, as he had so often done, and it comforted her that, even now, he still wished to see her, the habit of so many years strong in him — but oh, after marriage, it would stop, she knew that beyond a doubt.

'Yes.' He was restless, for him, standing up to look out of the window at the late May day, the year drawing on, and her life with it. 'She is well worth the speaking to; you first told me that nearly two years ago, and I did not believe you then. I do now. And you also once said that, contrary to my belief, she did not detest me, and you were right about that, too. But I do not know what her true feelings for me are — I do know that she likes talking to me, and you did say I could base a marriage on that.'

She wanted to say to him, If you feel as you do, then why not propose now? But she knew his damnable caution, his prudence, the way in which he weighed up possibilities, the virtues of him that made Canning and the others so respect his good judgement, the prudence she had once admired because it protected her. This judgement had led him to write home from Russia, during his embassy there, telling of his belief in the bad faith of the Emperor and his advisers, when those at home were deluding themselves and believing the opposite.

Had she spoken he would have said, I may be a master of diplomatic intrigue, but I detest it in private life. I feel that between you all I am being manipulated, to serve your ends and Lady Liz's, and I do not like it. What he would not have said to her, although he would have thought it, was, And I wish to remain my own man, as I have always been, not a handled tool used by others. And Harriet, from all that I have seen of her, and from what she has said to me, must feel the same. Our choices, the choices of which we spoke, are being pre-empted — and that, neither of us wishes.

Instead, he smiled, came over and sat down before her, consented to drink tea, spoke as though nothing had changed between them, and when she murmured as he left, 'And the Pearl, you are still serious about her, then?' using their cypher name for her, as they had used cyphers in all their correspondence, to fool both enemies and friends should it be intercepted, he answered, almost roughly.

'You may depend upon me to do the correct thing. I shall not compromise her, you may depend on that, too.'

And still the year ticked by, and Harriet waited and watched, hope deferred making the heart sick. Why does he single me out if he means nothing by it? If he spoke to a man as he does to me, no one would think anything, but I am not a man, and I am tired of being watched. It is beginning to become apparent that he is seeking me out to talk to me, nothing more, and if that is so I cannot bear it.

But being a woman, and helpless, she bore it, thinking

of all the women who bled internally as their hoped-for lovers hung back, or changed their minds. The only consolation was that he had abandoned any pursuit of Susan Beckford, and she must not, no, must not, complain, because since this February she had had him to talk to, had recovered the love she had lost and, if it were only companionship he was offering, she must settle for that, since, for all the gossip, his conduct to her was irreproachable.

They sat together, or opposite to one another at dinner, they talked and talked, exchanged books and confidences about philosophy, politics, music, even art — he was a connoisseur of beautiful things — but he said nothing that the whole world might not hear. And she wrote nothing to Hart of what was happening, had stopped confiding in Georgiana.

Once, Caro-William Lamb came up to her at Lady Melbourne's, looking more elfin than ever. She was wearing the palest lemon silk, beneath a cloud of gauze, a lemon silk ribbon was threaded through her lovely curls, a moon drop of a pearl depending from it. Her fan was lemon-coloured too, the feathers like a chick's down. She had made Harriet feel larger and clumsier than ever.

With a sidelong glance from her beautiful but treacherous eyes, Caro cooed at her, in a cruel imitation of Lady Liz, 'And when is the marriage to be announced, Haryo, dearest?'

Haryo could not bear Caro-William these days. Once they had been happy little girls together, but something had happened to that Caroline; she had gone for ever. Her naughtinesses, from being amusing, quaint almost, had become grotesque. One day, Haryo was sure, poor Caro would do something completely unforgivable, and their world would destroy her. She would drop out of it through shame and scandal, and be done for, as all were

who broke the iron-bound rules of conduct, unless you
were as thick-skinned as Lady Holland, whom Harriet
detested—and Caro was not thick-skinned.

'To what marriage are you referring, Caro?' she said
stonily. 'I know of none pending,' which she thought
sounded grand enough to deter anyone from questioning
her further.

But not Caro-William. She gave a shrill scream, hit
at Harriet's arm so strongly with her fan that she left a
mark there, and tittered her disbelief. 'Oh, you wicked
gel, Haryo,' and this time it was Lady Melbourne, her
mother-in-law, whom she was imitating. 'You know
perfectly well whom I mean. You and dear Lord
Granville, of course. How every lady in London will
weep when he finally leads you to the altar. I can think
of some very near home.'

And the sooner you are done for the better, for then I
shall not have to continue enduring your sillinesses, was
Harriet's inward response to *that*—a sentiment of which
she was at once heartily ashamed.

As it was, she said repressively, 'Do not be ridiculous,
Caro. Lord Granville and I enjoy conversing together,
nothing more.'

'Oh, so that is what they are calling it now.' And
Caro's shrieks could be heard all over the room. You
could hardly describe what she was doing as laughter.
Harriet could see her aunt's alarmed face, and there
was no Lord Granville present to calm Caro on this
particular evening.

Lady Melbourne, that worldly creature, looking
exactly like Madame de Merteuil in *Les Liaisons
Dangereuses*, came over to them. She detested her
daughter-in-law, and Caro-William detested her back;
the only member of the family whom Caro could stand,
beside her husband—and she could not always stand

him — was poor, kind, simple-minded Lord Melbourne, the lady's much-cuckolded husband.

'Are you well, Caroline, my dear,' she said coldly, 'or would you like some laudanum followed by bed rest?'

'No, indeed,' retorted Caro nastily. 'Why not take some yourself, if you consider it so efficacious for calming the nerves?'

Lady Melbourne's lips tightened, and Harriet, who did not particularly care for her, felt some sympathy for a woman who had daily to cope with Caro-William at her worst.

'My dear,' she said, in a voice so regal that it made Harriet want to giggle, distressing though this all was, 'you really must try to control yourself. If you cannot consider your own reputation you might consider William's.'

'Seeing that you never have considered either your own, or anyone else's reputation, madam,' retorted Caro, now quite outside of herself, 'I can think of no reason for taking your advice.'

This dreadful home truth nearly unmanned Harriet, who felt that if this continued further she was in danger of socially disgracing herself forever, particularly when Caro-William continued shrilly, 'All this pother because I was only asking dear Haryo when we could all expect Lord Granville to stop dilly-dallying, and finally pop the question!' This last vulgarism Caro-William had heard her nursemaid use, and it had quite enchanted her — and now she had found the occasion to use it.

Harriet's mixture of amusement and distress was only half tempered by the fact that, from past experience, she could expect Caro-William to call in the morning, at Devonshire House, to apologise for her dreadful behaviour — as though, thought Harriet, that excused it, wiped out everything.

Worse, Caro's unpleasant outburst had told her a

little of what people were saying, and she did not like it. Everything seemed to crowd on her at once. Lady Liz's scheming to marry the Duke, which had reached a fever pitch with mad hints being thrown in all directions, at everyone; her aunt Bessborough's solicitous, anxious face turned on her every time they met, almost-spaniel eyes following her and Granville about; Georgiana's pregnancy, difficult and unpleasant, as usual; her father, cold eyes on her, wishing some fairy prince would arrive to take his unwanted daughter away; Grandmama Spencer writing doleful letters full of advice, none of it helpful in her present situation; Selina uttering meaningful sentences and phrases about the wages of sin, and the dangers of making the wrong kind of marriage, her eyes implacable whenever Lord Granville appeared.

Oh, it was too bad! She was beginning to wish she had been born in a cottage when all that occupied her would have been survival — and this hothouse of emotions would not, could not, exist, for it was the result of being a duke's daughter and living in Devonshire House. And then her customary humour came to her rescue — oh, why suggest such a stark alternative? A shopkeeper's daughter would perhaps be the best, with enough of a competency to secure survival, and not enough to be troublesome!

'Haryo. . .' It was Georgiana speaking. They were sitting on one of the lawns behind Devonshire House, in the shade of some giant cypresses — Lord Granville had once said that it reminded him of Italy. Georgiana and her family were staying with Aunt Haryo, her children were all about her, and little George was on Aunt Haryo's knee.

The footmen had brought out a table and chairs, and tea, with nursery sandwiches and cakes for the little ones, which Aunt Haryo and Mama also ate, laughing and complaining that they would grow fat as they did so. The sun shone brilliantly, for they had reached the second of July, had gone past the turn of the year, and it will be Christmas next week, Aunt Haryo had told Georgie, and when he had cried 'Huzzah!' told him hastily that she was only funning.

'Oh, I like it when you are funning,' the little boy had said earnestly. 'No one is so amusing as you are, Aunt Haryo. Why cannot more grown-ups be like you?'

Harriet had laughed at that, a somewhat sad laugh, and that had occasioned Georgiana saying her name in a meaningful voice, and then adding, 'I have been thinking. Why should you not come with us all to Bure for a sea-side holiday? Sun, sea and sands would do you good. You have been in London too long.'

'Of all things the most pleasant. Of course I will come with you,' she said in answer, and was speaking the truth. Bliss to be simple-minded with Georgie and the children, and perhaps it was appropriate that at this moment Morpeth should come to them across the grass arm in arm with Lord Granville, both of them turned out *à point*. Morpeth had spent the night in town, at Park Street, and Granville, Harriet subsequently learned, had remained overnight with him. Both of them seemed full of something, Harriet's shrewd eyes noticed; both were so contained that they were almost uncontained, Granville particularly so.

Morpeth dropped a kiss on his wife's cheek, loving and anxious eyes on her, while Granville went through all the rituals politeness demanded of him.

'You have neither of you read *The Times* today?' Morpeth demanded.

'A novel query,' said Harriet naughtily. 'But no, we hardly thought it suitable for the children's amusement,' and she held tightly to George, who, on seeing his father, had begun to demand his attention, but it was

plain to her that both men had other things on their
mind.

'Then you have not heard the great news.' Morpeth
was cock-a-hoop, and not, it seemed, on his own
account. 'Then you will not know that there has been a
ministerial reshuffle, and that Lord Granville here was
yesterday gazetted Secretary of War in the new cabinet.
We may confidently now expect Bonaparte to be
defeated within the week!'

They all laughed at this, not least Granville, who
shook his head, and accepted the two women's congratulations with his usual calm, not even broken when
Lady Liz, hearing who had arrived, came rushing and
fluttering along to join in the celebrations.

'Office for you at last,' said Harriet to him, when the
servants had brought out chairs for them all, and more
tea, and they were all seated happily in the shade,
George now on his father's knee, demanding more cakes.

'Oh, indeed. A reward for hard work,' he drawled.
'That is, if you believe I am capable of any.'

'More than the world thinks, I dare swear,' said
Harriet shrewdly. 'But the blessing is not perhaps
unmixed.'

'You have not forgotten, then.' He turned the brilliant
blue eyes on her. 'No, but I shall try to master myself in
the House. Canning had promised me this, but I could
not believe it. You know, I wanted to be a soldier once,
but my father forbade it. Later, I tried to raise a
regiment of volunteers, but the King forbade that, and
now, I suppose, this is the nearest I shall ever get to a
boy's ambition — to order the doings of soldiers, if not to
be one.'

Another thing he was telling her about himself, which
she was suddenly sure he had told none other.

She laughed up at him, amusement, as always, giving
her the charm which she was unaware that she pos-

sessed, animating the plain face, giving it a playful mischievousness. The simple pale blue muslin dress which she wore suited her better than her evening gowns, he noted.

'A soldier, Lord Granville! Well, you have the necessaries to be one, stature and presence being the thing,' and oh, dear, she was complimenting him again, and had sworn she would not do so, 'but the post you have achieved gives you the pleasure of warfare, without the immediate pains.'

He took her up immediately. 'You have the right of it, and that shames me a little. I am not so old that I might not be useful on the battlefield, and I hate the feeling that what I may decide might affect the lives of men far from the office in which I merely write words on paper, while they spill their blood for me.'

Harriet became as sober as Miss Trimmer could have wished. 'Oh, no, I had no right of it. I should be ashamed. I was frivolous. I should have thought of what being Secretary of War means, and the dreadful responsibilities it will bring you, as well as the honour of the office. The second can hardly outweigh the disadvantages of the first.'

'No, indeed,' was his response to that. 'My pleasure must be tempered by that thought,' and he fell silent gazing across the beautiful garden.

'But you have seen war close to,' ventured Harriet. 'Your friend, Mr Canning, when he was last here, a few nights ago, told me that you were present at Austerlitz.'

'I fear that Canning likes to think so,' he replied, 'It is true that I went to Austerlitz and the Emperor Alexander received me there, giving me an audience in the open air, under a tree. He had commanded me to accompany him in this campaign against Bonaparte, who moved at such speed that instead of my meeting him at the palace of Prince Czartoryski the Emperor

NO COST! NO OBLIGATION TO BUY!
NO PURCHASE NECESSARY!

PLAY "LUCKY 7"
AND GET AS MANY AS SIX FREE GIFTS...

HOW TO PLAY:

1 With a coin, carefully scratch off the silver box opposite. You will now be eligible to receive two or more FREE books, and possibly other gifts, depending on what is revealed beneath the scratch off area.

2 When you return this card, you'll receive specially selected Mills & Boon Romances. We'll send you the books and gifts you qualify for absolutely FREE, and at the same time we'll reserve you a subscription to our Reader Service.

3 If we don't hear from you within 10 days, we'll then send you four brand new Romances to read and enjoy every month for just £1.80 each, the same price as the books in the shops. There is no extra charge for postage and handling. There are no hidden extras.

4 When you join the Mills & Boon Reader Service, you'll also get our free monthly Newsletter, featuring author news, horoscopes, penfriends and competitions.

5 You are under no obligation, and may cancel or suspend your subscription at any time simply by writing to us.

You'll love your cuddly teddy. His brown eyes and cute face are sure to make you smile.

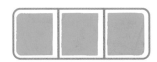

Play "Lucky 7"

Just scratch off the silver box with a coin.
Then check below to see which gifts you get.

YES! I have scratched off the silver box. Please send me all the gifts for which I qualify. I understand that I am under no obligation to purchase any books, as explained on the opposite page. I am over 18 years of age.

6A3R

MS/MRS/MISS/MR _____

ADDRESS _____

_____

POSTCODE _____ SIGNATURE _____

7 7 7	**WORTH FOUR FREE BOOKS** FREE TEDDY BEAR AND MYSTERY GIFT
🔔🔔🔔	**WORTH FOUR FREE BOOKS** AND MYSTERY GIFT
🍒🍒🍒	**WORTH FOUR FREE BOOKS**
🍒🔔BAR	**WORTH TWO FREE BOOKS**

MILLS & BOON "NO RISK" GUARANTEE

* You're not required to buy a single book!
* You must be completely satisfied or you may cancel at any time simply by writing to us. You will receive no more books; you'll have no further obligation.
* The free books and gifts you receive from this offer remain yours to keep no matter what you decide.

If offer details are missing, write to:
Mills & Boon Reader Service, P.O. Box 236, Croydon, Surrey CR9 9EL

Mills & Boon Reader Service
FREEPOST
P.O. Box 236
Croydon
Surrey
CR9 9EL

NO
STAMP
NEEDED

had joined his army straight away, summoning me to accompany him.

'On the day itself, the noise of the battle gave notice of what was happening at Olmutz where I was stationed. I wished to drive there, frightening poor Saxe to death, but met with the retreat, after which I, too, fled the dreadful scene of defeat and carnage.

'My companions in flight were Count Armfeldt, the friend of Gustavus of Sweden, and two noble Russian ladies who had accompanied their husbands to war — a thing I would never demand of a wife of mine — especially after what I saw of the aftermath of battle.'

Harriet had never heard of him speaking of his diplomatic missions before, and she remembered what she had said to her sister — how little women knew of the lives of men. 'You knew the Emperor personally,' she remarked.

'He was pleased to call me friend for a short time,' he answered, his expression a trifle wry, 'until Bonaparte's military skill persuaded him otherwise. This was in my first embassy, you understand, which was more successful than my second one, when circumstances compelled me to flight again, this time from Russia, without following all the formal diplomatic niceties which a good ambassador should carry out. Had I done so, I might be in Russia still! You see, I cannot allow you to think of me as some sort of hero; the truth is mundane enough.'

Morpeth had said of him the other evening, in answer to a question from Georgiana, that the man speaking to her had many claims to be considered exceptional as a diplomat. 'So much so,' he had added, 'that I doubt whether he will ever be encouraged to be a politician merely. I say merely, because there are many who will perform well in the House, or the Cabinet, but few who could do what Granville Leveson does when he is on a

mission. I saw him in action when I accompanied him
to Berlin — he was only twenty-five, no age to be a *chef
de mission*, but he was masterly, justifying Malmesbury
for having sent him there, despite some doubts about
his youth.'

'And should you like to be an ambassador again, or
would you prefer, one day, to be Mr Canning's Foreign
Secretary?'

'Now that I cannot tell you, for first it is mere
supposition that he would ever be Premier or that, being
so, he would nominate me for such an august post, and
secondly because as we grow older our circumstances
and our tastes change, and what we once desired no
longer attracts.'

Every now and then he gave her a glimpse of his
power of thought. He was not witty, in the way that Mr
Canning was, but his tempered calm, his ability to lay a
problem out, or, as he had just done, to sum up
possibilities so candidly and briefly, could not but
impress. She began to see why Canning respected him,
asked his advice, something which, knowing only the
social man, she had not been able to understand.

'And you, my dear Lady Harriet,' he said, turning
the conversation away from himself, and affairs of state,
'what are you proposing to do this summer, while I
slave at Whitehall? Morpeth tells me that your sister is
inviting you to accompany her to Bure. Loath though I
am to see you leave London, I cannot but think that a
holiday would refresh you, your year has been a hard
one. You have had many tribulations, many trials, and
you have borne them bravely. It is time you had
surcease from them.'

He paused, and, before she could answer him, continued. 'I am wondering whether it would please you to
join the Morpeths in their visit to my sister of Beaufort
at Badminton in late August. My other sister, Lady

Harrowby, with whom I believe you are already slightly acquainted, will also be there, and I hope to gain leave from my duties to be able to join in their welcome. It would give me great pleasure to show you Badminton, both the house and grounds.'

What could she say? He was being so particular that for the first time she allowed herself to hope a little. To invite her to meet his family was such a remarkable gesture from the reserved man he was — even though he had shown her a little of what lay behind his reserve — that it must contain a more than ordinary significance.

Harriet almost began to tremble, but she managed to control herself; she must. His kindness, and his under-standing of her difficult situation meant that she must accept his invitation gracefully. Lady-Liz-like trillings and quaverings of pleasure would not do.

'I should be honoured to meet your sisters, and to see Badminton, of which I have heard so much,' was her answer to him.

'Then I shall inform my sister of your agreement, and she will send you a formal letter of invitation. And now I fear that I must leave you. Being gazetted Secretary of War is no doubt a great honour, but is bound to make me short with my friends.'

Lord Morpeth, seeing Granville begin to stir, said to him, 'Yes, old fellow, we must be off, I know. Now be a good boy, Georgie — little men do not cry at Papa's departure, as I have told you before,' and he placed his son gently on Aunt Haryo's knee to comfort him, giving Lord Granville a last and pleasant sight of Lady Harriet Cavendish showing her delight at looking after little ones, George on her knee, and one of his sisters demand-ing to be seated there, as well.

CHAPTER TEN

'I WONDER,' said Georgiana thoughtfully to her sister. They were walking on the sands at Bure, near Christchurch, their parasols up, protecting them from the sun of early August.

'Now what do you wonder, Lady Morpeth?' said her sister teasingly. Harriet felt relaxed, 'as though,' she said later over dinner, 'I have spent the last few weeks in a warm bath, eating strawberries, and gazing at the heavens through an optic glass.'

'I wonder,' said Georgiana slowly, 'if, during our absence, Lady Liz has brought it off at last, is married to Papa by now?'

'Should you mind very much?'

'After all this time,' Georgiana said, 'I really don't know. Her living with him for so long has made it seem possible, never mind the insult to us, and to Mama — to Mama most of all.'

'I mind,' said Harriet, frowning. 'I have had to live with her, and her endless pushing forward of Augustus Clifford, and her attempts to manipulate me. Caro-George I don't mind, but Augustus — he has no sense at all, tries to act as though he were Papa's legitimate son, and Papa seems to care for him more than he does for Hart.'

'It is distressing, but true,' said Georgiana, and her mild voice made what she was saying sound even worse than it was, 'that Papa cares for the whole brood more than he does for any of us, or poor dead Mama. No, do not frown at me, Haryo, you know I am right.'

'I cannot bear the thought of her calling herself

132

"Duchess", and Aunt Bessborough seems to be on her side.'

'Of course,' said Georgiana wearily, 'and now, let me ask you another question. How serious do you think Lord Granville's intentions are, and would you accept him if he offered for you?'

'I don't know, to both questions,' said Harriet honestly. 'I only know that everyone in our world seems to think I ought to accept him without question, but that Selina Trimmer does not think that he is good enough for me.'

'Hardly the best of judges, Selina,' replied her sister, 'for all her many virtues.'

'Indeed,' said Harriet, 'but the real question is, is he serious? I have been asked to join him in your visit to Badminton, as you know, which might seem to suggest that he is serious.'

'You sound doubtful,' was Georgiana's only response.

'Because, oh, because. . .' Harriet twisted her hands together. She had lowered her parasol, put it on the sand, said, 'Once, when I was a little girl, I adored him without reservations; then, when I found out about him and Aunt Bessborough and all his other *belles amies*, I hated him; then, this spring, I. . .came to know him a little better. . .and to see how. . .complex he is, and I began to like him again—particularly to talk to. I'm not sure how great a hold my aunt has on him. Lady Liz wants me to marry him—to leave her with Papa, I suppose—and do I want a man so apparently swayed by others?

'But is he? So swayed by others, I mean. Morpeth and George Canning tell me what a superb diplomat he is, and I begin to wonder. Do other people control him, he who, I am assured, can so easily control and sway others? What is behind the charm, Lady Morpeth, tell me that?'

'I can't,' said Georgiana. 'Listening to you both talk, I am bound to say that you seem made for one another, so much at ease you are. But, of course, marriage is more than talking, and he has had such a procession of beauties, from the Queen of Prussia downwards, as well as being Aunt Bessborough's property for so long—you know, I suppose, that they have two little children, farmed out, I believe.' She saw by her sister's face that she had not known this, and added gently, 'Morpeth told me—they are being properly looked after, he said, which is a relief, for they are, after all, our cousins—where have I got to?' she asked plaintively. 'I have lost my way.'

'Lord Granville, his beauties and my aunt,' prompted Harriet.

'Ah, yes. It occurs to me that, although domesticity might attract, he could still have trouble with the idea of settling down.'

'Dwindling into a husband,' suggested Harriet, parodying the Congreve play which she had earlier quoted to Georgiana.

'Exactly. He has had all the benefits of marriage without the pains, as Morpeth once said of Lord Hertford.'

Harriet laughed at that—even though the laugh might be on herself.

'I suppose,' she said slowly, 'that that is why I am unsure about him. Will he settle down? Or shall I, like my aunt, be compelled to watch him charm and conquer others? I do not think I could bear that. I am not made for it. I have the unfashionable notion that my husband should love and care for me alone.'

'None of which helps you to make up your mind,' said Georgiana, being a little worldly for once. 'For where are you going to find this paragon whom you have described so movingly?'

'In a fairy story,' said Harriet, 'which is where I thought Lord Granville had strayed from when I first saw him.'

'Oh, yes,' said Georgiana fervently. 'I remember. He was so splendid, wasn't he? And still is, I suppose. Age has not diminished him. . .'

'Nor custom staled his infinite variety,' added her sister in a savage mockery of Shakespeare's great speech describing Cleopatra.

'Oh, you must marry him, after all,' said Georgiana, 'for you are both so clever. Think of the children you will have.'

Think, rather, of the ones he has already had, was Harriet's unhappy internal comment; two more to add to the list of sad unknowns whom Devonshire House had spawned down the years.

She knew that she had a half-sister at Howick, where her Mama's pretty child by Earl Grey, Eliza, lived, and the thought saddened her—and how like Papa, to place his own children in his nurseries, but compel Mama to let her poor child go to her father's family. How Mama must have suffered. It added one more to the count against him, and her own hope that one day he might be reconciled to her seemed but a fond delusion. . .

'I suppose,' she said abruptly, wrenching herself away with difficulty from her own distressing situation at home to the equally distressing one outside of it, 'that he really thinks of me as a friend, someone to whom he may usefully speak—about books, and ideas—not someone whom you actually want to marry. For that he will require a wife as beautiful and easy as himself, not plain, prickly Harriet Cavendish with the little eyes.'

'No,' said Georgiana, swinging round to face her sister. 'You are not to talk like that. I will not have it. You are a pearl,' she said, unconsciously echoing the name which Aunt Bessborough had invented for

Harriet. 'But you are a pearl still inside the oyster, waiting to be found. One day, someone will dive down, discover you, and hold you up as a trophy for the world to see. Do not ask me why I say this. I only know that I feel it — here,' and she placed her delicate hand over her heart, and turned her earnest eyes on Harriet, who stood transfixed at this strange and emotional statement coming so fiercely from the usually diffident Georgiana.

'And whether that someone will be Granville, or another,' she continued, 'I do not know, except that I also have the strangest feeling that it will be he who will cause the world to see the true value of the pearl.'

'Oh, if only what you say could come true — but in the meantime I must watch and wait, and I have done that for so long, Georgiana, that I am beginning to feel weary. I can quite understand Father looking at me with the expression that says, "What, you are still here?"

'Recently he reproached me for not taking Duncannon or Althorp, and I am beginning to wonder if he has the right of it — except that such repining is useless. I must think of the future, not the past — but I do not really wish to think of either of them. I wish I were a fish in the sea, dreaming merely of a fish's heaven, touching my fish husband only in passing. "There is nothing good or bad, but thinking makes it so," and, fortunately for them, fish do not think.'

She ended with a gasping sob, so that Georgiana drew her to her bosom, said, 'There, there,' patting her back, as though they were children again, and little Haryo had fallen down, and her sister was comforting her.

That evening, Harriet, Georgiana was pleased to see, had quite recovered her spirits. She remembered how in the old days Selina Trimmer was always complaining in her letters to her how rebellious, how naughty, how lazy

Harriet was. The new knowledge of life which Georgiana had gained from living for long periods at Castle Howard, with her difficult in-laws, informed Georgiana that Selina had never been quite fair to Haryo.

Selina could not accept that Haryo was not like the rest of us, she mused; not automatically good and obedient like me, but questioning, always questioning, and yet, at the same time, she has a stoicism which I do not possess, and which perhaps comes from the unsatisfactory nature of her childhood, given all the criticism from Selina and father, with only Mama to love her, and she had to share Mama's love — no, be fair, she said to herself severely, Mama's love was given first to Hart and myself — and only then to Haryo, and she must have felt it keenly.

Oh, I do hope that what I instinctively feel is correct, and that Lord Granville will, in the end, offer for her. I am sure he would be so good for her — for, like Haryo, she had seen the basic kindness which lay behind Granville's charming reserve.

Lord Morpeth had begged Haryo to play for them all, and she was now at the piano, playing the gay songs and rhymes in which the children could join in singing, as well as all the young people who were visiting them in the house which they had hired for the summer.

Her husband came up to Georgiana, and in the dusk, unseen, put his arms around her. 'You are fortunate, indeed,' he whispered in her ear, 'to have such an admirable and loving sister, so good with the children, such a pleasure to talk to. *There* is a treasure for a man of sense. I would not exchange her for the haughtiest beauty — neither Sally Fane, as was, nor Susan Beckford, as is, can hold a candle to her. A good heart and a bright wit waiting to be won.'

It was the nearest he had ever come to criticising his good friend and uncle, Granville, or the many men who had passed through Devonshire House — and passed her over.

Georgiana whispered back. 'He has asked her to go to Badminton with us, after we visit Paultons, and I am hoping that something will come of it. I am beginning to be afraid for her. Three years of coping with Father, Lady Liz and Aunt Bessborough are beginning to take their toll.'

'It would take its toll of me,' grunted her husband, 'and all I can say is, that if the Duke marries Liz Foster he will deserve her. *I* could not live with the lady, and I thank God, twice daily, that you do not take after her, that you are so like your dear Mama, as she would have been if the Duke had cared for her.'

Georgiana took his hand and kissed it. Despite her constant pregnancies, and the demands they made on her, she dearly loved her husband, and could only wish that poor Haryo could find someone to love her, and to value her. She would make a splendid maiden aunt, but she surely deserved more than that!

Lord Warwick, who was present, later turned the pages of her music for her, after all the children had been put to bed, and the adults had eaten supper.

At the end of her piece of Haydn, he led the applause, and then leaned forward to say, tact not being one of his strong points — he needed a few lessons from Lord Granville, both sisters later agreed — that music was a gift from God.

He fixed his eyes earnestly on Harriet, who was resting after her exertions, and added further, 'Such a gift, Lady Harriet, is a great boon; it supports us throughout life and enables us to bear its trials, consoles us for all our misfortunes.'

Harriet looked at him in wonder. What on earth would he say next? For his expression could only be construed as consoling her also — for what? 'I am fortunate,' he said, 'to know such gifted persons as yourself and Miss Beckford. Now she is a link between man and angel, sent here to prepare us for Heaven and teach us how to behave there!'

Between the notion of Miss Beckford mediating between God and Lord Granville, in the intervals of her preparing him for heaven, and the reality of the vacuous girl she was, Harriet was hard put to it not to expire in indecent mirth on the spot — the idiocy of the concept quite anaesthetised her from the pain of hearing her rival so eulogised.

Fortunately for her, she was saved from a reply by the sound of a giant clap of thunder, the weather having changed since the afternoon, and the whole party rushed to the windows to see the lightning playing above the Needles, and to admire the effect it had on the seascape before them.

Harriet, who hated thunder, peering at the scene between the stalwart shoulders of Lord Morpeth and Boringdon, could barely restrain herself from asking Lord Warwick to appeal to Susan Beckford to mediate for them between the earth and the god of the thunder, Thor himself, since anyone who was so much in the confidence of the one God reigning over all must surely be able to restrain the lesser ones in the Pantheon!

The only sad thing about the whole episode, she concluded later, was that she would not be able to share it later with Lord Granville, for she could hardly make such irreverent jokes about his latest target for marriage — if that was what Susan Beckford still was.

As it was, what with Lord Boringdon arriving with his second wife, Miss Talbot — his first having bolted with Sir Arthur Paget and been divorced — she was having the greatest difficulty in preserving her decorum. Her inconvenient irreverence was now prodding her to remark brightly something to the effect that bolting with other people's wives seemed to be catching, so far as the name of Paget was concerned. Fortunately, but only by exercising the strongest self-control, she managed to keep silent, and to say all the right things to the blonde and pretty bride, and the loving groom.

But when the company began to speak of Caro-William, who was staying over on the Isle of Wight at Ryde, the iron control needed to keep herself from speaking had her positively quivering. Caro-William, it was reported, was madder than ever, had publicly quizzed both her husband and his brother, Fred Lamb, about their relations with the noted courtesan, Harriette Wilson.

'Which,' Boringdon commented, 'is the outside of enough, since gossip has it that the lady is beginning to take her mother-in-law as an example, and in the direction of the servants at that—at least Lady Melbourne only aimed at the highest,' being a reference to her early *affaire* with the haughty Lord Egremont, William Lamb's father, and her later one with the Prince of Wales and its result, George Lamb, now installed as Caro St Jules's husband.

'Fred Lamb,' continued Boringdon, unable to resist telling a good story, 'told his brother that if he could not control his wife, then he ought to find someone who could. A keeper in a madhouse, he suggested, might be the best bet. That really set the cat among the pigeons, I can tell you. Feathers flew in all direction, Caro was screeching for William to defend her, and William obediently began threatening his brother. I suppose poor Fred found it too much to have to cope with Caro as well as his inamorata.'

Really, I should not be hearing any of this, thought Harriet, and pretended not to, bending over the book she had taken up—but was not reading. Georgiana was casting agonised glances in her direction, and Morpeth was trying to quieten his friend, but Boringdon, elated as a result of the joint consequence of enjoying his new love and having drunk a quantity of good wine after supper, roared on, entertaining them all with a description of a dinner party held immediately after the brothers had been on the point of fighting one another, in which no one spoke to anyone else, Caro having retreated to her room and poor Lord Melbourne, at the top of the table, unseeing and unknowing, quavering at his unruly family, 'Oh, we're all uncommon quiet tonight, ain't we?'

Trying not to laugh at what she was pretending not to hear was another difficult thing, Harriet found, but excellent for training the social muscles, and it was another good joke she could not share with Lord Granville. Oh, bother Lord Granville! How was it that he intruded in her thoughts all the time?

If she saw a good painting, listened to some new music, read an interesting book, heard a good joke, she instinctively thought of him — to tell him of it, to share with him the nonsenses and the paradoxes of the world she inhabited.

No, she thought. I cannot endure this, I cannot. For, if he means nothing, and we drift apart again, what shall I do? I can not bear to lose him now. For what I am beginning to feel for him transcends love — will last longer than love, if it is allowed to develop. It is true companionship — but perhaps he does not feel as I do, I must allow for that, and perhaps he is as shallow as Selina thinks him. . .but she did not want to believe that of him.

She tried to compose herself for sleep. She would be seeing him soon. How soon, she did not know, and the thought of that had her smiling as sleep claimed her. She would count the days, she knew that, but she also knew that he would walk in her dreams, and she was not sure that he deserved to.

CHAPTER ELEVEN

LORD GRANVILLE arrived at Badminton in a strange state of mind. The sense of being trapped, of being coerced was strong in him. He acknowledged that his own dilatoriness *vis-à-vis* Harriet Cavendish was partly responsible for the gossip which raged everywhere. He felt that his hand was being forced — by everyone from Lady Bessborough onwards.

The other evening, after he had eaten his supper at Roehampton and was talking to the Dowager Lady Spencer, Harriet's grandmother, with whom he usually enjoyed conversing, she had leaned confidentially towards him and said, a smile on her old face, 'It has given me great pleasure, Lord Granville, to learn that a match between yourself and my granddaughter, Lady Harriet Cavendish, appears to be imminent. I am assured that the Princess of Wales offered you her compliments on the subject.

'My dear Lady Harriet is a good child, as I am sure you are aware, and has been brought up in the best of Christian principles, and will guard her and your honour vigilantly. You could have chosen no better partner.'

Everything that was private in him, and he was a very private man, was offended by this. The notion that he was now the subject of every buzzing fool who lived in London was so distasteful that when the Princess had raised the topic during dinner at her own home he had smiled in his coolest fashion and had tried to turn the conversation, raising his brows, and commenting that all the world appeared to know his affairs better than he did himself.

But the Princess, who as he knew was both tactless and determined—and perhaps, he thought afterwards, she was roasting him a little, knowing his temperamental aversion to such gossip, whomsoever it concerned—had laughed, and said, 'Come, Lord Granville, you know as well as I do how correct the report is. Vain to deny it.'

He had ceased to try, but the determination to propose to Harriet at Badminton—where better?—faltered a little in the face of such determined pressure. He was no more forthcoming with Lady Spencer than he was with the Princess, although his manner to her was kinder. Looking at her, he could see in her old face, full of character, that in her youth her appearance and manner must have been very similar to Harriet's.

'My dear Lady Spencer,' he had said gently, 'the Princess was quite mistaken. Lady Harriet and I are close friends, it is true, but nothing is settled between us, nothing, and she would be as distressed as I am by the idle gossip which is running around London.'

He could tell how disappointed the old lady was, but she—and the rest—had no idea how much damage they were doing to Harriet's cause by exerting such simple-minded pressure on him.

So, all in all, driving to Badminton, instead of being excited at the prospect of seeing her, and renewing the happy intimacy which had come to exist between them, he felt—what did he feel? That he was being pushed into a corner, and that everything that he and Harriet did was the subject of unpleasant speculation.

Many years ago Lady Hester Stanhope had tried to corner him, had virtually announced their engagement, had even worn a ring which she claimed that he had given her, and the result had been, as he had written to

Lady Bessborough, that any feeling he might have had
for her was stifled at birth.

Now this was not Harriet's fault—he knew that she
was as private a person as he was, more so, for, despite
all, he was gregarious, and she was not, but inevitably
he could not feel offended by the brouhaha without it
affecting his feelings for her a little.

Or rather, he wished to propose, but not in such a
fashion that he might appear to justify himself to the
rest of the world. Well, he would take matters as they
came, and hope that here, in the country, with his
sisters, and his brother-in-law, the Duke of Beaufort,
and young Morpeth, he would feel more at home with
life, and less some staring gaby about whom the world
hissed.

Harriet knew none of this. Oh, she knew that there was
gossip, but not that it had gone as far as it had, or that
her grandmother, by trying to help her, might have hurt
her. She liked being at Badminton, and preferred the
country to the town, if Chiswick House could be called
town.

And the house itself was so noble, a Palladian pile of
such grand proportions that it was, she thought privately, almost a parody of itself, and she wondered
whether Lord Granville would be amused if she told
him so. She was sitting in one of the main drawing-
rooms, its glass doors open, showing a terrace with stone
urns filled with flowers, and beyond it the beauties of
the park, when Susan Harrowby came in, her lovely
face alight, to catch her sister of Beaufort by the hand,
saying, 'Come, my love, *he* is here,' reminding Harriet
of that day at Devonshire House when he had first
called, so excited were they.

Gossip had said that Granville had been the darling
of his family, the beautiful little boy of his parents' old

age, doted on by his sisters. Both women flew out of the
room, could be heard exclaiming in the vestibule, to
reappear again, virtually dragging him in, protesting
that he was tired from the journey, not fit, not properly
dressed to meet company, but they would have none of
it.

Except for the difference in age, thought Harriet
amused, it might have been herself and Georgiana
celebrating Hart — dear Hart, of whom she had seen so
little this year.

And of course, Granville did not look the figure of fun
which he proclaimed himself, was *à point* as usual, quite
magnificent in his many caped riding coat, which he
handed to the butler — his sisters had not even given
him time to remove it. Beneath it his bottle-green coat
with its brass buttons and long tails, his cream-coloured
trousers, and his Hessian boots were the finest that
money could buy, and his cravat was, as usual, a dream
of a thing.

He consented to seat himself for a moment, 'But only
a moment,' after he had done the pretty to them all, all
including Caro-George and Georgiana and herself, as
well as Borino's new wife — his manners were as perfect
as ever, to the degree that the greeting he gave to
Harriet was as warm as, but no warmer than, the one
he gave everyone else.

She felt her heart beating, so hard that surely he
could hear it, and for the first time she recognised the
strange sensations sweeping through her as the pangs of
desire, the flame of love, as the poets said, burning
brightly inside her.

She loved everything about him. From the long blue
eyes down to the varnished perfection of his boots. The
care which he took with his person, his cleanliness, and
the perfect order of his clothes pleased her beyond belief.
She determined to be more careful with her own clothes.

God would surely not mind her spending a little of her time on the vanity of dress!

But all of this was as nothing to the feelings which his presence was creating—if she had longed to see him, and now she must own she had—the violence of her emotions came to her as a shock.

He excused himself gracefully; did he ever do anything ungracefully? Rose and bowed, left the room with his sister of Beaufort who had her arm around him, petting him almost, so that later, after she had left Badminton, Harriet wrote to her brother Hart: 'The Duchess of Beaufort and Lady Harrowby are delightful. Lord Granville was there, and they love him, as we do you, which is not saying *peu de chose*.'

And then biting her pen, her throat tight, she merely wrote—for she could not tell Hart, or anyone else, the truth of what had passed between them at Badminton— 'So many people report that I am going to be married to him that perhaps it may be as well for me to begin acquainting my friends that I am not.'

She almost faltered, concluded, 'I do not wonder at the reports nor blame people for giving credit to them, and it is only from thinking myself a pretty good authority upon the subject that I take the liberty of contradicting them.'

Reading this, Hart cursed; he had thought the marriage almost a certainty, but, reading his sister's sad words again, the love he felt for her almost overcame him. What could have happened?

Harriet could have told him, but never did. 'Hope deferred maketh the heart sick', and all that week at Badminton she waited for two things, one desired, the other not.

The thing which she did not want to hear was the news of her father's marriage. Lady Harrowby had been told in letters from town that the wedding was due to take place any day. Granville, on arrival, informed her, so coolly that she did not pursue the matter, that he had heard nothing of a marriage before he had left town.

The days slipped by. Granville and she talked, read and ate together, played chess. He drove herself and the pregnant Georgiana around the grounds, and, Georgiana feeling overset, he pushed her in a little carriage, talking to her with such grave kindness that Harriet could not believe that this was the man who was dallying with her feelings.

For still he said nothing. Was it her aunt who was discouraging him? Was it because of her he spoke only of impersonal things, was impersonal in his kindness? And then, one afternoon, he came in to her where she was sitting in the garden-room, glass doors opening on to a scene of sun and flowers — she had a book in her hand, but had not been reading it.

She had left the others because, apart from his sisters, who seemed to approve of her, and whom she liked, they were all treating her as an invalid. His look was grave, determined, and, despite herself, hope flared in her breast.

Granville, for once in his life, had no notion of what he was going to say. Before he had sought out Harriet he had half brought himself to the sticking-point of proposal to her. His sisters had confirmed something which Lady Bessborough had half hinted at — that Harriet intended to break with her father if he married Lady Liz, would leave her home, rather than stay under the same roof as the woman who had replaced her mother.

Of all things, he must persuade her against this! Such an act would place her in the wrong, would estrange her from her father, perhaps even Hart; it could, he knew, do nothing but damage her. There was nothing for it; the caution which ruled him told him that he must point out the dangers to herself in such an act, and then, by proposing marriage to her, he could ensure that she would do no such thing.

But, walking towards the room where he had been told she was resting, the enormity of what he was about to do struck him again. For, in the end, was not the thing which was holding him back the loss of the freedom which he had enjoyed ever since he had left Trentham at fifteen to go to Oxford? Worse, it was his youth he was saying goodbye to, and this, allied to his other reservations had him, once again, in a mood so strange he hardly knew himself.

He saw her face change as he walked in, and the contrarieties of his nature and his mood were strong in him. He would warn her first, and then go on to the meat of the matter. Yes, he would offer, no doubt of it all. How could he doubt? Intellectually they were made for each other, and the marriage was convenient in every sense of the word.

'Lord Granville,' Harriet said, almost shyly, putting her book down, and rising.

'Pray be seated, my dear Lady Harriet,' he said gravely, remaining standing himself, until she said,

'And you, Lord Granville, pray sit. It is like having a guardsman on duty for you to tower over me. Let us chat together in comfort.'

He bowed and did as she asked him, though to be seated, he felt, constrained him.

'Lady Harriet, I venture to think that we are now on such friendly terms that I hope you will not feel it impertinent of me to raise some personal matters with you.' He paused.

Goodness, thought Harriet, looking at him, at his earnest face, what can he be going to say? If this is a proposal, it is an odd way to begin!

He continued, 'I know, none better, how difficult your

situation has been since your mama died, and how nobly you have borne it. You have faced the difficulties which the presence of Lady Elizabeth has created for you with admirable rectitude. Nothing so far has prevented you from behaving in a manner as sensible as it is noble.

'Judge, then, of my distress when it has been reported to me that the way in which you intend to act will result in you abandoning the principles which have governed your actions so far. . .'

Harriet listened to this nobly spoken farrago with mounting indignation. What could the man be speaking of? How do I intend to act? Does he know something about myself which I do not know? Has my aunt been filling his head with such nonsense that he can affront me by assuming that I shall behave recklessly—how recklessly? To what act can he be referring?

He ran on, unaware that Harriet was beginning to be consumed with a mounting anger, 'Such an act is calculated to inflame everything, will solve no problems,' and, Oh, God, he thought how do I finish this sentence without affronting her? Because every antenna he possessed was beginning to inform him of her annoyance at what he was saying, although he could think of no way of extricating himself from the pit he had unwittingly dug for himself.

He started again, dismally aware that the suave diplomat who had successfully mediated between great nations had made a dreadful cake of himself in trying to speak tactfully to an intelligent and high-spirited young woman. It was plain that she was beginning to resent every word he said to her.

'Our duty to our parents, must,' he insisted, and even to himself he sounded a pompous fool, 'come before everything else. The respect we owe to them must transcend our own personal desires, even if those desires——'

He was interrupted, and, God help him, it was about time. He had not thought to put himself into such a tangle, and only a half-hearted nodcock could have sunk himself so far into the mire without meaning to. . .or rather by meaning to offer helpful and useful advice to a young person who seemed to need it.

Harriet rose, white to the lips. How dared he? How dared he listen to gossip, and retail it to her, while protesting that he was advising her for her own good? Let him go back to Aunt Bessborough and make love to her, or the Queen of Prussia, or that woman in Russia, or Lady Cahir, or anybody on his long list of conquests! How could such a creature prate to her of duty, when she had thought that he was about to propose?

Who was the bigger fool? Lord Granville for talking such. . .bosh—or Harriet Cavendish for being foolish enough to think that he might be about to propose marriage?

'To what do you refer, Lord Granville, that you should speak to me so? I am at a loss to understand of what you are speaking. What is this act that will convey my disrespect of my parent, the Duke, to the world? Who has told you of such an act? On what authority do you speak? Pray explain yourself!'

She had the exquisite pleasure, even in her sense of loss and pain, of seeing him change colour, the polished diplomat beginning to stammer, at a loss, to say, 'I am pleased to hear that I have been misinformed. I had heard on the most reliable authority that you had determined to leave your home, should your father marry Lady Elizabeth Foster, and go and live with your Spencer grandparents. Such a breach between parent and child is as inadvisable as it would be morally wrong——' And he was dismally aware that, whatever else he was going to do after committing, with the best of motives, this wretched *bêtise*, it would not consist of a proposal to the white-faced Harriet opposite to him.

Oh, how dared he? Go to live with Grandmama and Grandpapa Spencer! Much though she would like to do so, she knew, had always known, that it would be wrong, both morally and socially wrong to leave Devonshire House and her father—had resisted the temptation to do so for three years.

'No, my lord,' she interrupted him again, as he paused for breath. 'How little you know of me after all, to believe such a thing possible. Not only have I never said such a thing, I have never considered it. My respect and affection for my father,' and at least, she thought, the first part of that sentence is true, 'would alone prevent me from taking such a step. I trust that I know, as you do not appear to know, that my conduct would be as correct as it has always been, whatever the depths of my suffering from the situation in which I find myself.'

What a fool he was! He had lost her, and, in the losing, he came nearer to desiring her for herself alone, for the gallant spirit with which she faced life, a spirit which he wanted suddenly for his own. But what was left for him now except apology and retreat? If he had behaved like this in Russia, God help the unfortunate country he had represented there!

His face a picture of the astonishment and confusion he felt, for he had breached his own rule of ignoring gossip, except that he had not thought that this was gossip, and had thought—but had he really thought at all?—to help her, he said, helplessly, 'Then I must beg your pardon for doubting your own good sense, and for believing that you could breach your own moral principles which I know, from conversing with you, are of the highest.'

Harriet, near to tears, to shrieking, all the hopes
which she had begun to entertain dead before her, alone
in the world, after all, with no kind friend to sustain her,
perhaps as far as marriage, bowed, said stiffly, 'You will
excuse me if I leave you, my lord. We cannot usefully
continue this conversation. The only comfort which I
take from it is to learn that you, like myself, consider
the tie between parent and child a sacred one. On that
we are of one mind, if in little else.'

Granville bowed again. He could do no more.
Chance, blind, brutal chance, created by his own folly,
his inability to come to a decision, which had resulted
in him approaching her with a divided mind, had
brought him to this pass. And now that he seemed to
have destroyed his credit with her irrevocably, desolation, a desolation as strong as Harriet's own, overwhelmed him. She was leaving in two days' time, and
would leave without an offer from him, for two days
would not be enough to repair what he had, without
meaning to, destroyed.

Two days to go before she left. How to endure them?
How to sit through dinner, make small talk, be pleasant,
smile through stiffened lips? Only the social training to
which she had been subjected through the whole of her
short life sustained Harriet in her misery.

Outwardly she was in total command; only the man
watching her, his own thoughts in turmoil, who now
had no centre left to his world, knew that she was as
distressed as himself. His own distress he could not
analyse — but he thought that he understood hers, and
was now helpless before it. The conventions of their
world stood between them. Had she been, or were he
planning, or able, to make her his mistress, he would
have taken her in his arms, caressed her, reassured her,
but he had only been allowed, permitted, to be alone

with her at all because of the chance that he was about to propose to her, and now that he had not they might meet again only in public.

He was even aware that the self-control which she was exercising was close to producing nausea in her — he knew that, because, astonishingly, he was sharing that sensation with her. What did his distress tell him? He shied away from its meaning.

And Harriet? What was left for her? Nothing, nothing but to suffer and endure as she seemed to have been doing all her life. Nothing to do but exist through the long evening, to go to bed, and then, only after Walker had left her, to sit there numb, and let the slow tears fall. To have thought that she might have found a friend to live with — she could face the fact that he might have come to her without passion — and now she was not even to have that.

She must face it. Her dream had been destroyed, and she was savage with herself for having dreamed it. Her mordant wit was turned upon herself; she could almost hear Emily Cowper saying, once the word got about that Lord Granville did not want her after all, so that she would be endlessly discussed, and mocked, 'Oh, I am not surprised that he spat her out. One can hardly say that she is of the first stare of beauty, poor dear Harriet. And one can quite see that all that wit might be tedious if one had to endure it over breakfast!'

She could imagine the letters which were leaving Badminton, Caro-George writing to Lady Elizabeth, to say that Granville and Haryo were not to marry after all, that she was surviving, single, to be a thorn in the flesh still, still a barrier to Lady Liz's plans to marry the Duke.

Was that all it was, the plotting and planning between those two unlikely allies, Lady Liz and Aunt Bessborough, to use him as a stalking horse to get her

out of Devonshire House? And had he balked at the
end, or had Aunt Bessborough changed her mind? Yes,
that was it, she thought feverishly, Aunt Bessborough
had vetoed the match, and he had fallen in with her
plans, and thinking so she slept at last, to dream
disturbed dreams which proved only that Harriet
Cavendish was thrice a fool, once to think a man might
come to love her, twice to think that that man might be
Granville Leveson Gower, and thrice that he might be
prepared to take her in a *mariage de convenance* — and he
did not even want that, so unattractive to him was the
notion of marrying her.

But Lady Bessborough, opening the latest letter from
Granville, sent from Badminton, half hoping, half fear-
ing that the match was on at last, the proposal made
and accepted, was shocked to discover that nothing had
happened, after all. His letter was written in the coolest
fashion, said nothing of marriage, simply that he had
seen Harriet and Georgiana, had spoken pleasantly to
Harriet on indifferent subjects. . .

What could he be at? In the end, she wanted him,
needed him, to marry her niece. She wrote despairingly
to him, reproached him when he returned to town, to
find him as calmly enigmatic as ever. 'I do not understand you,' she complained. 'I never shall; even after all
we have meant to one another, you remain in essence
closed to me.'

No, she did not understand him, nor did she know
that the letter which she had sent him, about the rumour
that Harriet was to leave home if Lady Liz and the
Duke married, had precipitated the strange state of
mind which had resulted in the debâcle of all Harriet's
hopes.

*   *   *

Other hopes were ruined that autumn. The reshuffled cabinet which Granville had joined as Secretary of War, under George Canning's guidance, fell, in the most dramatic and shocking circumstances.

Granville knew, none better, that by replacing the previous Secretary of War, Lord Castlereagh, by himself, Canning had made an implacable enemy, who continued to harass and oppose him all through that long summer.

Afterwards, long afterwards, he was to ask himself if the political tensions to which he was being subjected had spilled over into his private life, and had affected, if not caused, his disastrous behaviour to Harriet. Castlereagh, a man of high temper, and fierce decisions, often taken on impulse, boiling and burning at being superseded, at last considering himself mortally politically injured at being shunted sideways to the colonies, to run them, instead of the war, challenged Canning to a duel. A duel between two ministers of the Crown, supposed colleagues, fought at Putney Heath, at six o'clock on the morning of the sixteenth September!

'And what was I to do about his challenge?' confided Canning to Granville, when the whole sorry business was over. 'Refuse, to brand myself the jumped-up parvenu with no sense of honour? No, I was left to show that not only could I be as bloody-minded as my haughty lord himself, but as full of stupid honour as he is. Besides, I did not wish to be regarded as less than a man — one whose decisions might send others into danger, but would shirk danger himself. Never.'

'And what,' Granville said, smiling a little at his indignant old friend, who lay on a couch, his leg propped up before him, 'did you need to prove *that* for? I could have told them——'

'Oh, you,' retorted Canning. 'No, nothing for it but to oblige.'

'Damn it all, man,' Granville expostulated, 'you had never so much as fired a pistol in your life before. What a pity I was out of town and you could not call on me.'

Canning stared at him, his face wry. 'Could have done with you, but Charles Ellis there with me,' he finally said. 'Good fellow, too. Showed me how to hold the damn thing and fire it.'

'No wonder you missed, and a wonder he didn't. Had two gos at you, you say, one not enough. Never say you're not lucky, to be hit in such a way that your life was never in danger.' For Castlereagh's second shot had passed through the fleshy part of Canning's thigh, and he had even been able to walk away with Ellis supporting him, as far as Lord Yarmouth's house which was nearby, Yarmouth now having finished with his task of being Castlereagh's second!

Yarmouth said afterwards that on the way to the duel Castlereagh had been in violent high spirits, singing airs from the opera which he had visited the night before, roaring away about the wonders of Catalani as a singer. He praised Canning, too, for after receiving Castlereagh's second shot in the thigh he had coolly waved his pistol, and demanded to know whether Castlereagh wanted a third shot at him!

'So now it's all over, for both of us,' said Canning sadly. 'After that, my resignation must be sent in, and yours too, I expect, since depriving Castlereagh of the office you now hold started the whole damnable business off. In any case, Portland will want to jettison us both — too embarrassing — and he probably won't survive either. Little Perceval will probably be the man.'

He was to lose that, too, then, thought Granville, his face, as usual, betraying nothing of his feelings to his friend. It was an autumn of all the sorrows, to be sure. Later, when Canning had heard that Granville had not, after all, proposed to Lady Harriet, had possibly even quarrelled with her, gossip said, he knew, instinctively, that the constraint in Granville's manner, shown to the world in the aftermath of the duel, was not solely due to his natural disappointment at loss of office.

CHAPTER TWELVE

IT WAS difficult to tell which of the two parties was the more affected, behind the masks of propriety which both wore so well. Harriet wrote from Devonshire House in early October, when she had finished her long holiday, to Selina Trimmer, turning to her, as always, for advice in an emergency, telling her of her disastrous interview with him, and that she did not wish to marry a man who allowed his actions to be so swayed by others. Apart from that she said little to anyone, not even to Hart, her letters to him betraying nothing of her state of mind.

Granville's case was different. He was busy with his public life in the day, worked with others, played with others, although not on the gaming tables — the fit had temporarily left him — but when, at the end of the day, he was finally alone, what he had pushed to the back of his mind came to the front again, and taunted him. He had seen a *Phantasmagorie* performance when he had been in Paris in the peace embassy in the mid-1790s: it was some new kind of magic lantern show, and like others he had started and exclaimed as hideous images appeared and moved on a white screen set up in a dark room.

The images had left that room, and were now haunting the screen of his mind, appearing when he was alone, and one which swam again and again into his consciousness was the white tormented face of Harriet Cavendish.

Oh, he had wounded her, he knew that. Her conduct towards him was irreproachable, as it was to all the world. But the face he saw was a suffering one—had been since Badminton, and he knew, beyond a doubt, who had inflicted that suffering on her—and now he was beginning to suffer too.

He had thought that, after Badminton, he had settled it for himself. The convenient marriage was not to be; chance had willed otherwise. The meeting of minds was not enough to incite him to lose his freedom, he must gain more than that. What was it Lady Bessborough had said? He would be gaining a woman with whom he could converse, and perhaps that was not enough.

Then why was it that, in her presence, and out of it, he was beginning to feel such pain, as though it were her hurt he was beginning to feel, needed to assuage? It could not be love he felt for her, he knew it was not *that*—he knew what love and passion were only too well, he had held so many women in his arms, beside the one woman he had worshipped for so many years.

But if it were not love, what was it? A different kind of love, a new face to examine, one which he had not seen before, one which combined the lure of the body with something deeper? But surely he had felt that already, the deeper love, had he not?

Then what? Then what? He was pacing his bedroom, having returned home early from supper at Devonshire House where he had seen that face again, no longer being able to endure being with her, or with anyone. He had waved Saxe away when he had come to help him undress, pulled his cravat undone, eased himself out of his coat, kicked off his shoes, unbuttoned his shirt at the throat—he must not be physically constricted; his mental constriction, which he could not ease, demanded that his body be free.

The man who despised impulse, the deliberate man, the calmly aloof man, was on such fire that only energy would suffice to heal him. He must *do* something, anything to banish the phantoms which haunted a man in the night watches when he saw himself face to face at last.

He walked, almost reeled, downstairs to his study, although he had drunk little that night. He had begun weeding out his old correspondence; his cupboards had become cluttered, and that would never do. Order was all — without it the universe crumbled. He could not trust his secretary to do the job of deciding what to keep, what to throw away.

He pulled out an early box, dating back nearly twenty years, and began to sort through it, noting dispassionately that his hands were shaking. What a spectacle he must present, rumpled and tumbled, sitting there, unbuttoned, in his stockinged feet! He was like to have run mad, one might say, to put himself into such a pelter over a young woman, he who had selfishly bedded half the beauties in England without a second thought!

The smile on his face a sardonic rictus, Granville pulled out a letter addressed to him in a childish hand, no envelope, the paper folded once, and then into two, the small red seal which had closed it broken, Curious, he opened it. It was from Lady Harriet Cavendish, aged nine; the careful copybook characters informed him of her pleasure at his kindness in giving her the little book of the myths of Greece and Rome, and now she must express her heartfelt thanks to him, ending, 'your devoted servant, Harriet Cavendish'.

Reading it, he was back in Devonshire House again, a boy, seeing the plain child to whom he had presented the book. The child who had so amused him by her earnestness, so different from the rest of the little girls who had fluttered their eyelashes at him. He remembered that he had felt annoyance on her behalf when she had told him that she did not please Selina

Trimmer, that old dragon—who had, of course, been a young dragon, then.

And a hundred other memories of her assaulted him—all the occasions on which he had met her, and how her open adoration of him had amused and pleased him because it was expressed so differently from that of the rest. While she was growing up, he had begun to talk to her more seriously, challenge her to play him at chess, talk of books and—and then, at some point, she had changed towards him, become cool, aloof, almost antagonistic, and that, surprisingly, had hurt a little.

When was it, and why, that she had changed the first time? And why had she changed again, some time in the last few months, so that the friendship which had existed between them, and had been lost, was renewed?

The hand which held the letter clutched and crumpled it, he swore, smoothed it to try to restore the sheet of paper to its former state, put it down, walked to the sideboard where he poured himself a drink, his hand still shaking. She had trusted him, and he had forfeited that trust at some stage, why he did not know, and then she had trusted him again, and he had forfeited her trust again—and, this time, he knew why and how.

Because he had not felt for her that fierce desire which he had felt for other women, he had told himself that what she felt for him must also be lukewarm, at best, and that the failed proposal would not hurt her, but her face and manner told him that that was not so.

The clock struck three. He could not bear to hurt her. Was that love? He could not bear to lose her trust. Was that love? He could not bear to think that her opinion of him had been lowered. Was that love? He wanted her to talk freely with him again, and he to her. Was that love? He wanted to see her smile again. Was that love? He wanted to see her face turned towards him, unreserved. Was that love? He. . .wanted to be with her. Was that love?

If not, what was it? What. . .what. . .what. . .? Had Lady Bessborough been right? Had he, after all, not loved her quite as she had loved him? Had that yearning face she had turned towards him sometimes been inspired by the kind of hurt which he was feeling now, a hurt which he could neither analyse nor explain, he who analysed and explained everything?

Surely not. His feelings for her had been deep and true, he knew that, and, if passion had died, the friendship which had replaced it was still deep and true, so that the need to consult her, to talk to her, was still there. He remembered, he would never forget, the distress which had consumed him when he had left her to go to Russia in '04, how he had suffered.

He remembered that he had written to her in his agony, telling her so, and then later, torn from him, he had also told her that were she free he would marry her on the instant.

So, in what fashion did his feelings for Harriet differ from the ones he had experienced in loving the other Harriet, her aunt?

He knew, oh, yes, he knew what was different. For the suffering he had felt in '04 had been for himself— not for her!

Granville Leveson Gower, the man whose calm self-control was a by-word, a self-control so strong that many thought that no heart beat beneath it, lowered his head on to his hands. Oh, yes, he knew that he was something of an enigma to others; Lady Bessborough had complained of it occasionally, the last time when he had not proposed to Harriet at Badminton. She had told him that she would never understand him. He knew now that he was an enigma to himself.

Misgivings or no misgivings, love her or not love her,

he knew, without a doubt, that he wanted Harriet Cavendish for his wife, and at the earliest opportunity, when the occasion presented itself, he would offer for her.

Passion might be missing from what he felt, but the woman who inspired him to such a desire to protect and to console her, the woman to whom he wished to associate his life, would surely be more than someone with whom he wished to share a convenient marriage, the idea of which he had come to despise.

He picked up the letter. Took it upstairs with him, to place it on his night stand, to be a talisman against the dark, against the belief that Granville Leveson Gower thought only of self. For it told him that he had at last learned to suffer another's pain — as well as enjoy her pleasure.

Was *that* love?

CHAPTER THIRTEEN

FASHIONABLE London buzzed and roared. It was done. The Duke of Devonshire had given way, married the mistress who had shared his home these many years, made her his Duchess, in a secret ceremony at Devonshire House on October the nineteenth. Harriet Cavendish had not been sacrificed; Lady Elizabeth had gained what she had striven for without sacrificing anything or anybody.

'Oh, she has worn him down, never a doubt of it,' shrieked Caroline Lamb, who was the most bitterly opposed to the match of all the Devonshire House set, most of whom had been slowly worn down by Lady Liz's persistence and determination. 'Poor fool, he could not even lock himself away with his dogs, but she followed him there, cooing and wailing.'

For once, Caroline spoke the truth, as everyone knew; for every objection which the Duke had raised, his Liz had had a triumphant answer, even offering to waive the title of Duchess, if it would offend his mother-in-law, Harriet's Grandmama Spencer, who would detest to see her daughter succeeded by a person whom she regarded as little better than the Duke's whore.

Even Granville's failure to propose to Lady Harriet did not deter her, although it must have dismayed her. No matter; Harriet had told Lord Granville, it appeared, that she would not dream of leaving home if her father married Lady Liz!

Liz Foster hugged the news to herself. No, she need not wait. Canis was, must be, hers. For Lord Hartington, that kind and charming boy, who was to

164

grow into a kind and charming man, would not refuse
to know her — his opposition had been tied to Harriet's,
and, with that gone, the Duke had no piece left to play
on the diminished chess-board of his life. His black king
was well and truly cornered by the white queen, no
pawn, no piece left to protect him.

Did he really care whether his stern old mother-in-
law never spoke to him again? His Elizabeth had told
him that his daughters would not oppose the marriage
in the sense that they would not cut themselves off from
him, and a letter he received from them, jointly signed,
told him that she was right.

Numbly obedient, he copied the letter which she
wrote for him to send to the Dowager Countess Spencer,
to inform her that his mind was made up. He intended
to marry again, and, secure in her newfound glory, the
concession that she would not take his title was forgotten. Lady Liz Foster would be the Duke's second
Duchess at last, to the pleasure of herself and her
daughter Caro-George, and all her other children, legitimate and illegitimate.

'Imagine,' said Caro Lamb to her husband, William,
when the details were at last known. 'She married him,
with no witnesses but some tame toadies no one has
ever heard of, and one of Grandmama Spencer's favourite parsons — how that must have galled! And what's
worse, Frederick Foster, her own son, was at Chiswick
House at the time, and didn't even attend — what a
thing!' And then she sat down and wrote dear Hart an
angry letter on the subject.

She might have refused to wait for him to marry her,
thought Harriet when Hart later showed her the letter,
full of bile and rage, as though Caro had been personally
insulted; but she always turned to him in distress, as
Harriet did herself. He and Selina Trimmer were twin
towers of strength for her, as well as for poor Caro, the

only difference being that Harriet tried not to be too noisy in seeking their sympathy.

For now the deed was done, and the lady had what she had always wanted, the Duke and a kind of respectability, as Harriet told Selina Trimmer, first in a letter, and then in person. But she, what did she have?

And what did she want? In the first flush of anger and distress, she had written to Selina of her disillusion with such a man as Granville seemed to have proved himself to be, and later, in more reasoned form, but still bitter, she had railed against her aunt, who, she thought, had destroyed her hopes because she could not bear to lose her one-time lover.

She had to accept the new Duchess, but she could not like her, and to live at Devonshire House, and at Chiswick with her, knowing that the one escape from her — an escape which she would have carried out with loving enthusiasm, on her side, at least — was now closed made the future seem drearier than ever.

Harriet had never felt so alone. Selina, who might have supported her, was at Holywell; Georgiana, settled at Park Street, was heavily pregnant — she must not disturb her over-much, and her aunt, whom in other circumstances she might have sought out for help and comfort, was her enemy.

Returning to Devonshire House, in the end, was not as difficult for her as she had thought it might be. Lady Liz — no, the Duchess, now that she had won — seemed to have shed her worst characteristics with her illegitimate status.

She came to see Harriet as soon as she decently could after her arrival.

'My dear,' she said, embracing her stepdaughter — she was too wise to ask for congratulations, 'you cannot imagine how happy I am to see you returned to us. I know the Duke has missed you, and so have I. I had hoped that your news might be — better,' which was tactful for Liz, thought Harriet, allowing the kiss on the cheek.

'Oh, my news is good,' she replied with purposeful misunderstanding. 'Georgiana is well; Morpeth and the children are better.'

'Now, now,' said the Duchess, 'you know perfectly well what I mean.' Something of her old fluttering seemed to have returned at the prospect of discussing Lord Granville. 'I have invited him for supper and you are to be kind to him. He looks woebegone these days, they tell me. What with loss of office — and other things. . .' And her glance was almost offensively arch and reproachful, as though it had been Harriet who had turned *him* down, and not the other way around, thought Harriet, amused despite herself.

'You will be kind to him, will you not, dearest Haryo, for my sake?'

'I have never been unkind to Lord Granville,' she returned. 'My manner to him has, I think, been beyond reproach.'

'Oh, now I have said the wrong thing,' exclaimed the Duchess, 'but no matter. You are a good child, my dear, and will comfort him in his disappointment, I am sure.'

Child? Disappointments? What can she mean? I am so far from being a child that I am almost at my vespers, my last prayers. And his disappointments? What are they? That he has not secured Susan Beckford, or some other rich beauty? Or that my aunt has succumbed to old age at last? Despair was making her spiteful, she knew, and she damned the man who had caused it.

But all the same, she dressed herself carefully for the evening. They were all to have supper together, it appeared; the all not including Hart, who was still at Chatsworth, which he loved the most of all the possessions he would one day inherit.

Her dinner dress was of cream satin, high-waisted, and she wore a small circlet made of silk lilies of the valley on her hair, which Walker dressed high. Despair, rage, jealousy, anticipation, she did not know which, brought fire to her eyes, and a twist to her mouth which had Walker saying, 'Oh, you look beyond anything tonight, m'lady.'

So she did, and when he came in and bowed to her he looked beyond anything, too, no sign of the suffering of which Lady Liz had spoken. Nobody, indeed, appeared to be suffering anything—or, rather, all those who were suffering were not present. Her aunt Spencer, for instance, who had, in the most immoderate language, recommended Harriet to keep her language and behaviour pleasant and cool in tones and choice of words which would have shamed Billingsgate!

This dreadful but comic memory struck her as Lord Granville straightened up, giving her face even more animation than ever, so that he privately wondered at her. He had thought to find her distressed—remembering her appearance those last two days at Badminton—both by the marriage and what had happened when they last met, but she looked radiant, and her manner to him was more unforcedly pleasant than he had known it since. . .since the days when she had been a child and had run to meet him.

And then a thought struck him. No one could tell from his own manner of the depths of his suffering, so could it be that she, too, was in desperate straits beneath the brilliant social mask which she was wearing?

'I am pleased to see you in such looks, Lady Harriet.'

'My lord,' she said, and bowed back. Was it possible, after all that had passed between them, what she privately thought of him, that she was pleased to see him? Could it possibly be? 'One lives in the world,' she said, oh, so coolly; 'one must accommodate to the world.

Not all that happens to us is desirable, or pleasant, but one learns to accept it—as I am sure you already know.'

'You are practising to be a diplomat, Lady Harriet?' And the eyes on her were amused.

'No, no. A man's prerogative. Or, rather, men need to learn it, to practise it. We women may not be diplomats in public life, but in private, yes, in private, diplomacy may be considered the only art we use—and do not need to practise.'

'I think I understand you,' he said, and his smile was one of relief—relief that he was not to be reproached, either directly or indirectly, for the false position in which he had helped to place her, so that he added swiftly, 'And may I also say that I admire your conduct, which has been, and I am sure always will be, irreproachable? To surmount, as you have done, the difficulties in which you have found yourself since your mama died is admirable, truly admirable.'

Compliments! Compliments! Should she hit him with her fan as the Caros would have done? Or should she raise it and flutter her eyelashes over the top of it? Or should she clap him on the back à la Lady Holland, say, What a good fellow you are, after all, Granville? Or, or, should she say, And all that is no more than I deserve, after your own conduct towards me? But, instead she said—and what came out was pure Haryo, 'And thanking you for that, Lord Granville, is like thanking the parson for his sermon, what we hear being so much what we ought, or want, to hear that there is no merit for ourselves in admiring it.'

She should have been born a man, with that mind, he thought admiringly. What was it Lord Palmerston had said the other night, when they had all been half-cut, and indiscretion flowed as well as wine? 'By God, Harriet Cavendish is the shrewdest mind I know. Had her looks equalled her wit, Helen of Troy would have been hard put to it to exceed her, and she would have been Lady Palmerston by now!'

Harriet carried her wit and fire into supper with her, wondered what was giving Liz the megrims — she was not her usual self tonight — and the Duke, wonder of wonders, was publicly short with her, and when she cooed about the dogs which surrounded his feet, even during the meal, growled at her, 'Enough, Duchess, enough. The subject grows tedious,' and turned to Harriet, who had been placed next to Lord Granville, and said, 'How goes the puppy I gave you, my dear? You have not spoken of it since you returned.' Which, his daughter was sure, was said as a means of snubbing Lady Liz — no, the Duchess — rather than out of any genuine desire to speak to her.

But she also noticed that as she sat down to play chess with Lord Granville — 'You will do me that favour, Lady Harriet, I beg of you,' — her father's eyes were hard on her. Marrying her off, she supposed.

Later, however, in her own room, being prepared by Walker for sleep, seated beside the fire, alone at last, she found that all her thoughts about him were in turmoil again. What did he mean now? For his attentions to her were so marked that she was sure that everyone present must have remarked on them, and she could not bear it, no, not at all, if he meant no more by them than he had done before Badminton.

If he felt nothing it was grossly unfair of him to single her out so persistently. For the gossip would begin again, eyes would follow her, and him; every word, every action would be noted, spoken of, written about, and she would join the long procession of his women without even having had the pleasure of sharing his bed — which was a thought so gross that she shivered at herself. She was forgetting every moral precept which she had been taught, and Selina would be ashamed of her, but then Selina was not confronted by him; easy to be virtuous in act and thought when no temptation presented itself!

She could not sleep, so wrote to Hart instead, head bent over the paper in the candlelight and the rosy glow from the fire. Caro-George was as kind and tactful as ever, she began, then paused. But did she really know what Caro-George truly thought? Or, in the end, could one ever know anyone beside one's self? Did one truly know one's self?

Determinedly, she wrote on, asking Hart to come to London, to help and to advise her. The game had changed again, Lord Granville had moved forward his most powerful piece, himself, and appeared to be attacking her king again, after he had retreated when in a strong position—only to mount his assault once more, and this time, she thought more powerfully than before.

And, at the end, the letter sanded and sealed, her hands wiped clean, she knelt down by the bed to say her prayers, as Selina had taught her when she was a little girl in the nursery, and as she still did. She laid her forehead on the coverlet, lifted her joint hands to her lips, and addressed her Maker.

'Thy will, not mine, Lord,' she muttered. 'It is for thy servant to suffer and endure, not to question thee. But oh, Lord, I pray thee that it will please thee to ensure that Granville is not deceiving me again—but whatever thy will, I, thy servant, will obey it, and will do, in this life, as in that to come, what thou commandest me to do.'

She rose, slipped into bed, blew out the candle. She had not asked God to send her Hart, for she thought that two requests would be one too many. Besides, she did not think that she needed divine assistance to bring him to her, nor was she wrong.

CHAPTER FOURTEEN

IT WAS annoying that just as it looked as though Lord Granville might be winding himself up again, she and Georgiana were to visit Grandmama Spencer and Selina at Holywell. The weather was contrary, too, raining and windy, to fit her mood a little, but never mind; if he were serious her absence might prod him a little — or could it be out of sight, out of mind? She could not know.

'And do you really wish to marry Lord Granville, should he propose to you?' asked Selina, that day after the sisters had arrived, and were settled in.

Now what could she say to that? A true answer would be, I desire him most desperately, so that to see him now almost makes me feel ill, but, as to marriage to him, that is a different thing altogether. Selina would probably jump six feet into the air at such an improper reply.

She said instead something of the truth. 'Oh, Selina, I am so torn. In many ways, I should be most happy to be Lady Granville, but, to put it at its plainest, is there a want of principle there, a want not conducive to the happiest of marriages? The weakness which has kept him tied to my aunt, dancing to her tune, still doing so — *that* continues to worry me, as I know it worries you. Oh, let us not speak of it. I am sick at heart, have been since I wrote to you at Badminton, and all I can hope is that God will send me a sign — since no one else seems able to.'

And, returning to Chiswick, early on the fourteenth of November, all was still in the melting pot. Lady

172

Liz — she could not yet think of her as the Duchess — greeted her with a smile, and a breathless cry of 'Oh, my dear, so pleased to have you back. We must arrange some company for you. You must not be lonely!'

She was on her highest ropes, surprisingly so, for Walker had confided to Harriet that the other servants had told her that the Duke had, of all things, taken a new mistress! 'And after being faithful to her for so long, the moment he makes her the Duchess, he is off with someone else!'

Oh, thought Harriet, why should Liz trouble about the Duke's unfaithfulness? Being Duchess was all that counted, to be sure. And she prayed to God to forgive her for her cynicism.

She could not expect Hart to have arrived yet, and the Duchess's idea of company seemed to consist largely of eligible men. She came down to dinner to find a large company there, including the Bessboroughs, Lord Duncannon and his wife, Granville and Mr Ellis, among others.

Her heart sank, but she put on her most cheerful countenance; the Duchess had placed her next to Lord Granville, and beneath his usual imperturbability she could sense that his manner was distracted. He was even more splendidly dressed than usual, and, from what he said, he and Mr Ellis had been asked to stay to supper, and then overnight.

Surreptitiously, she examined him. So *à point* he was that the impression of nervousness he was giving off, could have nothing to do with worry over his dress. His frock coat was a deep blue with silver buttons, his pantaloons were of a light grey, his shoes were perfect too, light and flexible, almost slippers. His linen was spotless, his cravat a dream, and the chestnut curls brushed to perfection.

They talked of this and that. The sparkle of their

recent conversations had disappeared. Perhaps it was her aunt's presence. Whenever she saw Lady Bessborough she could not help thinking of how she seemed to be standing in the way of any future for herself with Lord Granville, and her manner was constrained, which made her aunt look unhappy, shooting agonised glances at Lord Granville, and yes, there was something odd about him today, no doubt of it at all.

Dinner over, the company dispersed, and Harriet, bored and a little bewildered, wandered into the library. The tensions of the house were beginning to affect her, and perhaps that was what was wrong with him.

There was a small and pretty room off the library, a little study room, it was called, although there was a fireplace there, an armchair and a sofa, and it really was not little, except by comparison with the library.

There were books of prints on the table, and idly she began inspecting one of them, only to hear the door open behind her.

She turned. It was Lord Granville, the strangest expression on his face.

He bowed, said, 'Lady Harriet, I am pleased to find you here, and alone.'

'Lord Granville.' Her voice was cool, as cool as she could make it. There was a mirror over the hearth and she could see them in it: the handsome man and the plainish woman, wearing a dress of toffee-coloured wool, with saffron collar and cuffs, which oddly, enhanced her, rather than diminished her — paler colours tended to kill her, she had found.

And what a thing to be thinking of, as he stood there before her so grave and still, as though he were about to address some congress of diplomats, ready to make grave decisions about the future of Europe.

He had paused, and the pause seemed eternal, although it could have taken no time at all. 'I think that

you may be aware of what I am about to say to you,'
and oddly, Lord Granville Leveson Gower, celebrated
for his self-possession, his perfect aplomb was, she saw,
unsure of himself, to the degree that she thought he was
about to stammer.

'We have long been friends and companions, you and
I, Lady Harriet, and recently, I think, we have become
more than that. In short, I have. . . I hope. . .' He was
lost, as he later wrote to Lady Bessborough; he hardly
knew what he was saying, could not remember afterwards what he had said. It was worse, proposing, than
rising to speak in the House, and God knew that was
bad enough.

What could she be thinking of him? He had virtually
insulted her at Badminton, and now he was incoherent,
and Harriet, wildly, could think of no way to help him
that would not look impertinent, as though she were
anticipating what was to come, for this was, at last, the
proposal she had been waiting for, and it was not at all
what she had expected—something suave and elegant,
she supposed, not at all like this.

He started again, simply, this time. 'Lady Harriet, I
have long felt affection for you—as you must be aware,
since we first met, when you were little more than a
child. . .' He was maundering, talking like a gaby. He,
who had always prided himself that, whatever his public
difficulties, in private none could touch him for *savoir-
faire*. . . 'That affection has become deeper with the
years, and later it has become such. . .' oh, Good God,
he sounded like a book of etiquette run mad. . .this was
worse than Badminton '. . . such that it has increased to
the degree that I wish to share my life with you. . .'

There, however ungracefully, it was out, and she
could but refuse him, he was not going to Madame
Guillotine, after all, could only be rejected. . .

And, suddenly, improbably, he did not want the

grave-eyed woman opposite to him to reject him. No, he could not lose her, now that at the last moment he had found her. He put out his hand, his beautiful hand, fixed her earnestly with his killing eyes; would they kill, now, for him, or had he destroyed himself at Badminton?

'Oh, pray, Lady, Harriet, I beg of you, allow me to . . .say that you will give me permission to ask the Duke, your father, for your hand in marriage?'

Love or no love, companionship and meeting of minds or merely a desire to settle, to sink into the arms of the same woman each night, to know security, stability, both of which the woman before him could give him, as well as being a fit mother for his children, he had said it. Not, I love you to distraction, for he had said that to too many women, and it had only meant that he wanted to bed them, and he wanted more than that from Harriet Cavendish, much more — although he hardly knew for what he was asking.

Yes, it was out at last, his declaration, and how feeble it was, compared with what he had said to others; it lacked the glib fluency of the Apollo who had. . .he would not think of that now, merely wait for her to answer him, and pray that the answer would be the one which he most desired.

It had happened at last, thought Harriet wildly, something which, if she were truthful, she had dreamed of since the day he had first walked into Devonshire House; her prince had seen her and picked her out from all the beauties who had surrounded him, occupied his mind and thoughts for fifteen years, to be his wife, his lawfully wedded wife.

And if, once, he had been the simple, spotless creature every young girl dreamed of before she knew the world, she now knew that he was something much more complex than that, a living, breathing mortal man, who could succeed and yet fail, could love and yet betray, be selfish, and yet could show unselfish kindness, be conceited, and yet know quite humbly his own limitations, and, what was more, tell her of them, be brave and yet cowardly, be deceitful, and yet, when Lady Luck called to him on the gaming tables, be rashly careless; yes, she knew all this of him, and more—she knew herself, as never before.

Here, at the last gasp, everything offered to her which she had once desired so fiercely, did she desire it—and him—now? Oh, yes, she fiercely *desired* him, but desire was not all; did she *love* him, love him enough to risk all, defy her own reason, never mind Raison Sévère, take the risk that the contrarieties of his nature would betray her, seeing that he could not truly love her, and that a marriage of convenience would not bind him?

Harriet hesitated, looked up at last, to stare into those amazing eyes which had won so many women—and resisted them. She would not close her own as so many had done; she would go to him open-eyed herself, aware of all the risks she was running, would take him because he was Granville, whom she loved, and would hope that her love would be enough to sustain her should betrayal come, that she would be as brave as other betrayed women had been, nay, braver, because she loved, and many of the betrayed women had not.

The enormity of what she was doing struck her; acceptance and denial briefly warred within her, and, in a sense, neither won, for what moved her, came as a revelation, was, oddly, a sense almost of duty, a duty owed to him as much as herself, that in marrying him she could bring to him what no other woman had done: a faithful heart, a heart not yet pledged or given to another; that she would go to him bringing nothing but her love and her own sense of integrity.

She would accept him because he was human, fallible,

as she was, and hope that together they could build on that, since she would take no deceits with her into marriage, and, judging by the way in which he was proposing to her, all suavity, all diplomatic sureness abandoned, his deceits might have dropped away, too.

And now it was her turn to stammer and look ridiculous, but she did not, and managed to say, her throat closing as she spoke, 'You do me a great honour, Lord Granville, by your offer, and I assure you that I shall be happy for you to approach my father, as you wish.'

And so it was said at last, what she had never hoped to say, and the strangest expression crossed his face— was it, could it be, relief? Relief that she had accepted him—had he, for all his fabled confidence, expected her to refuse? He took her hand, kissed it, and then moved towards her, took her chin in his hand, said softly, 'You will not deny me a betrothal kiss, Lady Harriet,' and, before she could reply, kissed her gently, not on the cheek as she had expected, but softly on the lips, a butterfly kiss, to which she could take no exception, and then, having filled her with the strangest, wildest sensations by so doing, he stepped back.

Of course, they must all have known what he was about to do, not her father, perhaps, but her stepmother, and, almost certainly, Lady Bessborough. They had known that she was alone, she had been watched: was she not the daughter of Dukes, and did they ever go unwatched? And knowing her to be alone, they had left her for him to find.

'I am sure,' she said, almost primly, 'that my father will take no exception to your offer, Lord Granville, but until you have spoken to him I shall say nothing.'

'And that will content me, too, Lady Harriet,' he said. 'For I, too, have those with whom I would speak, before the generality know of our betrothal, and I would ask you, if the Duke agrees, not to publish our news for forty-eight hours, while I speak to those members of my family in London.'

Harriet remembered that poor Hart had read of his father's marriage to Lady Liz in the newspapers before the Duke had taken the trouble to inform him of it. Oh, no, she was sure that, whatever else Lord Granville was, he was a man of honour who would not allow his near relations to be treated so cavalierly.

He held out an arm to her, to escort her from the room. Relief was written so plainly on his face, and yes, affection, that she knew that her judgement had been correct. He had been almost fearful at the notion of proposing to her, as she had been fearful that he might — or might not.

They reached the door. He turned to her, said earnestly, 'Forgive me, in my nervous excitement I had quite forgot. There was something which I wished to show you.'

Harriet allowed him to release her, he slipped his hand inside the breast of his perfect coat and took from an inner pocket a small piece of paper.

'Knights of old,' he said, 'used to carry into the tourney or the battle their ladies' favours. I brought this small favour with me, Lady Harriet, to sustain me this afternoon, and it is fitting that you should know that I did. Permit me to give it to you,' and he handed her the paper.

Intrigued, Harriet took it from him. He was closer to her than he had ever been before, as close as he had been when he had given her his passionless kiss. The scent of him was strong in her nostrils, the scent of clean man, clean linen, and the lemon fragrance which she had come to associate with him.

She was trembling a little, for how much closer would they soon be? And the enormity of what had happened struck her hard, the thought of having his arms around her, that he would. . . She banished the thought sternly, and the hands which opened the letter trembled, as her body trembled when she read it.

She had forgotten the letter, remembered what had occasioned it, but now, reading it again, the past returned, and she was writing it, Selina standing over her while she did so, and she remembered, too, how hard she had tried for it to be perfect, like him.

Harriet did not think him perfect now, for we are none of us, she told herself austerely, perfect; but she remembered how pleasing it had been to think him so.

He was watching her, head bent, as she read, and said softly, 'I remember that little girl, and how she pleased me, and you please me now, madam, but differently, and I hope to show you so, soon.'

'Soon?' she echoed, idiotically.

'Yes, soon,' he replied still gentle, as though she were fine china, taking the letter from her, to replace it carefully in his breast pocket again. 'We do not wish to wait, do we? I have wasted enough time, bringing us to this point, and so I shall tell your father — and we do not want a great brouhaha. This should be a private occasion; I do not want the world's tongues dirtying it, as they will try to do.'

Too much had been said about them already, Harriet thought. What Devonshire House did or did not do inspired gossip writers, memoirists, caricaturists, print makers, and the snake's tongues of the idle of the world who had nothing better to do but hiss of this and that, provided that she and her family were their subject. They had had a field day, a tattoo, with Lady Liz's marriage. She would try not to give them that pleasure.

'I should like,' she said, 'to wait for Georgiana's baby to arrive before we marry, if you are agreed, of course.'

'Your pleasure is mine, and your wishes are mine

now,' he said, taking her hand and kissing it, causing poor Harriet to shudder at the sensations in her produced by his touch. 'I know when Georgiana's little one is due. Would Christmas Eve suit you? — a fine day for a marriage, one might think.'

'If Papa and Heaton agree,' she answered, Heaton being the Duke's right-hand man, who would be responsible for all the arrangements, 'yes, most suitable.'

'A splendid Christmas present for me,' he said, and kissed her hand again. Did he know what an effect he was having on her, and if that was what his mere touch did to her what would his. . .loving do?

Another dreadful thought which she could not share with Selina. The day seemed full of them.

And when they walked back into the drawing-room, his hand protectively on her arm, she was sure that she wore a placard on her forehead which told the world of what had been said and done, but if the others knew they said nothing, for now it was all up to the Duke.

Granville, as he later wrote to Lady Bessborough, was so nervous he hardly knew what he was doing. He could not really remember what he had said to Harriet, could only hope that he had not made too great a fool of himself, and now it was to be done all over again.

But the Duke was missing, had gone, none knew where, although the new Duchess was aware of what he was about, but was not telling. So, it was after supper, a supper which neither of the principals could eat, before Lord Granville George Leveson Gower, DCL, PC, MP, could speak to his future wife's father, and even then he could tell that all his prospective father-in-law wanted to do was return to his puppies.

He had asked for a word with him, before supper, and the Duke had growled, 'Later, later, after supper, in my study.'

So, once more, the doyen of all the diplomats, the ex-ambassador, three or four times over, the confidant of emperors, kings, and princes, ex-cabinet minister, found himself trembling a little at the prospect of proposing all over again, as it were.

The Duke, slouched in a chair, waved him to another one. He was already unbuttoned, already playing with the dogs, all about him on the floor. The room stank of them, noisome smells coming from the odd corner.

'Of all men,' the Duke said abruptly, before Granville could so much as open his mouth, 'you are the one I would have chosen to marry my daughter Harriet; the one I most prefer. You are most fitted for one another's company,' and was that meant to be a compliment, or not? thought Granville amused, 'a son-in-law fit to take my daughter from me, to give her the companionship she needs.'

He fell silent, so that he was compelled to say, 'You are right, Duke. I have come to ask for Lady Harriet's hand in marriage, and your blessing with it. I see that I have that already.'

'Hmmph,' growled the Duke. He thought that the man before him had taken his time in making his mind up. He might have had the girl off his hands months ago — no wonder we weren't beating Bonaparte if my Lord Granville's hesitations were much duplicated in court and cabinet!

Granville felt compelled to say something. He rose, bowed — he disliked all this sitting about to decide things, it was slovenly, but then the Duke was slovenly, and the room. . .he must be running mad to think of such things at this juncture! — said earnestly, 'As a young man, I have had all of a young man's follies. May I assure you that now I am to marry I do not intend to persevere in them?'

It only occurred to him afterwards what a weaselling

speech that was, fit for a wily diplomat. He only *intended* to give up his follies! What in God's name had he meant by it — that he intended to give up women. . .or gambling?

Well, women he was sure he could renounce — if Lady Harriet was the woman he thought her to be — but gambling. . .and he shut his eyes to that, for it was something outside of himself, and, however often he had vowed when the fit was gone that he would never indulge again, when the fit took him. . .that was a different matter.

But he would try, now that he was to have a family, not to let it overcome him too much. And whatever he had said, the Duke seemed to be satisfied by it, forced port on him until his head reeled, and then, when he left, asked the Duke for secrecy until his family were informed. . .

Except, of course, that he wrote that night to Lady Bessborough, so that, reading his letter, she knew that her and Elizabeth's — no, the Duchess's — plotting had come true, and that in some way this letter was valedictory, for Harriet would be his first concern now. She knew him well enough to be aware that he would do his duty, and she hoped that that was all it would be, his duty, for she was human enough not to want her niece to take her place completely.

Harriet thought of none of this when she went to bed at last, having written to Hart, not to tell him of her great news, because she would do that when Granville had spoken to his family, but informing him merely that Granville was with them, and was staying the night.

All that filled her waking thoughts — and her sleeping ones, too, was that, in some fashion she could not have hoped for, her dreams had come true, and if there were reservations about what she had done that day in accepting him she kept them to herself for the moment.

She only knew that, for the first time, when they slept under the same roof she could think of him, and of married life with him, and that if he walked through her dreams again it would be as her affianced husband.

The little girl's dream had come true. The prince was hers — if prince he truly were. She had yet to find out — but, even if he was not, despite all she knew that she loved him, had done for years. Selina might deplore him, common sense might warn against him, but they were as nothing against the one fact. He was Granville and, for her, this, *this*, was love.

CHAPTER FIFTEEN

OH, HOW the letters flew about polite society when the news broke! And oh, how the gossip roared. Apollo, Antinous, caught at last, not by a beauty worth a fortune, not a beauty at all, but Harriet Cavendish, his former mistress's niece! But that aspect of the match was not the one which most occupied people — it was the apparent disparity between the two of them which engaged most people's thoughts.

Not all, however. George Canning, face aglow, came up a few nights later, at an all-male dinner party, to clap his old friend on the back, to shake him by the hand.

'Of all things the most sensible. I did not know you had it in you — to choose a wife so worthy of you, so fit to make you happy. A family man, at last. I see you, sitting there with materfamilias, paterfamilias in person, for what you really give your heart to you do well,' and as Granville laughed, a little embarrassed, protesting, he added earnestly, 'No, no, I will not retract what I have said — you do not yet know yourself, I think, but you will, you will. Pray convey my felicitations to the lady, but it is you who need them the most, for it is you who are winning the greater prize.'

'And so I am,' said Granville, thinking that he could depend on Canning to cut through to the heart of the matter. He had felt that some who had congratulated him had laughed behind their hands a little, but not Canning, never the friend of his youth. His delight was unfeigned.

That afternoon he had visited Harriet and walked

with her, alone, in the gardens, none to oversee them, for they were to be married, soon to be alone forever.

The day was cold, even for November, their breath smoked on the air, and Harriet had worn a calash, a giant hood lined with fur, to protect her against the cold, as well as a mannish coat, and he had worn a cloak which he had brought with him from Russia, with a fur collar coming high up, almost to reach his ears, a gold chain fastened it, and he knew, as he always knew, that it suited him, gave him an air of being something out of a Gothic romance.

This intense awareness of himself gave him, he also knew, an air of conceit, but the impression was not completely just — for he had that awareness of others, as well as himself, an awareness which years of diplomacy at every level had honed to a sharpness which sometimes disconcerted himself as well as the others.

He did not know that Harriet had registered this understanding, and had realised that it made him capable of the strange empathy which he conveyed to those to whom he spoke — that he was sympathetic towards them and their concerns — gravely caring, even.

Harriet had cast sidelong glances at him while they walked. He had admired the deer, keeping their distance from them today, and she had told him the story of their attack on poor Walker, which amused him, as she had intended. How strange to think that he was hers now, as she was his, and still she was not sure how she really felt. Delight, mixed with misgivings, produced an almost physical reaction compounded of nausea and euphoria.

'There is something of which I wish to speak to you, my dearest Harriet,' he had said, at last. She had been sure that there was something exercising him, and, as was becoming common, she had read him aright.

'It is about your aunt, Lady Bessborough. It is useless

for me to pretend; you must have been long aware of how much we meant to one another, how strong our attachment was. For years, your aunt was such to me that there was hardly a thought of mine I did not confide in her, a folly which I committed which I did not confess to her, God forgive me for that, but you must see how much she meant to me then—and still does, although after quite a different fashion now.

'Harriet, my dearest, I am also aware that because of that, and because of malicious gossip, you might have felt that she. . .tried to prevent my marriage to you, and if that is so then this must produce a constraint, possibly even a breach of confidence between you.' He paused, and Harriet made a small gesture of dissent; she could not speak.

As once before, she had the impression of being trapped in an engraving. The only colour in the landscape was that given to it by the warm face, the living body of the man beside her.

'No,' he said earnestly. 'It would be strange if you did not feel misgivings, but, of all things, I would wish that you and she might be friends again, for the truth is quite other than you might think. Your aunt, far from trying to prevent our marriage, did her utmost to promote it. If there was delay on my part. . .misunderstanding between us, that arose from my actions, not your aunt's. She reproached me, indeed, feared that I might wound you by my carelessness—as she saw it—for she loves you, I know from all she has said, as if you were her own child.'

Harriet turned her face towards him, stopped walking, and he turned to face her. 'She wished to promote our marriage?'

'Because she thought, as I do, that we could make one another happy, and the thing she wishes most in the world is to see the two people she loves so much, you and I, happy together.'

'Oh!' Harriet felt almost faint at this new and strange news. She had thought that her aunt must be jealous, and through jealousy would wish to see Granville and herself remain apart.

But this, this was love. To see the loved one happy, even at the cost of one's own happiness. 'Oh,' she said impulsively, as all the love and admiration she had once felt for Aunt Bessborough, destroyed on a day very like this one, rushed back into her heart again. She felt that she loved all the world. 'Pray tell her when next you write to her — for I know you write to her constantly, and I would not have you cease, for both your sakes — tell her that I love her dearly too, and will love and care for you as she would wish.'

For once she could not read the expression which crossed his face. Emotion rode on it, on the face of the man who never showed it, his pleasant smile a mask to conceal, not reveal.

'My dear,' he said hoarsely, 'you are an angel,' and he lifted his hands to pull the calash away to free her head, and then placed his left hand in her hair, the palm cupping her head, so that he tipped her wondering face towards him.

'Angels deserve a reward,' he said, and bent his head to kiss her on the lips, a true kiss this time, full of passion, and fire, quite unlike the one he had given her on the day of their betrothal.

Her passion, untutored but real, met his and matched it. She put her own hands up to grasp him by the arms, to steady herself against the dizziness which accompanied this initiation into true womanhood. The park, the world, disappeared.

Granville had meant to offer a kiss less innocent than the one he had already given her on the day of the proposal, but not truly passionate, but this kiss grew and changed, until he, knowing, as Harriet did not, what kisses like this led to was forced to stop; for, invading her mouth, his tongue had met hers, and she had given him hers, the pupil learning so rapidly from the master that the master had to run to stay ahead.

He stepped back, replaced the calash so that it framed her glowing face, the eyes giving him their message of love, of a desire for love to be complete, fulfilled. He kissed her again, on the forehead this time.

'As I said before, another pledge against our marriage,' and as she shivered violently, all the currents of love running through her for the first time, he misread her a little, said, 'Come, you are growing cold. I do not want the rest of the world, but we must return to the house — and the others.'

Disappointed, for Harriet knew that she now wanted more, wanted to hold Antinous and to lie fulfilled in his arms, even if the thought of what fulfilment would mean was a little fearful, as well as desirable. What she could not tell Selina was true; she had come to desire him, and as eating grew with the appetite, his caresses, brief though they necessarily were, were fuelling her desire for him.

It only needed Hart's arrival to complete her happiness; she had written to him again, urgently telling him of her news and her happiness, and could hardly wait to see him.

Returning to warmth and the fireside, she had found him waiting, standing before the window, impatiently looking out for her.

He was as unlike his father, the Duke, as a man could be. He had all his mother's charm, was tall and graceful, and, if not conventionally handsome, his expression was so sweet and loving that women turned to look after him, and his nature was as sweet as his looks.

Yes, he had come to love and to support her, for he strode up to them, to grasp Granville by the hand, to clap him on the back, to congratulate him on having the good sense to choose such a pearl, such a treasure, a bride who would fill his life with love. 'And wit,' he finished. 'Oh, you will never want conversation with Haryo around, and I know you, Granville, talk and reading are your twin passions, and she will be there to assist you in both. What a household! Master and mistress by the fire reading, and the babies bawling to be fed. "No, stay a moment, little ones, we must finish this delightful passage". I cannot wait to enjoy the spectacle!'

'Cease your funning, do,' retorted Harriet, delighted by this whole-hearted acceptance of their *fait accompli*, and they walked together into the drawing-room, to drink tea, to exclaim together, to kiss the new Duchess, as dear Hart did in his kind, good-natured way. Oh, how she loved him!

After they had enjoyed an early dinner, tea was a jolly affair. Granville and Hart liked one another, and they punned and laughed over the teacups, and Hart asked questions about the war, and George Canning, and Granville asked after Chatsworth, rather as though it were an ailing aunt, and Hart replied in kind. He thought that when he inherited his first task would be to restore it to its former glories. His father had sadly neglected it.

Only, the next day, his mood was grave. The lawyers had come, summoned by the Duke, to set out the terms of her dowry. Granville had been there, and Hart. Ironically, she thought, she, who was to take the dowry with her, was not there. The men would decide things.

The meeting over, Hart came to her alone, his face grave. Harriet rose, her own face suddenly white. 'Hart!

What is it?' For it was patent by his manner that something was gravely wrong. She could hardly speak, 'Granville. . .?'

'No, no, dearest Haryo,' he said, putting his arms about her. 'Nothing to do with Granville. He has behaved like a man of honour. He will always do so, Haryo, no fear of anything else. We agreed that what was to be said should come from me, because it is a family matter. No,' he said, almost violently for him. 'I told him that it was *my* duty to speak to you of this, seeing that the matter was none of his doing. Sit down, my dear.'

Something *was* wrong, she knew it, and her heart constricted. 'Come,' said Hart putting out his hand to her, 'it is bad enough, in all conscience, but one day, I promise you, I shall put things right. It is your dowry, dearest girl; Father will not give you more than ten thousand pounds — after he gave Georgiana, and then Caro-George, thirty thousand — and Caro-George is not even legitimate, and marrying George Lamb, who cannot hold a candle to Granville. Such an insult, such an insult. . .' And he was near to tears.

Harriet sat there, numb. It was not the money, although God knew that they could do with it, Granville being a younger son, and she having nothing to bring to him but the dowry. As their world counted poor, they would be desperately so — and yet, and yet. . . It was the knowledge that she meant nothing to him — less than Georgiana, she had expected that, but less than Caro-George, that hurt, that hurt so desperately that she thought she was about to faint.

Never forgiven, never, for having been a girl and not the heir he wanted. Never forgiven because before and after Mama died she had tried to act with integrity. Never forgiven, although she had tried so hard to bring herself closer to him in the years since Mama's death.

Never forgiven, because she looked so like the mother-in-law he detested.

And now he had informed the whole world of how little she meant to him. An insult, Hart had said, an insult. She could imagine the gossip, and the laughter that Granville had not only not netted an heiress, but the Duke had not even given his daughter a decent portion.

Hart thought that his sister was about to faint, she had gone so white. He jumped to his feet, swore, and when, shaking, she grasped his hand, saying, 'Oh, God, Hart, did he need to tell *everyone* how little he cares for me,' he kissed her, ran to the door, and called for Granville, who had been pacing the corridor outside while his future brother-in-law told his sister what their father had done to her — and to him.

Granville came in, dropped to his knees beside her, and, if Hart had possessed any secret doubts about what Granville truly felt for Harriet, they were dispelled immediately. 'No,' he said. 'No, my dearest, you are not to grieve. He does not know what he is doing. The money is nothing,' for she had begun to stammer.

'Oh, Granville, I am so sorry. . .'

He put his hand on her lips, so gently and lovingly, said, 'It is the hurt he has given you that I resent,' and he held her against his broad chest, all decorum forgotten, while she sobbed against him, Hart tiptoeing away.

'Damn the money,' he exclaimed, his usual calm gone. 'We shall manage somehow. Retire into the country. Damn Parliament, office, and society. I am sick of it. Nothing matters, but that you are not distressed. Come, let us go to town with Hart as soon as possible, tomorrow perhaps, buy your dress — and oh, I have a splendid present for you, I can hardly wait for you to see it — although nothing matters to you, I know, beside this. But it will pass, I promise you, it will pass.'

Gradually Harriet quieted, lying still against him, and he began to kiss her wet face, her eyelids, her cheeks, 'So salt, your tears,' he murmured. 'Attic salt.' Did he really say that? she thought afterwards, and why? He took out his handkerchief, spotless of course, wiped her face, and slowly, slowly restored her, murmuring, soothing and kissing her, as though she were a child again, until she lay, half asleep in the crook of his arm, he still kneeling.

'You will be cramped,' she said faintly.

'No, not while I care for my Harriet. See, you are better now. That was almost a smile. May I kiss the lips which smiled; am I permitted? Will Selina Trimmer drop from the chandelier to rebuke me, say that such impudence is no more than she expected from Lord Granville? Oh, if only I had a little more to live on, we could hand his money back to him, but no, my darling, we could not do that even if I had. It would be wrong. It would add to the gossip. No, you must be married from here, and we shall smile — shall we not? — and he shall not think that he has hurt you. . .if he thinks at all.'

Granville saw that she was recovered, that she was her usual stoic self again, would be able to leave the room and face the world. He leaned forward and kissed her on the lips this time, a gentle kiss, one to comfort a sad child, and was rewarded by a watery smile.

'Come,' he said, 'there are visitors, come to congratulate us. The tea board will have arrived. Hart will be so relieved to see you happy again.'

'Oh, you are so good,' she said, and, leaning forward, kissed him back, to his delighted surprise, a firm, honest kiss on the corner of his mouth.

'That is to defy Selina,' she said, 'and to thank you for not thinking of the money we have lost.'

'Oh, I think about it,' he said softly. 'But we are not

to have it, and to repine would be stupid, a waste of our
energies. We have better things to talk of—like presents
for the bride, and one for Selina, for she loves you
dearly,' and, talking gravely and pleasantly, he led her
down to their guests, the Bessboroughs and some
Spencer relatives come over to see her and, as he had
said, to congratulate her—and later to take the news
about the dowry back to chew over at their leisure.

CHAPTER SIXTEEN

So MORE letters flew about London and the great houses where the 'cousinry', the interrelated nobility and upper gentry of England, lived. Grandmama Spencer wrote to Lady Bessborough, commenting, as Granville and Harriet expected, that the Duke's generosity was so well known that his departing from it in Harriet's case was sure to be remarked on.

Harriet, as well as Granville, was happy that Heaton, the Duke's right-hand man, had said that the wedding could go ahead as rapidly as they had wished, the date fixed for December the twenty-fourth, for, despite the feelings which overwhelmed her all the time she was with him, away from him the old doubts were beginning to surface, despite the loving kindness he showed to her constantly after the Duke's decision over her dowry.

But with him, oh, that was bliss, even if it were only kindness which he displayed so constantly, teasing her a little, making her laugh, to forget what had been done to her by someone who should have shown her love.

Love in abundance was showered on her by Hart, as never before. He teased her, too. He came to her room to see her one afternoon, when Granville had driven to town, on a special mission, he had said mysteriously, nodding and almost winking at Hart, dropping his impassive mask a little — for her benefit, Harriet knew.

'Now, sis, why the long face?' For she was seated by the window, looking out, and offered him a pensive expression when he entered.

She had had a letter from Selina which had caused her doubts to surface again, so cautious was it in its congratulations, and she had asked herself again, Was she letting herself in for a long agony in which he ran after other women, treated her as so many husbands did — consideration for a few weeks, and then the habits of a lifetime reasserting themselves?

Something of her doubts showed on her face, even as she said, 'No long face, Hart. Pre-marriage megrims a little; everyone has them, I know Georgiana did. I'm also hoping that she has her latest child before the wedding. Granville arranged the date so that she has the greatest chance of doing so.'

'Oh, no,' he said softly. 'More than that, I think. You are troubled about him — and the future — are you not?'

She nodded. She could not lie to Hart. 'Then don't be,' he said energetically. 'You are made for each other, suit so admirably. There you sit each night, prosing the evening away. Such splendid *causeries* you will have when you are finally hitched, and he does not have to say goodnight to you, and leave. You may talk the night away.'

'There is more to marriage than talk,' said Harriet dubiously. 'He did not go to his. . .*belles amies*. . .for talk.'

'Oh, no, indeed not. One does not go to *them* for that,' replied Hart, as though he were a roué of sixty, instead of a very young man. 'Marriage is more than that. And if you are fearful about the other thing, which is not talk, you need have no fear. I have never heard a lady confess her dissatisfaction with Granville Leveson yet! Forgive me for saying so, dear sister, but it needs to be said. In that department he has no rival. You have no mama to help you, or advise you,' he offered gravely in defence of his frankness.

'I cannot imagine Mama saying any such thing,' protested Harriet.

'Not in my words, perhaps, but, depend upon it, she

was like to think of what I have said, and advise you accordingly. There, I have said it; it needed to be said. Besides, he is kind beneath all his flim-flam and grand manner. He is like someone left over from the nobility of France before the Revolution, but we shall not tell him so. I know he will be kind to you. In every way.'

'And that is all,' said Harriet a little despondently, 'kind?'

'*All*,' said her brother, 'what do you mean by all? Who has been so kind to you, dear sister, that you can afford to disregard kindness? It is more than most married women get.'

Harriet considered. 'Marriage?' she achieved at last. 'I have you and Georgiana; do I need marriage?'

'And I have my life, which is a man's, and you cannot share it, and Georgiana has Morpeth and her babies. No, he will care for you, and I think — no, I am almost certain — that when he marries you, he will settle down, Aunt Bessborough and the others well behind him. He has had his fun, and he will be such a family man as you have never seen!'

'I wish that I could believe you,' sighed his sister.

'Well, there is what I believe, take it or leave it, Lady Harriet, and only time will tell whether I am right to advise you so. Your little brother must fill the place of the mama you have lost and the papa — you never had.'

She leaned forward, her eyes full of love, and kissed him on the cheek. 'Oh, you are such a comfort, Hart, and have been since the first time I saw you. . .'

'Seeing that I was only a few hours old, I am sure that my advice was highly useful then,' he interrupted her, smiling.

'Oh, you cried at me, and held my finger tightly with your hand. It is one of my earliest memories. "And here is your new brother," Mama said. "You must love him, Haryo," — and I always have.'

'And by the by,' he said, before he left her, 'do not let Selina Trimmer advise you over-much. She knows neither you — nor the world.'

Going to town with Granville, Hart's words in her ears, was a delight. Never before had she shopped, gone about with such gay abandon. Poor they might be, but Granville behaved exactly like the *grand seigneur* Hart had dubbed him, and Hart, who went with them, and joined in the fun, was equally extravagant.

Granville's mysterious trip to town had been to arrange for her wedding present from him; he was giving her a necklace made from a diamond presented to him by the Tsar of all the Russias, worth no less than three thousand pounds. He also purchased many other, less expensive treasures for her and for their home. Hart went to Rundell and Bridges, the jewellers, to buy her a wedding present of equal magnificence, and gently bullied Grandmama Spencer into giving her something similarly extravagant.

Between them both, they were spoiling her outrageously. Hart behaved like the magnate he was, and Granville as though he were equally so; his taste was impeccable, and everything he possessed, Harriet discovered, when she visited his home at Stanhope Street, Hart chaperoning her, was exquisite. He and Hart got on famously together — another worry removed — and Saxe brought them all a cold collation at nuncheon, and they laughed and talked together after such a jolly fashion that Harriet hardly knew herself. To be with Granville was to savour the pleasures of life; he made everything easy.

He showed her his library: the bookcases were beautiful, specially made for him, and it was evident that his taste in dress was merely a public manifestation of the grace of his private living — which she was now to share.

That being so, Harriet took especial pains in selecting her wedding dress, although the nervous pangs which she was beginning to experience were making it difficult for her to do anything.

Such strange sensations gripped her. Later she was to understand that love and desire for the man she was to marry, mixed with fear of the immediate future, her wedding night, and the most distant future, when she would be his wife, had produced in her a mixture of indigestion, nausea and fright so strong that living through the last few days was like walking a tight-rope, fearful that if she fell she would descend into a pit from which she would be unable to rise.

The Duchess did not make matters better. Told of the news that first day, she had flung her arms about her stepdaughter as though she had been her dearest love, not an obstacle to be removed from her triumphant path.

'Oh, so happy for you, so happy,' she had trilled. 'Who better for you than Granville? Think, think, you will always have someone to talk to—no complaints there, I know—or anywhere else for that matter.' Well, she and Hart ought to get together to discuss *that!* was Harriet's inward and naughty comment to this typical piece of arch Lady Lizzery, and, as for talk, everyone seemed to think that that was all the bride and groom were fit to do, which, considering my lack of looks, is perhaps not a surprise, but surely he wants more from me than that?

Harriet was not to know that Granville had suddenly grown tired of waiting. He had thought that the time between the betrothal and the wedding was short enough in all conscience, but he had discovered in himself a dreadful desire to begin to initiate Lady Harriet Cavendish into the delights of love and married life.

This surprised him more than a little. Ever since he had comforted her on the day of the Duke's decision over the dowry, he had wanted to do so much more with her — wanted, indeed, to make love to her in earnest, and his new-found wish to be a faithful husband prevented him from seeking relief elsewhere, so that the wedding seemed to be aeons away, and time passed with agonising slowness.

Custom, his own stern sense of what was socially proper, consideration for her, prevented him from doing more than bestow light kisses, linger a little when he held her hand, and that was by no means enough.

They also visited Georgiana in Park Street. 'About to pig, at last,' she said cheerfully, after embracing Harriet and warmly congratulating Granville, who shook hands with Morpeth, his nephew of exactly the same age as himself, Granville being the child of his father's old age. Morpeth made jokes about what their relationship would be once Granville and Harriet were safely turned off, as he irreverently said.

'The table of relationships forbidding marriage will have to be carefully examined, too,' he joked. 'Not that I want to marry you, old fellow, but supposing our offspring should express a desire to tie the knot? Should we require a dispensation from the Archbishop of Canterbury, do you think?'

He looked tenderly at his wife, said teasingly, 'I hope you do not mind my arranging the new baby's marriage before it has done us the honour of being born! That would be taking the prudence I have learned from you, Granville, to extremes, no doubt at all!'

More spoiling of Lady Harriet Cavendish followed, led again by Hart, and supported by Granville, who held her hand surreptitiously, to her private delight at this breach of perfect decorum. Well, we may not be flirting in corners like the others, thought Harriet, he would never wear *that*, as I already supposed, but diplomatic discretion has its limits, I see.

Everything seemed to go well for them, as though Granville were arranging all life to suit their wishes. Georgiana's baby arrived, and Harriet took delivery of a little bracelet for Serena which was duly sent off, inscribed with Harriet's new initials, HLG, at Granville's suggestion.

But when the little parcel had gone, her love with it, she cornered him in the library — where else? — and said to him, 'A private word with you, my lord,' rather as though she were a junior clerk asking him for instructions.

'As many as you please,' he replied, turning those disturbing eyes on her, putting down his book and offering her his arm.

They took a turn in the long room. It was too cold to venture much outside. They were now well into December, and frost and fog surrounded them.

'Well, my love, or shall you still be "Lady Harriet" to me?'

'Oh,' said Harriet, delighted, 'it is about that of which I propose to speak. You should take a booth at a fair, and read minds — or did you read my face?'

He smiled. 'Neither — a lucky chance. Now, had we been deciding the fate of nations, you as Zenobia, Queen of Everything, and I as a visiting ambassador, I would have looked wise, and pretended that my lucky shot was meant!'

'Lucky or not,' she said gaily, smiling up at him, so that his heart lurched a little, 'I must tell you that when we are married, although form and usage says that I remain Lady Harriet, because of my father's greater eminence, and your lesser, I do not wish to follow form; I wish to be known as Lady Granville Leveson Gower; your wife should be no more — and no less.'

Her wit pleased him nearly as much as her consideration, and the expression of trust which she had given him. Harriet saw, that beneath his beautiful calm, and his murmured thanks, she had moved him. How much, she was not to know until later.

She was pleased that neither he nor she could read minds at the last great dinner before the wedding. It was bad enough to endure Lady Liz's — no, the Duchess's — falsities, but having to face her embattled relatives, all at one go — well, that called for courage above and beyond the call of duty, she thought.

She dressed herself with care in a cinnamon satin dinner dress, with coffee-coloured lace trim and inserts. Walker had made a circlet of silk autumn flowers for her hair — and something was beginning to happen to her, and she was not sure what was causing it.

The face she saw in the mirror before which Walker fussed her was not the one to which she was used. Despite all misgivings, all subtle fears of what this new life would bring to her, she had begun to change.

Oh, she would never be beautiful, but she was beginning to assume what in later years would be known as her presence, something which would endure longer than beauty, which would cause her still to be remarked on, when the young beauties surrounding her would be ignored.

Added to the upright carriage which she, of all Miss Trimmer's pupils, possessed the most, it gave her something intangible, which more than one of the guests assembled remarked on and wondered at.

They were all there, her beautiful half-sister, Mrs George Lamb, Caro-George; her lovely cousin Lady Caroline Lamb, Caro-William; Emily Cowper, divinely beautiful and divinely something else, which Harriet did not care for. Their husbands, and the Bessboroughs, with Duncannon, who had once been her half-hearted suitor, whom she had wholeheartedly held off.

The Bessboroughs! Her aunt, whom she welcomed with the most loving of kisses, for her to stand off and say anxiously, 'You are happy? Oh, yes, I see you are happy!' And the pang which went through Harriet Ponsonby, Lady Bessborough, Lord Granville's great love, but now only his adviser, struck her to the heart.

For she alone, looking at her niece, could see what was beginning to happen to her.

Under *his* tutelage, *his* affection, Harriet Cavendish was beginning to blossom, becoming the woman she was meant to be, something quite unlike the immature, prickly girl who had been created by lack of love and care. Lady Bessborough knew at once that she could not compete with this Harriet; the man who loved talking to clever women would love in time, if he did not already do so, the witty, poised woman Harriet was turning into.

And kind Uncle Bessborough, who had always had a loving word for Harriet, who in her turn had always shown her interest in the world of art and painting in which he had immersed himself—a refuge from the world in which he was compelled to live—could also see the change in her, and was pleased at it.

Lady Melbourne was there, her worldly face amused. This marriage had something which she also recognised as rare and different, and looking across the table at her old friend, who had enjoyed her handsome young lover for so many years, she recognised and understood the agony through which that old friend was going.

The Duke was unable to attend—or so he said. Gout had struck him down. Hart would take his place, he ordered, and so my Lord Marquis of Hartington sat at one end of the table, his stepmother, the erstwhile crocodile, at the other end, smiling sweetly at him, her status confirmed by this first great event of her marriage — an event which she had so desperately wanted, and had tried to bring about. She was happy above all that Hart had offered her his friendship, which meant more to her than mere recognition.

'Oh, how can you, Hart, how can you?' spat Caro-William at her cousin, who was determined that all should go well — for Harriet's sake.

'How can I what, dear Caro?' murmured Hart, his charming smile growing broader. He still loved Caro-William to distraction, and thought that had she waited for him, instead of falling in love with William Lamb, and marrying him, he would have prevented or controlled her follies, and her life — and his — would have been very different.

'Endure all this, of course. The crocodile at one end, grinning her death's head grin at you, her little serpent of a daughter sitting halfway down looking as though butter wouldn't melt in her mouth. . .'

'Can crocodiles hatch serpents?' queried Hart lazily.

'Oh, you know perfectly well what I mean,' said Caro crossly, 'and Granville marrying Harriet. What a turn-up! What will be the end of that, I wonder?'

'Good, I should think,' shrugged Hart, determined that nothing should mar Harriet's send-off.

'And Emily Cowper grinning that poisonous grin — did you hear her? "Dearest Haryo, how you are to be congratulated, such a prize", when you know, as well as I do, that she will be spreading malice, like incense, about poor Haryo all round society. She should be the devil's acolyte, she should, she should!' and her voice rose alarmingly, so that heads began to turn.

Hart said, his voice soothing, his eyes concerned. 'Come, Caro, compose yourself, for Haryo's sake. And as for marrying Granville, what could be better? She loves him to distraction, but does not know it yet. You

are my dear girl—are you not?—and will not let Hart
down, I am sure of that.' And gradually Caro lost her
nervous look, and began to smile, a watery smile, and
behaved herself, so that Harriet, relieved, began to enjoy
herself, and felt free to admire the magnificent spectacle
which was Lord Granville Leveson Gower in full fig, as
though he were about to confer with the Tsar of all the
Russias, instead of readying himself to marry Lady
Harriet Cavendish.

She could even endure Emily Cowper's falsities, and
her mother's no less ambiguous compliments, and was
happy to think that Granville had stipulated that the
wedding would be quite private, with few relatives—
one more grumble for Caro-William, as she let Hart
know.

Even George and William Lamb behaved themselves
and did not get at the wine—or let the wine get at them,
thought Harriet, talking to William—who, for all his
odd manner, she was sure meant to be kind. And
Duncannon congratulated her, so that all in all the
evening was far from being the ordeal she had feared it
might be, and she could feel as well the approving looks
she was winning from the man who was going to be her
lord and master.

'Oh, I can see that you will be a splendid diplomat's
wife,' he told her at the end of the evening, when their
guests were leaving.

'Now, what do you mean by that, my lord?' she
wondered.

'Oh, the diplomat you are fast becoming should not
need to be told,' he riposted. 'Not that you do not need
some lessons, Lady Harriet, but not in that line—in a
line where I shall be pleased to be your teacher.' And
the blue eyes left her in no doubt as to what he meant,
and she did not ask him to explain.

Granville was amused and pleased by her response;

most young women, had he cared to speak to them so, would, he knew, have had a simpering answer for him, pretending that they were innocent, but showing by their manner that they were well aware of his double meaning.

But Harriet simply said briskly, 'You know that I have survived for the last three years, while walking the tight-rope, here in Devonshire House, and we have even managed to eat our way through our celebratory dinner without anyone, including poor Caro-William, doing anything to overset us, me least of all, so that after that even being entertained by the Grande Porte in old Constantinople will be as nothing to me. You may make me your senior adviser on your next mission — I would make nothing of such Byzantine negotiations after surviving Lady Liz — I mean, the Duchess!'

He could have kissed her glowing face then and there. It was not Granville Leveson Gower who was changing her, it was happiness.

'Not long to wait now,' was all he could say, and he wondered for the first time if she was as impatient for him as he, improbably, was for her.

All that they now had to survive was the wedding!

CHAPTER SEVENTEEN

AND suddenly, the wedding ceremony was behind them, and they were alone together driving to Woolmer in Hertfordshire for their honeymoon, the house lent to them by Granville's half-brother, the Marquis of Stafford.

Behind them stretched a small train, with Walker and his man Saxe, and other servants in one of the Devonshire carriages, and grooms as outriders; Lord and Lady Granville on the first journey of many.

She sat beside him, so conscious of him that she could hardly breathe. They had not spoken since they had been handed in, since the wedding guests, Hart leading, had cheered them off.

He stirred, suddenly put an arm around her, to pull her close to him, said, 'Lady Granville, you are very quiet,' and there was — could it be? — a slight mirth in his voice. . .and something else.

'Yes,' she answered, inanely, but it was all that usually articulate Harriet Leveson Gower could find to say.

'Lady Granville,' he repeated, and then, 'You do not know how much you have pleased me already, madam.'

'I have?' And her throat had closed, she could hardly speak, seemed doomed to monosyllables.

'Such an honour as you have done me, to take my name, Lady Granville,' he said again, and the something in his voice was pleasure at what she had done. 'Lady Granville must be rewarded,' he said softly. 'Now, what reward can I better give her than a loving husband?' And he took her hand and kissed, not the back of it, but the palm, so that shudders of delight rose in her to quell her fear and wonder at what she had done.

She had been so low, that last twenty-four hours, all the questioning renewed. Hart had seen, and helped her, had been light, but supporting, and all through the ceremony she could almost feel him murmuring, Courage, and the presence of her sister's children had helped, little George piping 'You do look fine, Aunty Haryo,' and then, 'We have a new little brother; are we not lucky?'

Hart and Granville had arranged that only their immediate relatives were there, his sisters Lady Harrowby and the Duchess of Beaufort, who had been kindness itself, and everyone had laughed when George's sister, little Harriet Howard, had suddenly announced halfway through the ceremony that she was very tired, and were they going to marry her? For she did not understand what was happening to Aunt Haryo and Uncle Granville — who had, of course, behaved throughout in the most impeccable fashion.

Nevertheless, the whole thing had been quite unreal, and Harriet would have liked to say at the end, Thank you, this is all very interesting, will you excuse me now? and go to bed with a good book, instead of being dressed by Walker in her smart blue wool, with the pelisse trimmed with grey fur, and preparing to go to bed with Lord Granville.

'You will like Woolmer,' he said suddenly, loosening his grasp of her a little, sensing her nervousness. 'It is one of my brother Stafford's prettier homes, and I know everything will be in perfect order, so that you need have no worries on that score.'

Oh, her worries were not on that score. Not at all. They were on the score of whether she, plain, inexperienced Harriet, could please him after he had enjoyed so many lovely and experienced women.

Suppose he took a disgust to her — she knew that such a thing had happened — or she took a disgust to him, when they were at last alone together, the door closed behind the last servant, and she must be truly a wife.

She remembered that Caro-William had been distressed on her honeymoon. No one had talked to her directly of it, but she had been aware of the whispers and the gossip. 'Married life is a trial,' she had overheard women say. 'If they are not too demanding, then they are not demanding at all,' and then she thought of all the marriages she knew, beginning with both of her father's — and shivered.

'You are cold,' Granville said. 'Come, let me warm you a little,' and he chafed her hands, and pulled her closer to him again, so close that she could feel the strong beat of his heart, was aware of his body as she had never been before.

For before he had always been something to be admired, like a piece of china, or a beautiful painting, or a sculpture, but now he was something else altogether. He was a man, a living and breathing man, who would shortly make certain demands on her that no man had ever made before. She could no longer confine herself to admiring him from a distance; they would soon be as close as any two human beings could ever be.

Harriet shivered again, desire mixing with fear, and this time he read her aright. 'Do not be frightened,' he said softly. 'For my wish, Lady Granville, is only to please you, to make you happy, and feel how my heart beats at the thought,' and he took her hand and placed it against his breast, so that she could feel it beating, strong and steady, beating so hard for her, Harriet!

After that, she dozed a little against him, soothed by his gentle kindness and the movement of the carriage, tired after the excitements of the day, to be awoken

when the carriage stopped. Dazed, for an instant, she
could not remember where she was, until she heard him
say, 'We are here, madam,' releasing her, and then
assisting her out, into a world where flambeaux flared,
servants ran before them, doors were opened, and the
world of consequence enveloped them, destroying the
pleasant quiet which she had enjoyed alone with him.

Later, supper over — and what she had eaten and drunk
she did not know — they were alone together again.

Or rather, Harriet was alone, having been undressed
by Walker and slipped into a magnificent nightgown,
more trimmed with lace and ribons than many evening
dresses, so that she felt foolish in it — but the Duchess
had given it to her, and she could not refuse it — and sat
in the bed awaiting him — he being readied for bed by
Saxe in the adjacent dressing-room.

And now it was her heart beating furiously, especially
when she heard the door open, heard him say 'Goodnight,' to Saxe, heard Saxe reply,

'God bless you, my lord,' and then he was with her.

She hardly dared to look at him, not sure whether
what she felt was fear of what they were about to do —
or desire for it. He was wearing a robe over his
nightgown, so that she saw less of him than she had
ever seen before.

He walked slowly to the bed, saw her eyelids flutter,
such a small betraying sign. She waited for him to get
in the bed, but he did not, sat on it, near to her, took
her hand; it was stone-cold again, and surely he could
feel her trembling as it lay in his large one.

No, Harriet did not know what she felt. Inside her,
the busy intellect which informed all her doings and
sayings was remarking sardonically, Since your mama
and your aunt, and everyone else, enjoy what we are
about to do so much that they risk reputation and

honour to do it with whom they please, why should you fear the act of love?

Because that is why I fear it, and oh, he has had so many women, and suppose I do not please him? For that was the real fear, the ghost which had haunted her since she had accepted him, and oh, if she did not, it would be the end, the very end, she could not bear it! Such a fine gentleman as he was, so discriminatory — she feared that Harriet Cavendish might not be to his taste after all.

Nothing showed, only her hand, slowly gaining warmth from his, quivered a little.

Granville spoke, his voice so low that it was at the edge of being unheard. 'Do not be afraid, my Harriet. I shall try not to hurt you this first time, and I promise you, I shall not go too fast. Your pleasure is what I wish to ensure, Lady Granville.' And he said her new title so lovingly that simple pleasure, not lust or desire, ran through her.

' "Patience, and cut the cards",' she said, her ever-ready humour breaking through.

'Yes,' he said. 'You are cold, I see. I hope to warm you. But not yet.'

He rose, tall in the candle light, the perfect profile sharp against it. *Il bel uomo*, Sir Thomas Lawrence's ideal man, now, improbably, her husband. He was leaving her! She watched him re-enter the dressing-room, and, before disappointment could touch her heart, he came out again, carrying a silver salver with a bottle and two tall glasses on it.

Harriet watched him set the salver on the night stand. He looped the bed curtains further back, poured sparkling white wine into the glasses, two waterfalls of amber liquid, handed one to her, and took one for himself — they had each drunk one glass of a rich and fruity red at supper.

'Come, Lady Granville Leveson Gower. A toast to our marriage. Drink up, madam, no heel taps!'

She drank the wine, her eyes on him, and when she had finished, his eyes on her, he drank down his own, in one greedy swallow, not at all after his usual elegant and mannered self, throwing his head back, and saying when he had done, 'A true libation to the gods requires a little abandon, madam. They do not like our fine manners, and we must humour them tonight.'

He took the glass from her, refilled his, but not hers, and took her hand again.

He was going so gently with her, and her hand was now warm, and the rest of her body, and she did not know whether it was desire for him, or the drink, or his refusal to leap on her and seize her — how could she have thought that he would ever do any such thing, he, of all people? — but all this had relaxed her, and his touch this time had the strangest effect on her.

It was as though an impulse, a wave of heat had passed from him to her, ran up her arms, into her body where her breasts quivered at it, passed finally into the pit of her stomach, setting up strange vibrations there.

She had seen an anatomy folio once, showing a man's body flayed, nerves, arteries, and veins displayed, and his touch had revealed to her her own possession of such senses, and the sensation which stimulation of them created.

Granville leaned forward, took her head in his hands, brushed back a wandering tendril of her hair, and then kissed her gently, first on the forehead, and then, her eyes having closed at the pleasure of his touch, on the lids, and finally, a butterfly alighting, on her mouth.

They were chaste kisses, no passion in them, Harriet knew that, and did not know how she knew it, but, perversely, the very lack of passion inflamed her, so that as he withdrew she shivered a little.

He said, instantly and still gentle, 'Don't be frightened. I promised, remember,' and then, 'Let me teach you, Harriet, what a man feels for his wife, and how he demonstrates that feeling. You will be an apt pupil, I am sure; the child who so eagerly wished to learn, the woman whose discipline has been so nobly displayed, will want to experience all that life has to offer, and it will be my pleasure to teach you what pleasure can mean to a man and woman both. Do not be afraid, I beg of you.'

Oh, it was not fear she felt, not simple fear, but fear mixed with desire, and when he leaned forward to take her in his arms again, she still in the bed, he still out of it, she said hoarsely into his neck, where the male scent of him, strong above the scrupulous cleanliness of his clothes and person, overwhelmed her starved senses. . . Oh, yes, the fear was there, a strange fear, and she must tell him. . .

'I am afraid that. . . I may not please you. I am only plain Harriet Cavendish, after all.'

Granville made a little sound in his throat. Her nearness, the feeling of perfect trust in him which she gave off, despite all her reservations, her natural modesty, was having a strange effect on him.

'Oh, no,' he said softly. 'You please me already, my wife, have done so for longer than I can remember, and as for pleasing me here, in bed, why, it is for me to please you, and in the doing we shall please each other. Believe me, my pupil, I shall prove to you how much I love Harriet Leveson Gower who is my wife. There is no Harriet Cavendish now.'

How kind he was, Harriet thought with wonder, when he sat back a little, to smile gravely at her, the long blue eyes doing his work for him. Whatever else he was, rake, adroit politician, cunning diplomat, gamester, man of a

corrupt world which laughed at God, he was nevertheless kind, as Hart had told her.

And he was going to be kind to her, she knew. No, he
was being kind to her, and if, perhaps, that kindness did
not include true love, the passion which he had felt for
her aunt and his other women, it would have to do.

It was more than she had ever hoped for, more than
anyone else had ever given her. No one, no one, had
ever spoken to her in that tone of voice, shown her such
loving consideration, put her interests first, above all
others, as he was doing now, not Mama, not Father, not
Georgiana, not Selina Trimmer, not Hart, nor anyone
in the world in which unconsidered Harriet Cavendish
had lived for twenty-four years.

He was going to take her, if not in perfect passionate
love but in loving kindness — which might be better, for
perfect passionate love in her world had so often led to
such perfect passionate misery.

Something of what she was thinking reached him as
she stirred in his grasp; he had left one hand holding
hers, their only bodily contact. He released the hand
and, seeing her about to speak, put his finger on her
lips.

'No,' he said, 'no words yet — the first lesson, I think.
The A of the alphabet of married love. This time,
Harriet, I shall kiss you as a man should kiss his wife,'
and he bent his head, but not before she had looked into
those killing blue eyes once again, those eyes which had
done such execution on men and women alike, binding
the men in friendship and the women in love. She
drowned in them, and felt his lips on hers.

'A child's kiss first,' he murmured, pulling away after
giving her another butterfly to play with, and then, 'but
something more is needed, I think. Let us progress to B,
my pupil,' and this time he kissed her more firmly, and,
her mouth remaining closed, his opened, for his tongue

to tease her mouth open, pushing and probing gently, until she felt his tongue touching hers, creating a sensation so powerful that she shuddered and gasped beneath it, opening her own mouth still wider, following his lead so swiftly that he was suddenly roused beyond his expectations.

'You must not beat the teacher at his own game,' he said, pulling away, laughing at her a little, 'but perhaps you ought to try. Suppose I suggested, only suppose, that a wife might invite her husband and teacher into bed with her, seeing that learning the alphabet might be easier, if we were nearer together.'

Harriet stared at him, her eyes alight, her whole body on fire, threw back the bedclothes, said, 'A true wife must show obedience to her lord—and since you are doubly my lord, my obedience must be absolute. Welcome, my lord, so that we may proceed to C.'

She watched him rise, throw off his dressing-gown to reveal that he was wearing night-rail as fine as, if not finer than hers, a choirboy's collar of lace around his throat. He put his hand to the buttons of his nightshirt, stopped, said, 'Not yet,' and then with one lithe movement was in bed beside her, to fit her into the crook of his arm, her head on his right shoulder, and now he kissed her.

'A pause, a rest, for us to jump even further when we attempt C—so that we might reach D,' and oh, he was tantalising her, for although the feeling of his hard body against her soft one was almost frightening, the sensations which coursed through Harriet told her that she welcomed him, that desire was beginning to outrun fear. After blessing her with more kisses than anyone had ever given her in her whole life, he said softly, 'If you are ready. . .'

She whispered, Yes.'

He murmured, 'Allow me to inform you that the

game of love is more satisfactory the fewer clothes there
are to impede one in the performance. You will allow
me,' and, taking her mute nod for an answer, he began
to unbutton her nightdress, and his mouth, which he
had placed on hers, left it and began to travel down,
down, as far as the cleft between her breasts, which was
all that the opening at her neck allowed.

Harriet shuddered with pleasure, needed to embrace
him, put up her own hands, to put them on each side of
his head, to stroke him, something which she had
wanted to do for as long as she could remember.

What was more important was that she needed his
mouth to do more than simply kiss her exposed neck
and throat; her breasts had begun to ache, and the ache
was travelling down her body, so that when he said,
'Beautiful though this is, do you really want it on?' she
made no effort to stop him slipping off her night-gown,
indeed, shamefully helped him, so that presently, he
then removing his, they were like two of the stone gods
in the gardens at Chatsworth, all the trappings of
civilisation gone, and she at last saw the perfection of
his body.

And when he began to stroke her, gently, oh, so
gently, the whole of her, from top to toe, saying, 'You
have my permission, madam wife, to return the compliments I am paying you,' even as first his hands caressed
her breasts, and then his mouth, and finally her flanks,
so that she cried out, and found her own hands stroking
him, no fear, fear gone, only desire so strong in her that
he laughed soundlessly, raising his head to say, 'Does
the pupil need a teacher? So apt you are to learn.'

Harriet only knew that the kinder he was to her, the
more slowly he went, the more the fire of passion began
to consume her. Had he forced her, gone swiftly, tried
to push her towards consummation without waiting for
her to awake, to respond to him, she would have frozen,

and what would have consumed her would have been fright, distaste for such intimate handling and loving.

But, paradoxically, his very gentleness—for it was plain as their lovemaking proceeded that he only went as far with her as she was willing to let him go, pausing if he thought she was taking fright, then slowly, patiently taking her along with him, by degrees, even though his own desire for consummation had become so strong that only by an act of will was he able to treat her with such tender care—his very gentleness inflamed her, until she began to cry out, calling his name.

'Oh, Granville, Granville, have we reached E yet, or is this F?' Her active, witty mind informed the body which was beginning to learn a new wit, so that even in his growing passion he laughed soundlessly into the stomach he was then kissing, his mouth travelling ever downwards, until, upon his reaching the desired goal, she gasped and rose against him, crying out again, so that now he soothed her, still waiting, still not willing to push her to the final act until he was certain that her need for it—and him—was so great that she would welcome him, demand him, find it easy to accept him, and he would serve her needs, not his.

Harriet did not know what she wanted. Only that she wanted more than she was being given. She clutched at him fiercely, and when she called his name again, he whispered, 'Yes, yes, I know, I am here; a moment, and we shall be together as you wish,' and he turned her on her back, rising above her, her arms around his neck, his eyes on hers, the desire for fulfilment now so strong in him, so aroused by her willing response, the look of perfect trust she gave him, that he could contain himself no longer.

'Now, my wife, now, and oh, do not be frightened,' he muttered hoarsely, 'if I hurt you a little at first, forgive me,' and he finally entered a woman so on fire for him that pain seemed like pleasure, and to Harriet what was happening to her was so strong, so powerful that her senses reeled, and the sensations which began to course through her were so intense that at the moment of complete fulfilment she was almost mindless, and together, her arms around him, his around her, one being — as much as two could ever be one — they felt together what was given to few: a perfect harmony and fusion, a complete loss of self.

The selfless patience that her husband had shown her had not only rewarded Harriet, it had rewarded him. Her gratitude, once the first transports were over, and they lay separate again, panting, was so great, so lovingly expressed, that the rake, the roué, the man who had enjoyed so many women, found that giving his young and virgin wife pleasure at the expense of his own selfish desire for consummation was itself so pleasurable that he, too, had experienced an ecstasy greater than any he had felt before.

'Oh, oh,' said Harriet rapturously showering him with kisses, leaning over him, so that it was his turn to be loved, 'Oh, thank you, thank you. If this is G and H, what can Z be like?'

'I have not hurt you?' he asked tenderly.

'A little,' she said, 'but then. . .oh, I had not dreamed such pleasure existed. How kind you are, how kind, to be so patient with your novice bride.'

He sat up, took her in his arms, felt her heart beating against his own, still rapid, her eyes on him brilliant, and then she began to cry, slow silent tears running down her face.

'Oh, I *have* hurt you,' he exclaimed, feeling such tenderness for her as he had never felt for any woman, seeing once again the small solemn child who had stared at him with such worship the first time he had visited Devonshire House.

'No, not hurt,' she sobbed. 'It was so. . .perfect. To be with you like that. There should have been music at the end, to celebrate such ecstasy. The gods themselves could not have enjoyed such harmony as I felt with you.'

'And I with you,' he said, and the smile he gave her was not the one with which he usually rewarded the world, it was one for her alone, tender, and — dared she think it? — loving.

Harriet was suddenly shy. Should she really be saying these things to him? What etiquette governed behaviour in the marriage bed? No one had informed her of *that*! Selina had left that out of her many lessons. She giggled at the thought, tears forgotten, her face coming alive as it always did when wit reigned supreme.

'I had not known. . .' she began. What had she not known? What was knowing? This, this, was feeling, thought had no place at the time, it came afterwards.

She said so, ending, 'I had not understood that men and women could experience what we did,' and she kissed his hand in love and thankfulness.

'It is not always so,' said her husband, lying back, and enjoying the play of expression on her face, 'but, seeing what pleasure we enjoyed together this night, why, I can only say that I hope we may experience the same joys again. But not tonight. Another night, when your body is recovered. And then we shall celebrate without the need for learning alphabets of any kind — for I think that shortly the pupil and the teacher will be fairly matched.'

Saying so, he leaned over to kiss her, and whispered something in her ear which she did not understand, and, gazing at him with a solemnity which had him on fire for her again, so different was she from the other women with whom he had made love, she said, 'Pray what is that you tell me, husband? Is it Greek you offer me?'

'Nearly,' he said, smiling, for he knew that her passion for knowledge would inform all her words, and deeds, even in the marriage bed. 'It is Russian, a proverb which says that a satisfied wife crowns a man's endeavours.'

'Russian!' exclaimed Harriet delighted. What new talent would he show her next? 'And where did you learn that, pray?' and, even as she spoke, she was admiring his perfect body in the candlelight.

'A lady taught me,' he said lazily, 'a little, only a little, but I remembered that.' His eyes mocked and teased her, so that she did something entirely uncharacteristic, something the Caros and Corisande would have done—struck at him playfully, a light slap. 'You are not to tell me of your other women, sir. I know enough about them already.'

'Allow me to inform you that the lady in question was not of an age, or an appearance, to be "one of my women",' and then seriously, sitting up to take her in his arms, 'Oh, Lady Granville, there will be no other women now. You are my wife, and my wife shall have no cause to doubt me, ever. You do believe me?'

Harriet, in his arms, where she had always longed to be, looked into his eyes, said, 'I believe you, sir, but, as the Scotsman said, an ounce of proof is worth a ton of promises.'

'And what Scotsman was that?' said her husband naughtily, 'One Lady Granville has just invented, I dare swear.'

Harriet's laugh was genuine and unforced, throwing her head back a little, so that he kissed her again, at the base of her throat, so that she regretted that she must wait another night for further joy. 'Oh, you are beginning to know me, I see.'

'And now, you must sleep,' he said gently, 'for you
have had a long day, and my Lady Granville must be
ready to enjoy another.'

Harriet went to sleep in his arms, enriched, fulfilled.
Never before had she felt so happy. She was not to know
that such ecstasy was given to few, and that she and he
had achieved it because of his self-sacrifice, and her
humble acceptance of it.

Granville did not sleep immediately, but watched
over her until she was suddenly warm and quiet in his
arms. An angel, he thought, I have married an angel,
and I must look after her, for pearls like Harriet
Cavendish are rare. Passion and wit combined; what
could a man ask more?

He had not told her how much he loved her, for that
coinage was debased for him, having too often been
expended on less worthy objects.

And, if he walked through Harriet's dreams, for the
first time she walked through his.

CHAPTER EIGHTEEN

GRANVILLE awoke the next morning, not quite sure where he was, or who he was. There was a woman lying in his arms, her head on his chest, and his first thought was, Good God, I have overslept! I must be away from here! And then, the present claimed him.

The woman in his arms was his wife, who stirred sleepily, and brushed his chest with her lips, muttered, 'Granville,' and slept again, the sleep of the fulfilled. His wife: no need to protect her by deserting her.

He hardly knew himself, or recognised his thoughts as he kissed her hair and tightened his grip on her a little, so strange were the sensations sweeping over him.

He only knew that he wanted to protect her, that she was his, and his alone, and that, if once forbidden fruit had seemed the sweetest, that was no longer true. In his arms, beneath him, she had enjoyed her first transports of love, and he was sure, knowing her, that only in his arms would she ever feel them again, so good and true was she. She was his, and his alone.

Was that love he felt? And, if so, he asked himself again, what had he felt for Henrietta Bessborough? For sure, he had thought that it was love, but it was quite different from this, and now he knew, not intellectually, but to the depths of his soul, that love had many faces, and the one which he was being shown was a new one, and a welcome one.

Harriet stirred again, turned her face towards him, blind with sleep, and, as in a transformation scene in a pantomime he had seen in Naples, all had changed. He had once, he remembered with shame, dismissed her as

222

plain, smiled a little when he had heard men joke about her lack of looks, her difference from her mother, her aunt, her half-sister, her cousin.

But what did he see now? As the mime's face in Naples had changed in a trice, so that beauty succeeded ugliness in a flash, so had she changed, and he could not grieve for her that she was plain and to be pitied, because he no longer saw her face, only knew Harriet, whose spirit transformed the fleshly envelope which contained it.

In their previous night's loving her wit had informed everything she did. The novice had met the master on his own ground and matched him, and, in the final ecstasy, she had whispered hoarsely in his ear, 'Ah, this is why men love and women weep.'

Holding her to him he felt faint at the mere idea that she would disport herself thus with other men, and for the first time knew a strange distaste for the man he had been, who had used other men's wives so lightly, for he knew that he could not bear another man to touch the treasure he had found. . .

Harriet, too, awoke to strangeness. To the scent and warmth of another body, the consciousness of being held and cherished.

'Granville?' she queried. 'I thought you might have risen.'

'No,' he whispered, his lips on her cheek. 'Not today. Today is ours.'

'It is Christmas Day,' she answered, her lips caressing him.

'A time of birth,' said Granville, 'a season to celebrate a new life. Shall we celebrate ours?'

'It would not be wrong?' was her question to him.

'Not wrong,' he replied, 'but right after the best fashion. We pledged ourselves to each other, and to

God, yesterday. He cannot frown on us today, so recent are our vows.'

'You said once that you were not witty,' she murmured into his chest, as he turned her beneath him, 'but I think you have glanced at wit, and she has blessed you.'

'I am married to wit,' he said, 'and if you cleave to me, as you should, then your wit is mine, and I am blessed beyond most men.' He paused. 'If I hurt you, you must tell me, and we shall delay our celebrations a little.'

Sensation overcame her again. Harriet did not know whether she was hurt or not. Such sweet ecstasy was itself almost pain, pain lying in delay, and sweet flooding pleasure in fulfilment. She cried out beneath him, and he held her so close, so close at the climax of their loving, that it was hard to tell where Harriet ended and Granville began. Harriet was suddenly able to perceive what passion did to its devotees.

What reason, what common sense, could cope with this? No rational argument, no call of conscience or duty was strong enough, she almost feared, to combat this. Fortunate the man and woman who celebrated their pleasure inside the bonds of marriage. For the first time she truly felt for her aunt — and for him.

'Oh, yes,' he whispered, lying beside her in their mutual afterglow, holding hands, legs entwined, her hair across his face, his mouth against her cheek, passive, but still so utterly aware of each other, 'today is truly ours — let us seize it, for those who neglect the day for the morrow may pay for it a price they might not like.'

And so it was, truly theirs, and the rest of the honeymoon as well. They played together as though they were nymph and satyr, making love one evening on the big sofa before the fire, their clothes falling away,

'As though,' said Harriet, 'we were a hero and heroine of all those French novels I was not allowed to read.'

He had ordered every chandelier lit before the servants left them, their supper on a small table before a giant fire, and then he had said, 'The eye must be satisfied in love, as well as the body,' and they had made love ferociously, Harriet for the first time beginning to plumb the depths of passion, discovering that so far she had only paddled in the shallows.

His kindness was so great that she could only marvel at it. He seemed determined to spoil her in every way. One afternoon he gave her a splendid fur-lined cloak — wolfskin from Russia, he said, pulling the cords of its hood together, and fastening them for her, treating her as though she were the finest beauty who had ever walked into the ballroom of the Prince Regent's barbaric home at Brighton.

Every day she discovered a new treasure for her delight, a necklace, a brooch, a handkerchief, a fur muff with violets pinned to it, a small illuminated book, with a quotation on every page, decorated with flowers and animals. On the first page were the words *amor vincit omina*, love conquers everything, and Harriet thought that it had conquered her — she was not so sure about Granville.

One morning she found a package on her dressing-table, opened it to find a cobweb of fine lace inside, and a note in his rapid script, 'Would Dr Johnson approve, d'you think?' reminding her of their conversation earlier in the year.

She found him downstairs, drinking coffee — it was snowing slightly outside, and the room was full of a strange light: he had risen early, and was reading *The Times*, which he put down as she entered, holding the cobweb before her. 'Oh, it's beautiful, Granville, beautiful, but you should not spoil me so, it's bad for me.'

Granville put on an expression which she had come to know, one he rarely employed, except when something annoyed him and distressed him—an expression so delicate many would not have registered it.

His mouth thinned a little, the fine eyebrows rose slightly—she had first seen him do this at Devonshire House, she remembered, when she was small, and had told him that Selina was frequently displeased with her, and she wondered what provoked it now.

'And you have been spoiled so much and so often, Lady Granville,' he said, and it was plain that his displeasure was not for her, 'that you think that a little from me is unnecessary? I cannot remember that any went out of their way to please or to consider you over-much.'

Harriet thought with a little shame of the years which she had spent demeaning him—and which he had spent watching and regretting, not unkindness to her, but thoughtlessness towards little-considered Harriet Cavendish.

'Oh,' she said helplessly, 'but only think, Granville. It has not prepared me to be pampered like this.'

'Then my wife must learn to be pampered, for I intend to spoil her a great deal—there is much leeway to make up, Lady Granville, and I intend to see you cosseted as much as you were neglected.'

'No one was unkind to me,' she offered.

'No, indeed, and not particularly kind, either.'

'It was good for my character.' This offering was made with a smile.

'True, and I get the benefit of it, but I do not have to like the memory of your treatment by others, myself included.'

It was useless. She had discovered before that where he was set in his opinion, he had an answer for everything. It was not that he was obstinate, but he would only change if convinced that he should change, by the power of the argument you presented. In this case, little she could say moved him. He had only to see her flower and alter under loving kindness to know the depths of her previous suffering, however lightly she had borne it.

Harriet was unaware of how much she had already changed by the time the honeymoon was over. She did not want it to end. Would he change when they left Woolmer, would he become slowly indifferent to her, as so many other husbands did after the first transports were over? Oh, she did hope not.

On the contrary, once they were home at Stanhope Street, he was, if anything, the kinder. He drove her to see Georgiana and the baby, Morpeth greeting them with a smile, and, once alone with Granville, clapping his uncle on the back, saying 'Well, old fellow?'

Granville replied, 'Very well, as you see, both blooming,' and then began to talk of other things, but Morpeth, a little surprised, saw how his eyes followed Harriet, watched her, and foresaw and tried to fulfil her lightest wish.

Georgiana exclaimed over Harriet, who wore her new cloak, refusing either to undo the hood or take it off until she had shown it to her sister.

'Oh, Georgiana, he has been so kind and he has given me so many pretty things, and oh, Georgiana, you never told me how delightful marriage is, oh, I know it will be harder when the babies come, but at the present. . .' and she gave a great sigh.

Georgiana could not help noticing how much Harriet had improved, as though Granville had used sandpaper to smooth her rough edges away. She had suddenly acquired poise and a new confidence; she would never be a beauty but was developing a presence which would make heads turn as much as beauty would, and would last longer than that, or prettiness, both ephemeral things, as her sister was beginning to realise, looking at what was happening to those around her as the years sped on their way.

'Yes,' she said in her gentle fashion, 'he has made you happy. I can see that. Oh, Haryo, I am so pleased for you.'

'If it lasts,' said Harriet, suddenly anxious. 'Oh, Georgiana, it is like a dream. I think I shall wake up soon. The only thing that worries me is the way we are spending money, but Granville says that we are to hire a house in the country, and live on the cheap. We are only being extravagant for the present.'

'Granville, live on the cheap!' spluttered Georgiana. 'Forgive me, but what a turn-up that will be.'

Harriet began to laugh too, thinking of her husband and his irrepressible love of everything that was fine and rare. 'Yes, I know, but we shall try. After all, I am little better. I have no idea at all about such things as living within one's means, seeing that I have never had to.'

'The trials of being a Duke's daughter,' joked her sister. 'But enjoy yourself, my dearest love. You deserve a little happiness.'

And even if it doesn't last, thought Harriet later, writing a letter to Georgiana, when she and Granville had started on a round of country house visiting — one way to live on the cheap, she supposed, being to live on others, although all these visits would have to be returned when they hired a home of their own — what I have at the moment is more than I dared to hope for.

As Granville had written to Lady Bessborough from Woolmer of his happiness with his 'perfect angel, Harriet' — since she had wished him success in his marriage at the last dinner, and had begged him to write to her, if he were happy — Harriet wrote in her letters to her sister of Granville as an angel of kindness and goodness to her, showing her every consideration, laughing at herself tenderly as she did so.

And what, she thought, shall I be writing in two or three years' time? *That* will be the test. . . How will I have fared compared with all the others who have been married from Devonshire House? What will the coming years bring me? 1811, 1812? Where shall I be? And Granville and I? What shall we be doing. . .?

CHAPTER NINETEEN

TIME turned back on itself. The woman in the study, Harriet, Lady Granville Leveson Gower, sighed, put her past behind her for the moment, rose from her seat by the fire, and returned to her escritoire — taking a loving look at the man in the painting above the hearth — and continued her letter, dating it May the eleventh, 1812: that date which was once the future, was now the present, and soon would be the past.

She wrote to her brother, once Hart, now William, the Sixth Duke of Devonshire, at Chatsworth, of Caro-William, who was conducting an *affaire* with the poet, Lord Byron, so publicly and recklessly that Harriet feared that at any moment she would do something so finally outrageous that her long-suffering husband would demand the separation or the divorce which his family and friends urged on him. To this had the love match come!

Harriet had felt nothing but exasperated pity for Caro-William for many years, but the contemplation of her headlong career brought tears to her eyes. She blinked them away.

'And Caro-George,' she wrote, 'has asked to come to see me later today, and I am fearful of what she may be about to tell me.' For there, she thought sadly, laying down her pen again, was another love match gone sadly awry.

For loud, large, boisterous George Lamb was not only impotent, unable to consummate his marriage, but rage and shame were making him mistreat the one-time Caroline St Jules to the degree that her delicate beauty was becoming clouded. She had grasped at Harriet the previous evening, when both had been at one of Lady Jersey's receptions, and said, 'Haryo, dearest Haryo, a rock of strength in the sea of misery which surrounds me. May I come to you tomorrow, I desperately wish to speak to you, privately, I beg of you. Do not tell Granville.'

'He will be out tomorrow, after one o'clock,' she had replied. 'Come to see me then.'

'I will, I will,' Caroline had said fervently. 'Oh, you do not know how fortunate you are, and to think that when you married. . .' Politeness and propriety prevented her from completing the sentence, and the look she gave Harriet as she left her was an agonised one.

Harriet's arm was scarlet where Caro-George had clutched at it in her despair. 'How fortunate you are,' Caro-George had said, and she supposed — no, she knew — she truly was.

For Granville's loving kindness to her had not stopped with the honeymoon, had continued, and still, today, his care for her was paramount in his life. The question she had asked herself when she had returned to London after Woolmer — How long would her happiness with him last? — had been answered in the best possible manner as the years slipped by.

She had become pregnant very soon, and the pregnancy had not been easy — but he had done everything in his power to make it so. They had lived mostly in the country, and in those last difficult months he had done all that he could to make her comfortable. She remembered the long afternoons when he had read to her, had pushed her about in a little wheeled chair when walking became difficult, drove her everywhere, held her hand, comforted her and generally made her life as happy as possible.

And after dear little Susan had been born — and how

pleased that had made him — they had rented Tixall, a house not far from Trentham, where his brother lived in such state that Harriet averred that the houses for the pheasants were better than those for the peasants, and they had begun to entertain all those whom they had visited in the early days of their marriage.

If possible, her life became even happier, and his loving kindness greater. Under such tutelage she blossomed and changed dramatically, becoming a hostess of such note, running such a pleasant establishment that to visit Tixall became the object of most people's ambitions.

Between Granville's charm and friendliness and her own new-found abilities to please and to organise, plus her delight that country living kept them close together, Harriet began to feel that she was living in Paradise. All those early painful years seemed like a bad dream. Tixall and its happinesses had been made possible by dear Hart, who had raised her dowry to thirty thousand pounds after his father's death — the first act of the new Duke of Devonshire being to ensure that Harriet and Granville's lives were made financially easier.

She watched Granville ride past the window, his exercising of the ponies — and himself — over. They were off to Tixall soon; she was expecting her second child, and Georgiana was to join her there, to be with her.

Meantime there was Caro-George to see, and luncheon to eat with Granville before he left for the Foreign Office.

'To talk about Russia again,' he said, over their cold collation. 'Otherwise, I might be off to the House. But they seem to think that I can be of use.' And he shrugged his shoulders. 'Well, we shall see.' He put down his knife and fork. 'You will not be lonely?' he said, a little anxiously. He was never completely at ease when she was pregnant.

'No, indeed,' she said. 'You are not to trouble about me. Caro-George has proposed herself for the afternoon, and we shall chat about all those things women love and men despise!'

He dropped a kiss on her head as he left her, said, 'I hope to be early home this evening. A quiet supper by the fire, d'you think?' and then was gone; she heard him calling for Saxe.

Harriet was thoughtful as she waited for Caro-George. It seemed an odd thing to think, in view of everything, but did he really love her? He had never said so, in so many words, but if actions were words then he did.

But she could not be sure. Was kindness love? Was paying her every attention love? Was praising her continually, for her wit, her conscientiousness love? Was his constant thoughtfulness, the little presents he showered on her love?'

She shook herself when she heard Caro-George's carriage arrive. What a fool she was, to question what she had. Who cared if it was not the grand passion, the heroic *affaire* he had had with Aunt Bessborough? Grand passions were uncomfortable things, and her life with Granville was so comfortable that it was as though she lived in a perpetual feather bed, coddled in the softest down. She was stupid to wish that it might be more, that he felt for her what he had felt for her aunt, whose eyes followed her so wistfully these days.

The door opened and Caro-George almost shot in. Her eyes were wild, and her clothing, usually so neat and careful, was in such disarray that Harriet was taken aback, surprised, but did not show it. To control such discomposure her own composure must remain absolute.

Caro-George came across the room in one bound, had seized her by both hands and was looking deep into her half-sister's eyes. 'Oh, Haryo,' and the diminutive moved her, such a reminder of the old days, and their old nursery was suddenly all about her, never mind that the beginning of her own nursery was upstairs — probably demanding to be fed if the French clock on the drawing-room mantelpiece told true.

Harriet disengaged herself gently, moved away, indicated a chair to Caro. 'Yes, my dear,' she said. 'What is it that has distressed you so?'

'Oh, never say that you are not aware. All London is a-buzz — even you must know! It is as bad as Caro-William with Byron! And I must tell you that I am innocent, quite innocent! But I must also tell you how tempted I am, and I do not know what to do for the best! There is no one, no one, to whom I can turn, you must know *that*! Mama is on the Continent, and his mother is the last person to whom I might go for help, even if George were not her son!'

Harriet ignored this comment on Lady Melbourne, while acknowledging its truth. 'I cannot help you,' she said carefully in response to this cascade of exclamation marks, 'unless you tell me what your trouble is.'

'I want to be good, oh, I do want to be good,' said Caroline convulsively. 'But it is so difficult. I do so want a child — you all have children, all of you, even Caro-William, and poor Georgiana has too many. . .could she spare one for me, do you think? No, I shouldn't have said that, but I am going mad, quite mad.'

She looked defiantly up. 'You do know why I can't have children, don't you?'

'Yes,' said Harriet steadily. 'George's little trouble, I presume.'

'George's little trouble! What a way to put it! To think that I was so mad to marry him, couldn't wait, would not listen — and now, he is not even a man, cannot. . .' and she broke into a passion of weeping, so

that Harriet went perforce to sit by her, and offered her
her handkerchief, not a dainty one for the pocket but a
large sensible one — like me, I suppose, thought Harriet
sardonic even in the face of Caro-George's very real
misery.

'There, my love,' she said, taking her into her arms
and rocking her. 'Cry, it will do you good.'

Caro sat up, glared at her. 'Nothing will do me good!
Nothing!'

How like her tiresome mother she was at times, was
her half-sister's reaction, but she said aloud, 'Think of
poor George and *his* misery. You still have him.'

'Oh, I don't want him, and I cannot have what I do
want, a man who will truly love me and give me
children. You do not know how fortunate you are. So
easy to say, "You have George", when you, you have
Granville, and the whole world knows how he adores
you, and what a remarkable turn-up that is, not at all
to be expected.' And she broke into fresh wailings, after
adding brokenly, 'And now you have your own little
darling girl, and, what's more, she is lucky enough to
look exactly like him. . .'

Instead of me, her plain mother, thought Harriet with
amusement. Obviously, Caro-George was beyond tact,
and nearly beyond behaving herself according to
society's tenets.

Her next words proved this beyond a doubt, for
Harriet already knew, as did all polite society, and had
told her brother that Caro-George was deeply engaged
with the rising young lawyer and politician, Henry
Brougham. 'Oh, I'm afraid I shall bolt with Henry,
without meaning to,' she announced tragically, 'and
that would be to ruin me, and damage his prospects,
and the only person with any common-sense whom I
think could advise me properly, is you. So I trust you to
tell me what to do.'

'Oh, the only sensible thing to do, since I am apparently doomed to say it,' replied Harriet, trying to restrain her normal caustic self, 'is, that you must stay with George, and behave yourself. Think how little our own mothers' and aunt's conduct answered. Happiness rarely flows from sin.'

'It did for Granville,' moaned Caroline, irrefutably.

'Well, he did give it up first,' replied Harriet. 'What an improper conversation we are having, to be sure.'

She was a little dazed by it. Caro-George's firm declaration that Granville loved her, adored her, and what a surprise that was for everyone, given her lack of looks and her upright character, she had made violently and tactlessly plain. 'A remarkable turn-up', she had said, and so she supposed, it was, with Granville firmly and improbably a faithful husband into the bargain.

Could she really believe her? Was it true? Was the care and devotion which Granville showed to her daily more than that of a naturally kind man, who liked to see those about him happy, because that made him happy? She would like to think so, but dared not.

She would think about it later. It was not her happiness that was at stake here, it was Caro-George's; she must be reassured, sent away to do the right thing, not the wrong thing.

Harriet rose, rang the bell, ordered sherry, coffee and biscuits — one or more of these ought to help quieten Caro-George — while she spoke gently to her of impersonal things, asked if she had recently heard from her Mama, spoke to her of music, books, the opera, anything to take her mind off her one dreadful problem from which all the others stemmed — poor George's impotence.

And after that, before she left, must come gentle

advice, plus a recommendation to read the right books,
speak to the right people, ignore what her mama might
advise, and try to disappoint all those who would be
amused to see another member of the Devonshire House
set ruin herself irretrievably.

CHAPTER TWENTY

LONG after it had grown dark, Harriet sat alone, her book on her knee unheeded, thinking of her life, and of *him*, the man who had changed it beyond any reasonable expectations.

To someone who had thought herself doomed to spinsterhood, or a loveless marriage undertaken principally because of who she was, a Duke's daughter, and not because of what she was, the last two and three quarter years had seemed a paradise. The only flaw in their life was his gambling, which no resolution he made could ever check, for once the fit was on him, nothing sufficed but that he must feed it — the prudent, cautious man changed and grown reckless. She could forgive him that, although it worried her, for in all else he was what a man should and ought to be, to his wife and child, to his and her family, to his servants, to his friends, and to his country.

She was blessed among women, and if she had his love, as well as his care, esteem and friendship — for she knew that she had the last three — then she was doubly blessed, for in the world in which she lived few women had even one of them — and she had them all.

The world! She laughed at herself, for their world was so small a part of the other world which lay all about them: a world beyond the cousinry. Her world was that of affairs, politics and social consequences, and of that other world she knew little, and if she tried to enter it she knew that her arrival there would seem as big an intrusion as their attempt to enter hers would be.

An intrusion, because that other world was as alien

238

to her as the wastes of Siberia, or even the half-barbaric Russian court of which Granville had told her, which brought her back to where her wandering thoughts had started—to him, and to their world's belief that he adored her. . .as she adored him.

Nothing showed. She had spent the rest of the day since Caro-George had left wrapped in the serenity which she brought to everything. A serenity which increased every day of their marriage—and which was so unlike the manner of the girl she had been—wrapped her around, never left her.

She had written, read, embroidered, seen the housekeeper, ordered the supper for which he had asked, 'Not too much to eat,' he had said to her recently. 'Domesticity will make me fat if I do not take care. We all risk it as we grow older, and my family seem to risk it more than most.'

'Because you are already large,' she had mocked him gently, 'and fair, and muscle turns to fat with age,' but oh, looking at him, his figure was as trim as ever, and, although neither of them knew it then, he was to preserve his good body and his handsome face into old age.

He knew her well, and could hear the affection beneath her gentle mockery.

'Oh, I know that I am older than you are,' he had replied gaily. 'No need to remind me.'

When he had left her, he had said that he would not be late, but the evening drew on. She had a sudden fear that he might be gambling again, but thought not. He had shown none of the signs he displayed when that loomed. The slightly *distrait* manner, his behaviour never less than perfect, but oddly disengaged, as though his body was with her, but his mind was elsewhere. No, it was not that, she was sure of it. Besides, he rarely broke his word to her in matters such as this, being punctilious about his promises to her.

It was dark before she heard him arrive, heard his voice in the entrance hall, knew that before he came to her he would repair the damages of the day; he always came to her *à point*. She rang to tell the butler to be prepared to serve their supper, picked up the *Morning Post*, tried to pretend that she was engrossed in it. Not good for him to think that she was burning for his return, which she was.

As soon as he entered Harriet knew that something was wrong. She had learned to read him, as though he were her second self, as to some extent were her sister and her brother.

His speech to her was strangely formal. 'Lady Granville,' he said gently, and took her hand, 'Lady Granville, I have something grave to tell you, for I think that you should hear it from me, rather than from another, or from the public prints. Pray sit down, for the news is shocking.'

What could it be? Was it Georgiana or Hart? Oh, no, not that! Not that!

Granville read her too, said, 'I have been clumsier than I intended, dear Lady Granville. I should have told you that this is not a family matter.'

Then what?

'This afternoon,' said Granville, 'the Prime Minister, Spencer Perceval, was assassinated in the lobby of the House of Commons, by a crazed Russia merchant called John Bellingham. He died immediately, being shot through the heart.' He paused. 'It happened at five o'clock. I was summoned to the House after he had been arrested. Poor Perceval, it appears that Bellingham went there intending to shoot me. He blamed me, as ambassador in 1807 and 8, for his business being ruined by, as he saw it, the treaty I concluded then and my supposed inaction in his own hopeless legal case against the Russian government, although I had done what I could for him. Not finding me, he shot poor Perceval instead!'

'But Perceval could have had nothing to do with his case,' said Harriet faintly.

'No, indeed. But in his madness—which he had begun to show in Russia—he probably thought any member of the government a legitimate target. I must own that I have been greatly moved by this. By the horror of Perceval's death, and by my own fortunate preservation... Had I gone to the House this afternoon...'

He shuddered. 'Oh, Lady Granville, the ways of God are mysterious indeed. I can only thank Him that he chose to save me, but poor Perceval...and *his* grieving family which might have been mine...and Bellingham's wretched wife and little children.'

Faintness overcame her. How could she have borne it if God had chosen to take him? Even as she thought this, there was a knock on the door. 'The food!' she exclaimed, pointing to the small round table set ready for them by the fire. 'Is it possible that you could eat and drink a little? You look hagged to death,' for his face was white and sombre, but after all, prosaic though it might be, life had to go on.

'A little, I suppose,' he said. 'I have touched nothing since I left you at midday, and it is now eleven of the clock.'

Then you must try to eat, my dear lord,' and she summoned the servants in, saying, 'Leave us for the night, when you have finished bringing in supper. My lord has had grievous news, and we do not wish to be disturbed again.'

'You are always thoughtful,' he said, and, picking up the bottle of wine, poured two glasses from it. 'Come,

Lady Granville, drink with me, I beg of you. And when
we have eaten, I have something to ask of you, which
this day's events have made more urgent.'

They both ate and drank sparingly. The news he had
brought with him shocked them. Not that Perceval had
been a friend — but that the Prime Minister of England
should be shot dead in the House he graced was a
sobering thought.

'Anarchy and chaos have flourished around us since
1789,' Granville remarked, after they had finished
eating, and he had poured himself another glass of wine,
Harriet refusing one. 'The Revolution in France was so
powerful, so great, that it could not remain within
France's boundaries, and Napoleon inherited it, to take
it across Europe, even into the East, which means that
many who might be content with their lot will seek to
improve it by revolution, even if by the means they use
they destroy the very basis of the civilisation which
sustains us. And the madmen, like Bellingham, are
encouraged to exploit their basest instincts.'

It was the moderate man's creed he was expounding,
the creed of a man who believed that change was
inevitable, but should proceed gradually, so that old
institutions should be reformed, and not destroyed. He
was to say something of this, later, when Canning died,
in his eulogy of his old friend, but, talking to Harriet, he
saw other implications in what had happened: personal
ones, involving himself and his family.

'Lady Granville,' he said, next, 'I wish to speak to
you of a most serious matter. One which I have been
refraining from raising with you — for many reasons.
But today's events have brought something home to me.
If I had been the one lying dead in the lobby, then two
lives might have been destroyed with me, because of my
dilatoriness, my moral cowardice.'

His formality, the gravity of his manner, disturbed

her, but Harriet gave no sign of her worry, merely inclined her head.

'You have my full attention,' she said.

'And that I always have,' was his reply. 'You spoil me. You are too good for me in every way. Which makes it difficult for me. . .'

He rose, walked away from her, stared at a small Canaletto. His hesitation, so unlike him, disturbed her a little. What in the world could he be leading up to? He was usually so quietly confident, so serene in everything he did — part of the grace which he brought to living, and which some mistook for lack of feeling. And strange, too, she thought that a man so gregarious, so happy to be with others, should yet remain so private.

As though he realised what she was thinking, he gave her a rueful smile, said, 'You will wonder what I am at. I hardly know how to raise this matter with you, such a thing as it is, but I must. In honour, I must speak to you; in honour, I should not. You see what a pother I am in.'

She did indeed. She said, in her usual slightly amused but composed manner, 'Yes, I see that. Most unlike you, I own. But, I am all attention, "all ears", as the poet says.'

He had half turned away from her, said, in a stifled voice, 'It is a favour so enormous that even you, in your angelic goodness, of which I have had so many proofs, might find it hard to grant.'

Harriet tried to help him, since help was so patently needed, said briskly, 'Unless you tell me what it is that troubles you, what it is that you want of me, I can make no answer, either of consent or dissent.'

Granville at last managed a smile, said, 'Despite your protests that you are too frank, too dismissive, I sometimes think that you should be the diplomat, not me.'

'As to that,' replied Harriet, 'I cannot judge. You

244 AN UNEXPECTED PASSION

may try, I suggest, to imagine that I am another diplomat, a lesser one, a Levantine, perhaps, and you may find it easier to address me.'

'So, madam,' he said, his voice suddenly as formal as though he were addressing the Emperor Alexander himself, the Tsar of all the Russias, 'this is the matter. She and I, she being your aunt, Lady Bessborough, I mean, are both troubled, about. . .' And he paused, to begin again immediately, 'Our children. You know, I collect, that we do have children. Such a thing cannot be hidden.'

'Yes,' said Harriet, 'I know, have known for some years, although it is not a subject about which I gossip, or encourage others to do so.'

'Exactly,' he said gratefully. 'You are the soul of discretion, as I well know, and that discretion is absolute. A boy and a girl, George and Harriet Arundel Stewart, the latter being my mother's name, since I could not give them my own.' He did not say that Mr Arundel was the pseudonym which he and her aunt had used in their secret loving—it had pleased them to be nobodies, plain Mr and Mrs Arundel, and they had used the code in their letters. 'They live, not in hiding, but in something like it, and all that they know of their parents is that I am their guardian, and they my wards. Of their mother they know, and can know, nothing.'

He stopped, turned away from her. She had seldom seen him so moved. He was usually so contained, so controlled.

'They have no real name, no station, no position in life as they are. She. . .your aunt. . .saw your half-sister, Eliza Courtney, when she visited Howick, the home of her natural father, who has taken her in. Your aunt. . . was so distressed. Eliza has nothing, is nothing, is little more considered or thought of than a governess, or a servant. For the first time it brought home to her what it meant for our children—such a half-life, not to be borne.'

'But inevitable,' said Harriet steadily, 'given their unfortunate circumstances.'

'Indeed. And you must know that I was. . .thoughtless as well. I cannot evade my responsibility for their existence. And she can never have them with her, but, situate where they are, she may visit them occasionally, give them presents, love them a little. Alas, that is only at the expense of never giving them a decent living in the future—for should anything happen to her, neither her husband nor her legitimate children have any interest or care for them. Whereas I. . . I. . .if I. . .we took them in. . .can give them that—but of course, were we to do so, she would lose them. She is prepared to make that sacrifice to see them cared for, their future assured.'

Harriet said nothing. It seemed politic not to. He was wrestling with himself, more than with her, faced for the first time with the consequence of unbridled pleasure, and not liking it, so harsh was that consequence for the innocent victims of it.

He swung around, fell on his knees before her, took her hands in his, and kissed them. 'If you would consent, we might. . .adopt them, make them part of our household. . .such a thing to ask of you, when you have already given me my first present, our daughter, and are about to give me another, perhaps my heir.'

Harriet disengaged herself gently, rose, walked away. It was her turn to be moved. 'It does you honour,' she began, 'only honour. . .'

'Honour?' he exclaimed, staring after her, straightbacked and upright as ever, her carriage the most remarkable thing about her, the one sign that showed she was the daughter of Dukes, betrayed that she was the child of privilege. 'You say that of the proofs of my dishonour which I ask you, my wife, to take into your home and to care for as your own.'

'Honour,' she repeated firmly. 'Not to wish to abandon them — or her.' She said this with difficulty, remembering as she did the resentment she had felt towards her aunt, coupled with a strange shared feeling of affinity. The final and ultimate affinity, she had thought, was her acceptance of the man who had been her aunt's lover for so long. How wrong she had been! This, this was the final affinity, to accept their children, give them a loving future, security, and not the half-life which otherwise awaited them. How better could she demonstrate how much she loved him — after God, of course — than to do this for him?

'If my aunt wishes an honourable future for them at the expense of losing them, and God knows, now that I have had Susan, I know what a sacrifice *that* is, then I am willing, for the love I bear you both, to take your children. And think, she has already lost you. Such desolation — and I know that you love her.' She said this last with some internal agony, none of which showed.

'No,' said Granville painfully, 'I loved her once, almost to distraction. I was obsessed, would have given up my career, my future prospects for her, if that had been necessary to secure her love. But the boy I was then has long gone, and the nature of my love and hers has changed, inevitably so, with the passing of the cruel years. Because of the love I *once* felt, and because of the consequences of that love, I ask you, my good angel, to do this, not for me, but for them.'

'And I will do it,' said Harriet, and had no difficulty in so agreeing to take them, although, not long ago, had he or another made such a suggestion she might have recoiled, shocked, so strong was Raison Sévère's teachings.

But all that she could think of was two stricken

children, and her own half-sister, pretty little Eliza
Courtney, thrown away, despised.

'I might suggest,' she added, 'that at first we take one
of them on trial only. Perhaps Harriet, who is, I collect,
the older of the two, could visit us, and we may see how
it answers. After all, she may not take to me.'

'Impossible,' said Granville, impetuously for him. 'I
would not ask it of you, were it not to relieve them —
and her. Your aunt is old and ailing. . .when I think of
what she was when I first saw her all those years ago in
Italy. . . I should not speak of this to you. . .but I must.'

'If you wish to speak of the past. . .' said Harriet,
putting out her hand to him, for he had risen and was
standing before her, so that she could see the suffering
plain upon his face. So strange to see it on him, the
perfect diplomat always, grave, controlled, his presence
so calm that to be with him was almost to be charmed
into believing the world a perfect place, an Arcady,
peopled with happy creatures — like himself. 'Do so, if it
comforts you. You can neither offend me nor hurt me.'

'Oh, you are too good, too good. I said that I loved
her. . .when I first saw her. . . I was just past twenty. . .
a boy. . .a spoiled boy. . .the pet of the family. And she,
she was in the pride of her beauty. . .and it was a *coup de
foudre*, a thunderclap. There were others, during the
long years of our loving, I confess it. . .but they were
nothing. . .for years there was no one else but her. . .it
was a kind of marriage, almost. I would have married
her on the instant, had she been free, but she would not
leave Bessborough, nor blight her children's lives by
such a desertion — as she saw other lives blighted. When
I had to go to Russia in '04, it quite broke me to leave
her. . .and she, and she. . .'

His voice had thickened at the memory, remembering
how they had clung together, and wished that the gods

had not placed them in an impossible situation, duties and convention keeping them ruthlessly apart.

'And then. . .when it was plain that at last I must settle down and marry, that the differences between our ages, as well as her marriage, was such that what we had enjoyed together must end, she it was who said that we must part for me to marry. . .and then she suggested you for a wife. . . I was reconciled to second-best, to milk and water after the finest Falernian wine — you see I am being candid with you — and when I asked you to marry me, it was with no expectations at all. . .beyond dull comfortable domesticity and friendship. . .'

He was looking away from her, so hard it was for him to speak, and she replied, trying to keep the anguish from her voice — he must not know how she felt about him, even though she knew that the whole world was aware. . .and laughed a little, 'Yes, I knew that, Granville. I married you, knowing that.'

'Oh. . .' he said, and now the anguish was in his voice, not hers. 'But did you know what then happened? "Springes to catch woodcocks", the Bard said. And I was caught. The girl I had taken as second-best, to share my bed, to give me an heir, to run my home, to be a wife. . .merely a wife. . .not my love. . .was an angel, come to me at last. Not merely someone good and true, but someone whom I could love after a fashion I had not known before. To mock me, to show that there is in love something beyond desire, fulfilled lust, the satisfaction of the body. . .but a love which is mind and body both. . .which is sacrifice of the self. . .the loved one being so important that passion itself becomes secondary if passion prevents the loved one's interests being served. . . I could not, cannot, hope that you feel for me what I feel for you, with all my imperfections on my head.

'Harriet, I love you to distraction, can only hope that

you feel for me, a little, what I feel for you. For sure, a
man cannot be loved twice by two women as peerless as
those with whom I have shared my life. And now this
latest favour which you have done me. . . I do not
deserve it, or you.'

Harriet was stunned, overcome, said, and hardly
knew her voice, 'You must not deceive me by speaking
so. Such a poor plain thing after all——'

'No,' he interrupted her violently, and caught her to
him. 'Never say that, Harriet. Never that. You are my
star, my good angel, and what you look like matters
nothing beside what you are. If once I thought that
collecting beauties was the game of life, I have learned
that nothing matters beyond the treasures which you
bring me — goodness, and a constant loving heart such
as I have never known before, and, beside all that, the
fact that you please me more than any other mistress I
have known is quite beside the point.'

He meant it. By all the gods in the pantheon, by the
one God whom she worshipped, he meant it. She, poor
plain Harriet Cavendish, was the love of his life. The
girl he had taken in convenient marriage, to round out
a successful life, was his true love. She could not believe
by his speech, by his manner, the expression on his face
that he was lying to her.

Granville caught her to him. His lips were in her hair,
his hands caressed her. The self-contained man that he
was had for once revealed himself, and in doing so had
crowned her life.

'Oh,' she said, 'you need have no fear. Do not you
know that I already love you to distraction, but would
not bore you with my adoration? For you to express
such doubt. . .my heart. . .my only love. . .' And when
he lifted his head to look deep into her eyes she knew
again that he was not lying about the depth of his
feelings for her.

Caro-George had told her nothing but the truth. Unlikely though it was, Granville loved her. Of all the women he had loved and known, she was the only one to whom his heart had been truly given. If she adored him, then the adoration was mutual — and that she could not have hoped for, had never expected.

She held him to her heart. She knew him well enough to know that he might never make such a revelation again, that her willingness to look after his children had brought from her a declaration which he might otherwise have never made so starkly.

She thought of her aunt with pity, knew the agonies through which she had passed when she had lost her beloved, because she herself had suffered them after Badminton, when she had not known that he would come to her again, that she would possess what her aunt had once had. Except that Granville was offering her what he had never truly offered her aunt: his inward self.

Harriet was not to know that her aunt had written this in her journal, had seen the way in which he looked at Harriet, and had thought, He never looked like that at me, for all our protestations of love. Giving him to Harriet had seemed a way of keeping him, so unlikely was it that he would ever feel for her niece what he had felt for her.

But what Granville felt for Harriet transcended that. And Harriet knew it. She had come home at last. For she had been granted what she could never have expected: she was the first in someone's mind and heart. Not second as she had been with Mama, with Georgiana, with Selina Trimmer, even with Hart, but first. She was the pole star of the man she had married, and, as Caro-George had rightly said, What a remarkable turn-up that was!

She remembered with a smile what she had written

to her sister, late in the second year of her marriage, 'Granville, adored Granville, who would make a barren desert smile,' and oh, the perfect bliss of knowing that she had made a barren desert smile for him!

Later, lying in his arms, secure in his love—for he had been so careful and gentle with her in her fifth month of pregnancy—as he was secure in hers, she turned towards him, and traced his sleeping features with her hand before she, too, fell into the deep sleep of the fulfilled.

The future lay all before them, and she had no doubts, no doubts at all. Together they could weather anything; neither time nor chance could touch the eternal core of them, for, in the words of the book he had given her on their honeymoon—and that alone should have told her what he truly thought of her—*amor vincit omnia*, love conquers everything, and at last, loving, she knew that she was truly loved.

EPILOGUE

And was Harriet, Lady Granville Leveson Gower— later Harriet, Viscountess Granville, and later still Harriet, Countess Granville—correct in her belief?

Yes, for sometimes fairy-tales do come true, even in real life, and to Harriet and Granville it was given to live as happily together as is ever given to mortal men and women to do. Years into their marriage we find them expressing undying affection for one another.

So much so that when, at last, Granville—now Earl Granville—died, full of years and honour, Charles Greville, writing a eulogy of him in *The Times*, said that the most remarkable thing in his long and prosperous life — he was ambassador to first Holland, 1823–4, and then France, between 1824–1841 — was his happy marriage to Lady Harriet Cavendish.

All their children, apart from one who died young, lived happy and successful lives, and Harriet and George Stewart, too, were happy with their adoptive parents. Harriet made a grand marriage; George remained a bachelor, was appointed his father's private secretary and after Granville's death looked after his adoptive mother devotedly.

Finis coronat opus: the end crowns the work.

SELECT BOOKLIST

The author consulted many books and newspapers
before writing this novel but these are the basics —
unfortunately, some of them have long been out of print
and may be very difficult to track down.

Granville George Leveson Gower, 1st Earl Granville

Castalia, Countess of Granville (ed.), *Private correspondence of Lord Granville Leveson Gower, 1781–1821*, 2 volumes, John Murray, 1916.

Granville, Harriet Leveson Gower, Countess

Leveson Gower, (Sir) George and Iris Palmer (eds.), *Haryo: the letters of Lady Harriet Cavendish, 1796–1809*, John Murray, 1940.

Surtees, Virginia (ed.), *A second self: the letters of Harriet Granville, 1810–1845*, Michael Russell, 1990.

Askwith, Betty, *Piety and wit: a biography of Harriet, Countess Granville*, Collins, 1982.

Calder-Marshall, Arthur, *The Two Duchesses*, Hutchinson, 1978.

An Unexpected Passion
by Paula Marshall

W e always try to ensure that our Masquerade books are just what you want to read. To do this we need your help. Please spare a few minutes to answer the questions which follow and, as a special thank you, we will send you a FREE novel when you return your completed questionnaire.

Don't forget to fill in your name and address, so we know where to send your FREE book.

Please tick the appropriate box for each question ✓

1 Did you enjoy AN UNEXPECTED PASSION by Paula Marshall?
Very much ☐   Quite a lot ☐
Not very much ☐   Not at all ☐

2 What did you like best about it?
The Plot ☐   The Hero ☐   The Heroine ☐
The Background ☐   The Cover ☐

3 What did you like least about it?
The Plot ☐   The Hero ☐   The Heroine ☐
The Background ☐   The Cover ☐

4 Do you have any particular comments you'd like to make about this book?
_____
_____

5 AN UNEXPECTED PASSION is based on the lives of real people, would you like to read other books of this kind?
Often ☐   Occasionally ☐   Never ☐

6 **If we publish more real-life stories is it important that they have happy endings?**

They should always have happy endings ☐

I would prefer them to have happy endings ☐

I don't mind, they should reflect the true historical facts ☐

7 **How often do you read Masquerade books?**

Every month ☐   Every 2-3 months ☐   Every 4-6 months ☐

Less often than every 6 months ☐   This was the first one ☐

8 **Which historical periods/settings would you enjoy reading about?**

_____

_____

9 **From where did you get this book?**

Mills & Boon Reader Service ☐   New from the shops ☐

Other (please specify): _____

10 **Are you a Reader Service subscriber?**   Yes ☐   No ☐

If yes, what is your subscription number: _____

11 **What age group are you?**

16-24 ☐   25-34 ☐   35-44 ☐   45-54 ☐   55-64 ☐   65+ ☐

THANK YOU FOR YOUR HELP

Please send your completed questionnaire to:
Mills & Boon Reader Service,
FREEPOST, P.O. Box 236, Croydon, Surrey CR9 9EL
NO STAMP NEEDED

Please fill in your name and address to receive your FREE book:

Ms/Mrs/Miss/Mr _____ MUP

Address _____

_____

_____ Postcode _____

DIRECT MARKETING ASSOCIATION

mps MAILING PREFERENCE SERVICE